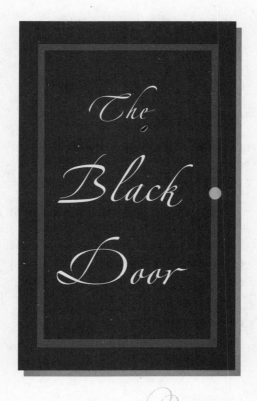

The Black Door

Velvet

ST. MARTIN'S GRIFFIN   NEW YORK

This is a work of fiction. All of the characters,
organizations, and events portrayed in this novel are
either products of the author's imagination or are
used fictitiously.

ISBN-13: 978-0-7394-8034-2

The Black Door *is dedicated to my agent, Sara Camilli, who saw the vision before it was in focus! Thank you so much for your love and support. You're the best!*

acknowledgments

I'd like to thank the following people, who helped make *The Black Door* a reality:

My St. Martin's family, Matthew Shear, John Murphy, my editor Monique Patterson, one of the best in the business, and Emily Drum (her right hand!), Anne Marie Tallberg, and Christina Ripo.

Denise Milloy and Bill Boyd, thanks for a wonderful photo shoot! Billy at Plush Chicago, thanks for letting me use your cool club for the shoot. Saunté Lowe, thanks for the celebrity hook-up. Amy Olsen, thanks for your friendship!

And to the following muses (sans full names for obvious reasons) who add flavor to the pot: Kevin M., Paul M., Lou M., Andrew M.S., Jack M., Michael N., Michael F., A. Mense, J. Sasson., C.E.W., H.K.W., David H., F. Collier, Bill C., T. Crown, Frank M., I. Allen., A. Phillip., Phillip W., Steve A., W.S., and Daryl M. (just to name a few!).

And lastly to the readers, thank you for your support, and I hope you enjoy reading *The Black Door,* just as much as I enjoyed writing it!

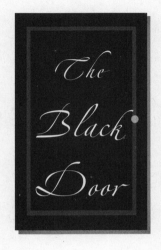

The Black Door

prologue

"A HUNDRED and Fifty-sixth and Riverside Drive," she said to the driver, then leaned into the backseat of the black stretch limousine, closed her eyes, and envisioned the titillating night ahead.

She was on her way to The Black Door, a private club. Not your typical members'-only club, The Black Door was an ultraexclusive adult playground, catering solely to the carnal needs of women. She could feel her juices begin to flow at the thought of the possibilities that lay ahead. Within minutes, they were pulling up in front of a nondescript brick building with a polished, pitch-black, ten-foot-tall door.

She stepped out of the car and balanced herself on candy-red, six-inch spike heels. As she teetered toward the entrance, the night breeze swept through the sheer silk sheath that she wore underneath a black, ankle-length cape. She cautiously tapped on the door. After a few seconds, a masked, six-foot-tall, muscular hunk of a man opened the door to decadence and demanded the password.

"Wet 'n' ready," she whispered in a soft, seductive voice through her half mask.

The doorman stepped aside and she glanced down at his large package, which was wrapped tightly in a black leather G-string. She walked into the foyer and removed her cape. The temperature in the room was frigid, and she could feel her nipples harden. She looked down and saw the imprint of her large round areolas beneath the sheer sheath. The doorman licked his lips at her beckoning breasts, then walked behind her and tightened her patent-leather scarlet mask. As he stood close, she could feel his erect member pressing deeply into her backside. She gasped with pleasure and instinctively stuck out her rear to meet him. They began a slow, seductive grind in the middle of the foyer. He reached around with one hand and massaged her full breast, while his other massive hand reached underneath her dress and found her pleasure pot.

"Ohh . . ." she moaned, as he stuck his large finger inside her moistness. His aggressiveness took her by surprise and she flinched slightly, but quickly recovered and gave in to his seductive touch.

When she was near orgasm, he stopped suddenly and said, "Now you're ready for The Black Door."

She could hear people mingling in the inner sanctum and walked slowly toward the closed ornate door. With each step, her heart began to race . . .

ARIEL SAT at the polished oval conference-room table, along with her colleagues, and listened halfheartedly as the managing partner gave his weekly billing spiel. Ariel Renée Vaughn was one of three female partners at Yates Gilcrest, one of New York's leading law firms, with offices in every major city in the world. Bob's speech on revving up the firm's revenue didn't apply to Ariel, since she had two of the top billing clients on her roster, so she crossed her long legs and gazed out of the huge picture window. From her twentieth-floor vantage point, she could easily see the treetops of Central Park. With fall in full glory, the robust rust, ruby, and citrine hues of the leaves decorated the sky like a painter's colorful palette. Ariel's mind drifted off into a daydream.

She had come a long way from being that little foster-care girl living in a crowded house with five other parentless children. Her mother had given her up for adoption at birth, but she had never been adopted. Ariel spent her childhood drifting from one foster home to the next, until landing in the home of Mrs. Grant, a big-hearted widow who encouraged Ariel to study hard and make good grades so she could get into a good college and land a good job. And that's exactly what Ariel did. With a 4.0 grade-point average and stellar SAT scores, she landed a four-year scholarship to Columbia University and studied prelaw. Months before graduating from Columbia's law school, she was recruited by Yates Gilcrest as a junior associate, and worked diligently over the years, slowly making her way up the ranks. After ten years of hard work, Ariel had finally made partner.

With a hefty six-figure salary, a two-bedroom luxury condo in the ritzy part of town, and one of the most powerful judges in the city as her man, Ariel should have been on top of the world, but she had become restless lately. Something was missing, and she couldn't quite figure out what it was.

"And in closing"—Bob looked around the table at the bored faces staring back at him, waiting impatiently for him to wrap up the meeting—"let's not forget about the annual Lancaster benefit on Friday."

The Lancasters were one of the wealthiest families in the city, with a net worth approaching $1 billion, and the bread and butter of the firm. Every year, the matriarch of the family hosted a gala at the prestigious Waldorf-Astoria to benefit the Boys & Girls Clubs of America. Attending the black-tie dinner was a must for all of the partners and their significant others.

"With that said, this meeting is officially adjourned."

Ariel gathered her notes and stuffed them into a thick leather-bound legal portfolio. As she stood, she smoothed the narrow pencil skirt that had gathered at her hips. Her figure was voluptuous with a perfectly round sister-girl butt, a full, overflowing C-cup, and a pair of knockout Tina Turner–type gams. Since she worked in an old-boy company with gray-haired staunch Republicans at the helm, Ariel hid her body underneath tailored blazers, buttoned-up blouses, and oversize sweaters to keep the attention focused on her brain instead of her body. She quickly buttoned her suit jacket to conceal the too-tight skirt and marched down the corridor to her corner office.

"Ms. Vaughn, here are your messages," Ariel's assistant said, handing her a stack of pink slips.

"Thanks, JoAnne," she responded, taking the messages.

Ariel closed the door to her office, parked herself behind the masculine mahogany desk, and thumbed through the telephone messages. One was from her Realtor calling about a pricey beach-front property for sale in the Hamptons; one was from her foster mother, Mrs. Grant, with whom she still maintained a close relationship; two messages were from her best friend, Meri; and one was from Judge Hendricks. Ariel and Preston Hendricks had been dating for years, and though they were in a committed relationship, the sheets had long since cooled off. He was like a worn-in pump—comfortable, without pinching your toes. Besides, they were the perfect match on paper. Both were financially secure and well respected in the legal community, and it was just a matter of time before Judge Hendricks threw his hat into the political ring. Ariel would be right by his side all the way to Washington.

She picked up the phone and dialed her foster mom's number. "Hey there, Mom," she said.

"How's my favorite daughter doing?" she asked, using her usual greeting.

"I'm good. Did you get the check I sent?" To the dismay of her foster mother, Ariel sent a monthly check that not only covered household expenses, but was enough for her to treat herself to anything she desired.

"How many times do I have to tell you to stop sending me money?" she scolded. "I get more than enough from the state for taking care of these babies."

"No offense, Mom, but you're getting too old to be changing diapers and running around after those kids."

"Well, if you gave me some grandbabies I wouldn't have to rely on my fosters to keep me company."

Ariel rolled her eyes. Since she had turned thirty a few years ago, Mrs. Grant had been hounding her to marry Preston and have a family. "Mom, I don't have time for babies, I've—"

"Well, I hope you have time for Judge Hendricks," she interrupted. "That man is going places. I saw his picture in the paper yesterday; he was at some kind of fund-raiser. He sho is one good-looking man; sort of reminds me of Mr. Grant when he was that age." Mrs. Grant's husband had died many years ago from a sudden heart attack and she never remarried. "You need to stop working so much and give that man more attention; men like him don't come around every day, you know."

Ariel had heard this comment more than once, and she was getting tired of the mild browbeating. "Yeah, I know," she simply said.

Mrs. Grant could hear the annoyance in Ariel's voice. "Look, baby, I don't mean to be a nag. I just don't want you to end up old and alone like me. Hear me when I tell you that being without a man is no picnic."

"Don't worry, Mom. I'm not going to let Preston slip away. I promise." She smiled into the receiver, trying to comfort the old woman.

"Judge Hendricks is on line one," JoAnne said through the intercom.

"Speaking of the devil, that's him calling me now."

"Well, get off the phone, baby, don't keep the man waiting. I'll talk with you later."

Preston's baritone voice boomed through the speakerphone. "Good morning, Ms. Vaughn."

"Judge," she responded. This greeting was part of their routine, and a reminder of how they met.

Ariel had been clerking for one of New York State's top judges, and on occasion would see a distinguished-looking gentleman rushing through the corridors of the courthouse with his black robe flying open and floating in the breeze. She learned that his name was Preston Hendricks, and he was a recently appointed judge. Though he was older, Ariel was attracted to his assertiveness and often sat and listened in the back of his courtroom.

From Preston's perch on the bench, it was hard for him to miss the attractive young woman with the mouthwatering breasts who hung on his every word. Divorced, with a grown son, he was ready to jumpstart his stalled love life, and she fit the bill perfectly. During a chance encounter in the elevator, he introduced himself as Judge Hendricks. And from that day on, they greeted each other formally until they began dating three weeks later. Though Preston was fifteen years her senior, he was a tiger in bed, showing her positions she never knew existed. She had only been with inexperienced younger men, and being with a more seasoned man was thrilling. His appetite for her was insatiable. He would bury himself between her thick thighs and suck her clit until her body shivered from one climax to the next. He would then fill her slippery wet vagina with his hard, thick shaft and pump them both into another realm of ecstasy.

Early in their relationship, they made love on a daily basis, often three times a day—morning, noon, and night. His ex-wife had been a rail-thin size four, with hardly enough tush for the push. So he absolutely loved Ariel's full-sized, curvaceous body, especially her plump, melon-sized 38-Cs. Often he would call her into his chambers, lock the door, and make her take her bra off underneath her tight sweater. The outline of her large, hard nipples pressing against the fabric drove him absolutely crazy. He would sit in his chair licking his lips and masturbating until he was on the brink of orgasm. It was like having his very own personal porn show. He would then pull her close and lift up the sweater. Ariel had a bright red rose tattooed on her left breast; the flower looked so real that he was always drawn to touch it before sucking and biting on her nipples, until he turned her over his desk, spread her legs, and fucked her from behind. But as the years passed, Preston's focus shifted from his sexual desires to his political agenda, and now if they made love once a month, that was a lot.

"How's your day going?" he asked.

"It's going. I just got out of a boring staff meeting, and Bob reminded us about the Lancaster fund-raiser on Friday. Remember? I had you mark your calendar last month."

"Yes, I remember. But I won't be able to attend."

She exhaled loudly. "What do you mean? All the partners and their significant others will be there, not to mention the Lancaster clan. And I refuse to show up without an escort," she fumed. Lately Preston had started putting her on the back burner and she didn't like it, especially since she was trying to be understanding and supportive of his career.

"I'm sorry, but I have to fly to Washington for a dinner meeting with Senator Oglesby. I know I promised you that I'd go, but the senator's office called just an hour ago, and when Senator Oglesby calls, you go, no questions asked," he explained.

Ariel knew that Preston's political aspirations were a priority, and that allying himself with the right party could take him all the way to the Supreme Court, but she still didn't like being put off at the last minute. "I understand," she conceded, with a tinge of sadness in her voice.

"Now, don't sound so heartbroken; I'm sure you'll have a great time without me on your arm. Look, honey, I've got to get back to court," he said, rushing her off the phone.

Ariel sat holding the receiver. She hadn't expected Preston to back out of the fund-raiser, and wanted to try and persuade him to push his dinner to the next day, but he didn't give her a chance. Now she was dateless with no prospects in sight. She decided to call Meri; maybe she had an extra man on the side that she could loan out for the evening.

Meri Renick was a golf-widow, though not the typical wife whose husband golfed in his spare time leaving his wife alone to fend for herself while he spent hours on the links with his friends. No, Meri was actually a widow, whose husband died on the ninth hole. He had had a massive heart attack on the golf course, leaving her his vast fortune. With no children to support, Meri spent hundreds of thousands of dollars overhauling her assets, until she once again had the perfect thirty-year-old face and matching body. Most evenings, Meri could be seen at a swank restaurant having dinner with a stunning hunk or two, or strolling down Madison Avenue with a beau on each arm. She offered no excuses about the younger men who kept her bed warm at night and even during the day.

"Daarliing," Meri purred into the receiver. "I was just thinking about you."

"And what where you thinking?"

"I was thinking that I haven't spoken to you in a while, and that it was high time we caught up over lunch and cocktails." They usually had a girly chat session at Meri's penthouse at least once a month.

Ariel had known Meri for ten years. They met when Ariel represented Meri in a divorce from her first husband. Initially, Meri was skeptical of the brash young attorney with the killer boobs and knockout body, but Ariel had come highly recommended, and after she negotiated a hefty settlement for Meri, they became fast friends.

"Sounds good to me." Ariel thumbed through her datebook. "How does next Tuesday sound?"

Meri hesitated for a moment, "Hmmm, let's see . . . No, next Tuesday isn't good. I'm having dinner *and* dessert with Paul."

"And who is Paul, pray tell?" Ariel hadn't heard that name before.

"Only the most delicious man I've ever tasted. He's got the biggest cock I've ever seen. It must be at least twelve inches long, and as thick as a roll of half-dollars. I nearly choked to death the first time I went down on him," she said, without shame, as if talking about sex was the most natural thing in the world.

It amazed Ariel how free Meri was with the details of her sexual exploits. Meri was in her late forties, but had sex more than most twenty-year-olds. "Speaking of men, I need one for—"

"Don't tell me you and the good judge have finally called it quits. I've been telling you for years that he's just too old for you. Trust me. What you need is a young stud to rock your world on a daily basis." Meri was a proponent of sex; she believed that a regular romp in the sack kept the mind *and* the body young.

"My world is perfectly fine, thank you very much, but I do need a date for the Lancaster benefit. Preston is going to be out of town and I don't want to go alone. You know how pretentious that bunch can be. Everyone will have a date, and I don't want to be the odd woman out," she explained.

"Well, my dear, you've called the right person. Do I have the perfect solution for you!" she squealed gleefully, "You have to use my escort service; they have some of best and brightest, not to mention some of the finest, men in the city."

"Escort service?" Ariel asked, shocked. She knew that Meri lived on the edge, but didn't expect that she'd be involved with a seedy escort service.

"Don't sound so shocked. It's extremely classy, totally aboveboard *and* legal. I use them all the time," she confessed.

Ariel leaned her elbows on the desk and listened intently. "So tell me, exactly how does this work?" She had only heard rumors about this type of service and was intrigued to find out how they actually operated.

"Well, my dear, it's really simple. You call the private number and tell them the type of event you're attending and what type of man you need to complete your evening. Give your credit card information and the details of the pickup location," she said, rattling off the details as if she were giving her the ingredients for a casserole.

"Meri, you say this so casually, as if I'm shopping for a new pair of shoes, or a purse."

"In a sense, you *are* just shopping for another accessory. Except this accessory comes with fringe benefits!" She laughed.

"When you said aboveboard, I assumed you meant sex wasn't a part of the arrangement. I'm just looking for an escort, not a mating stud," Ariel said, making it perfectly clear that she didn't want to get involved in some kind of sordid affair.

"This is a strictly platonic service, but if you need a little maintenance, I have the connection for that too," Meri said slyly.

Ariel didn't want to admit it, but the truth was that she needed a tune-up in a big way. That was probably why she'd been so antsy lately. The last time she and Preston had had sex, it was purely uneventful. He just rolled on top of her in the middle of the night, slipped in his penis, half-humped a few times, and then rolled off and went back to sleep. She missed the passion that they once shared, but knew Preston was preoccupied. Besides, sex wasn't everything, she kept telling herself. "Are you sure this is a reliable service?" she asked skeptically.

"Remember the man I was with at the Whitney Biannual?"

"You mean the Richard Gere lookalike in the tailored Armani suit?"

"That's the one. Well, he wasn't a shipping magnate from New Zealand like I previously said. He was an escort," she said proudly.

"Shut up!!" Ariel was stunned. The man she met at the Whitney Museum was poised, well spoken, and a complete gentleman. If he was the definition of an escort, then she was sold, no more questions. "Okay, what's the number?" she asked, reaching for a pen and a piece of paper.

Meri spouted off the telephone number from memory. "Trust me, you won't be the only woman in the room with a date for hire. As a matter of fact, I'm bringing one of my old standbys. And as usual, I'll craft an impressive persona for him, and nobody will be the wiser. I suggest you do the same."

Ariel felt a little uneasy, and began to question her decision, "Meri, are you sure this is totally safe? And what if someone asks why I'm there with another man, instead of Preston?"

"Yes it's totally safe. And if anybody asks about Preston just tell them that he's out of town on business; which is true, but then add a little white lie, and tell them that your date is an old family friend. The term 'family friend' always sounds more appropriate, or should I say platonic, than an old friend from school. Trust me, darling, you have nothing to worry about. Look, I've got to run, my lunch date is here, but I'll see you at the benefit," she said, hanging up the phone.

With Meri's reassurance, she felt a little more at ease. Settling into her decision to employ the escort service, Ariel decided to use her middle name for a little anonymity. She jotted down a believable background for her "date," along with a list of attributes: smart, well versed, attractive, well dressed, and most of all, discreet. She underscored the word *discreet* twice, because the last thing she needed was for Preston or the partners to find out that she was using a male escort for the evening.

2

WARM SCENTED bath bubbles caressed Ariel's body as she submerged herself deep in her Jacuzzi tub. She took a sip from the wine goblet that sat on the marble edge of the tub, leaned back on the headrest, closed her eyes, and let the jets ease her aching muscles. The water felt so relaxing; she could feel a week's worth of anxiety leave her body as she let her mind drift from the details of her daily life into the realms of fantasy. The Cabernet and soft music playing in the background were making her horny. What she wanted more than anything else at the moment was to get fucked, but with Preston away on a business trip that wasn't an option, so she slipped her middle finger between her legs and found the tiny bit of flesh that held so much pleasure. She slowly stroked her clitoris with one hand while massaging her nipples with the other. Ariel soon brought herself to a satisfying climax, finished bathing, and stepped out of the tub. She wrapped her body in a terry-cloth towel and padded into the bedroom.

Laid out on the bed was a black YSL gown with a plunging neckline, matching scarf, and sexy fishtail hem. Ariel let the towel drop to the floor, walked over to the dresser, picked up a jar of creamy moisturizer, and began conditioning her skin. As she smoothed the cream over her chest, she looked in the mirror and had to admit that she had an amazing rack. Though her breasts were large, they were not the least bit saggy; her erect nipples were the size of thumbnails and seemed to be made for sucking. She did a little wiggle and watched as her titties bounced up and down. Preston loved it when she danced for him. He would watch from the bed with his tongue hanging out of his mouth as she pranced naked around the room and danced to a slow hypnotic groove. She made a mental note to perform for him once he got back from Washington; it was high time they brought the sizzle back to their relationship, because she couldn't go much longer without having sex. Though she had no problem bringing herself to a pleasurable climax, there was nothing like the heat from a man's body between her legs.

Ariel walked back to the bed and put on a strapless bra to harness her lethal arsenal, but it only enhanced her cleavage. After dressing, she looked into the mirror and noticed that the neckline revealed too much of the rose tattoo on her left breast.

She had gotten the tattoo while in college when it seemed like such a cool thing to do, when everyone on campus was getting either tattoos or navel rings. Now she regretted the positioning of the rose, because it limited the type of necklines she could wear. In the corporate world, it was anything but cool to expose such a personal statement, which was why she wore buttoned-up blouses and turtlenecks most of the time. But in private, most of her lovers were drawn to the lifelike flower, and loved to touch and kiss the surreal petals.

She readjusted the dress so the rose was covered, but the neckline was still too deep. Unlike her business suits, Ariel didn't have any conservative evening gowns. Usually she attended black-tie functions with Preston, and he liked to show her off (like most men who paraded their women around like trophies). She would just have to wrap the gown's matching scarf around her neck to conceal the tattoo and her cleavage. She then sat at the vanity and expertly applied her makeup, and spritzed her wrists and neck with her favorite scent, ENJOY.

Once she was powered and primped, she made her way downstairs to the waiting Towncar. She had decided to tell the escort service that she would pick up her "date" in front of The W Hotel on Lexington Avenue, which was just around the corner from the Waldorf. Even though Meri gave the service high marks, Ariel was still a little skeptical. She didn't want him to meet her at her apartment building just in case he was some nut job who stalked women for sport. She'd recently heard on the news that a delivery guy from a grocery service was arrested for stalking his female customers. But on the other hand, she didn't want him to meet her at the hotel, because it would be obvious that they had not come together, and that was the whole point in hiring an escort in the first place.

As the car cruised down Lexington toward The W, she began to fidget with nervous energy. She had never even gone out on a blind date before, so meeting a stranger for a night on the town was beyond her comprehension. She suddenly thought about canceling the date and going solo. She took out her cell to call the escort service, but it was too late. The car eased to a stop in front of The W Hotel, and standing near the entrance was the finest man that she had ever laid eyes on. He was at least six four and cocoa brown, with a shaved head and a manicured goatee that framed his chiseled features perfectly. Even through his tailored tuxedo, Ariel could see that he was well toned and had broad quarterback shoulders.

He casually strolled over to the car and mouthed, "Renée?" using her middle name, which she had given the service.

Ariel cautiously rolled down the window halfway and asked,

"Mason Anthony?" The escort service had provided his name, and she wanted to make sure that he was the right person before she opened the door.

Beaming a wide smile with two rows of perfectly straight white teeth, he responded, "The one and only."

Ariel unlocked the door and let in her date. The intoxicating scent of his cologne filled the backseat of the car, tantalizing her sensory memory the moment he got in. If she was correct he was wearing Issey Miyaki, a sexy hypnotic cologne, which she loved, that Preston wore in the beginning of their relationship but had stopped wearing long ago. She took a deep whiff on the sly for a cheap thrill. Ariel's eyes fluttered, but she quickly snapped out of her reverie and went over the script with him, so he could play out his role without any glitches.

"It's common knowledge that I'm dating someone else, but at the moment he happens to be out of town; that's why I needed an escort for the evening," she said, feeling the need to explain her situation so he wouldn't think that she was some desperate chick looking for love. "I'm going to introduce you as a friend of the family, who happens to be in town for a conference, and—"

He interrupted, "What type of conference?"

"Hmm." She hadn't given that little detail much thought. "A medical conference. The medical profession should be safe, since most of the people in the room will be legal types."

He chuckled slightly. "Actually, that's perfect."

"And why is that?" she asked, looking confused.

"Because I'm a third-year medical student at Columbia, so that won't be a stretch," he said confidently.

Ariel gave him a look of disbelief, as if she was having a hard time swallowing his story. He looked more like a model than a med student. "And I suppose you're working as an escort to pay for school?" she asked skeptically.

"I know it sounds like a cliché, but it's true. I don't want to be saddled with a ton of student loans once I finish school, and the service pays me a nice salary for a few hours of work." Actually, the service only paid him a minimum wage, but some of the more generous clients made up the difference with a hefty tip at the end of an enjoyable evening.

Ariel winced at the mention of money. She had shelled out a cool five hundred dollars for the pleasure of his company. Though she could more than afford the fee, the thought of paying for a date made her cringe. "Glad I could contribute to your education," she said with a sarcastic edge. "Anyway, just remember that you're a friend of the family who happens to be a doctor from Chicago," she reminded him again.

He could sense that she was uneasy and put his hand lightly on her knee. "Don't worry, I won't forget. I'm a professional, remember?" He winked.

Ariel felt a jolt of electricity surge through her body at his touch; she imagined his hand roaming up her thigh, only stopping once he found her pleasure point. Her heart began to beat a little faster at the delicious thought. "Get a grip," she told herself. Though he looked good enough to eat, he was a platonic escort, not a gigolo lover.

The limousine rounded the corner onto Park Avenue and filed in line behind at least a dozen other black Towncars that were headed for the same destination. Ariel clutched her bejeweled Judith Lieber evening bag as the driver parked in front of the gold-toned ornate entrance to the landmark Waldorf-Astoria hotel.

Mason opened the door and reached inside for Ariel's hand to help her out of the car. Once inside, he held her by the elbow, like a perfect gentleman, as they made their way up the grand staircase toward the party. The elegant ballroom was abuzz with a healthy majority of New York's philanthropic community dressed in their finest. The men wore the customary penguin suits, sans tails, while the women were draped in ice and donning one-of-a-kind designer originals from Valentino, Krizia, and even vintage Coco Chanel.

Meri made her way through the throng of people with her date in tow. "Darling, there you are. I was beginning to think that you changed your mind," she said.

Ariel air-kissed her friend on the cheek. "We were caught in traffic." Ariel noticed Meri eyeing Mason and decided to rehearse the spiel on her friend before going cold turkey. "Meri, I'd like to introduce you to Dr. Mason Anthony, a friend of the family," she said with a straight face.

Meri extended her hand as if she expected him to kiss it. "Nice to meet you, Doctor." She winked, and then turned to her date. "And may I introduce my dear friend Jean-Marie Baptize, from Paris," she said, referring to the handsome European standing close by her side.

"Bonjour," he greeted them in a heavy accent.

Ariel wondered if he was actually from France, or a dial-a-date. There was no doubt that he was from a foreign country, or was he? Reflecting on the conversation she had had with Meri earlier in the week, she assumed not. "Nice to meet you."

"Let's find our seats," Meri said, leading the way through the crowd.

En route to their table, Ariel ran smack-dab into Bob, one of the managing partners from the office. "Wow . . ." His eyes drifted from her face directly to her plunging neckline. "You look amazing."

Her colleagues were accustomed to seeing her all buttoned-up and straitlaced. Suddenly she felt self-conscious, and she was sure that he could see the outline of the rose tattoo. "Hello, Bob," she said, readjusting the scarf around her neck.

Though the scarf covered most of her cleavage, Bob still seemed to be mesmerized by her ample breasts, and he licked his bottom lip as if he could taste the forbidden fruit. "I'm so glad you could make it out tonight." He grinned.

I just bet you are, she thought. "Bob, you know Mrs. Meri Renick, a good friend of mine and last year's chairwoman," she said, redirecting the conversation.

He snapped out of his lust-induced trance. "Meri, it's so nice to see you again. How have you been?"

"Fine, thank you. How's your wife?" she asked, reminding him that he was a married man and shouldn't be ogling her best friend.

"She's fine." He quickly glanced around the room, making sure his wife hadn't caught his wandering eye. He turned back to Ariel and looked at Mason. "And where's Preston?" he asked.

"He's in Washington on business." Sensing that Bob was waiting for an introduction, she said, "May I introduce Dr. Anthony, a friend of the family. He's in town for a medical conference and lucky for me, he agreed to fill in for Preston."

"Nice to meet you," Mason said, shaking Bob's hand.

Bob shook his hand in return, then said, "Well we better be seated before the presentation starts."

In a sense, Ariel was glad that Bob had been overwhelmed by her breasts, because his preoccupation kept him from asking a million and one questions about her date. They found their table and settled in for a long evening of cocktails, dinner, and mundane speeches on the importance of giving back to the community.

Three hours and four bottles of wine later, they were as giddy as a couple of kids on prom night. "That wasn't so bad, was it?" Meri asked, giggling, once the last speaker stepped down from the podium.

Ariel glanced at her date and thought that the evening had gone quite well. No one had suspected the truth, and if they did, they didn't let on. It made her wonder how many other women in the room had hired an escort for the evening. "Painless." She smiled.

"Let's go over to the Four Seasons for a nightcap," Meri suggested.

"I think I'm going to call it a night. I've had a long week and I'm bushed," Ariel said, declining the offer. Then, as if on cue, Mason got up and slid back her chair.

Meri clung to her date's arm. "Come on, darling, I have a chilled bottle of Cristal at my penthouse and we can cap the night off in private," she said suggestively.

"As you wish, *mon chéri*," Jean Marie replied in his thick French accent, kissing the back of Meri's hand.

Ariel's earlier assumption was correct. Mr. Frenchman was indeed on the clock, and knowing Meri, he would be working overtime tonight. "I'll call you tomorrow," Ariel said, before turning to leave.

The limousine driver had timed their departure perfectly, and was pulling up in front of the hotel the moment they stepped through the revolving doors.

"Can I drop you somewhere?" Ariel asked Mason.

"Just take me back to The W, if you don't mind. I'm meeting a friend there."

Ariel wondered if he was going on another date, or just having a casual drink at the Whiskey Bar. "Sure, no problem." She looked into his brown eyes. "And, Mason, thanks for a lovely evening."

"It was my pleasure, Ms. Vaughn." He smiled warmly.

"Please call me Renée."

He reached inside his breast pocket and took out a business card. "Renée." He said her name slowly, letting the syllables roll off of his tongue. "What a beautiful name for such a beautiful woman."

Her cheeks warmed from the compliment and she blushed. "Thank you, Mason."

He slid the card into her hand. "If you're ever in the need for more than an escort, please call the number on the back and tell them that I referred you."

Ariel didn't know what to say, so she just said, "Thanks."

Before getting out of the car, Mason brushed the side of her face with a soft kiss. "Take care, Renée."

Ariel put her hand to her cheek once he was gone and savored the feeling of his touch. His parting words rang in her ear, and she looked down at the business card he had given her. The front was highly glossed in black with a picture of a door, and nothing else. She flipped the card over, and on the back was a telephone number embossed in scarlet lettering. "What a unique-looking card." She fingered the smooth surface of the card and thought about throwing it away, but slid it into her purse instead.

MASON BREEZED through the lobby of The W as if he were the owner of the trendy boutique hotel. He bypassed the Whiskey Bar on the left, where singles mingled trying to pick up fresh meat for the evening, and the Lobby Bar on the right, where out-of-town businessmen huddled over cocktails, and made a bee-line straight to the bank of elevators that led to the guest quarters. Alone in the elevator on the ride up, he retrieved a key card from the breast pocket of his tuxedo jacket, looked down at the piece of plastic, and fingered it lightly.

Earlier that evening before his date with Ariel, he had gotten a call from another date. Well, it really wasn't a date, per se. She was an old client who was in town for the weekend. Mason had just stepped out of the shower when his cell phone rang.

"Well, hello there," she whispered seductively into the receiver.

Not recognizing the voice, he looked at the caller ID, but didn't recognize the phone number either. "Hello yourself," he said in a deep baritone voice, trying to hide his uncertainty.

"Do you still look as good as you sound?" she asked, wasting no time.

Mason half smiled and unconsciously ran his hand across his ripped abs. "Even better."

"I'd like to be the judge of that," she said, with an overtly sexual innuendo.

"Is that right?" He grinned.

"That's absolutely right. I remember the first time I gave you the once-over. You had just started working at The Black Door and were as green as The Incredible Hulk." She chuckled slightly.

The moment she mentioned The Black Door, he knew exactly who was on the other end of the phone.

IT HAD BEEN his first week working as a "server" at the club. Though he had had several lovers in his lifetime, this was the first time that he was being paid to perform and the thought made him a little nervous. Rock, a seasoned server, was showing him the ropes when two older women came into the Leopard Bar, one of the club's signature lounges. Mason notice how her peachy pale skin was in stark contrast to the flowing black chiffon chemise that she wore. Her platinum blonde hair was cut short, which enhanced the black mask with paved crystals. And to complete the look, she wore a pair of black stilettos. She was a combination of sex, sophistication, and class, and he noticed her immediately.

Nodding in her direction, Mason asked Rock, "Who's that?"

"She's one of our elite clients from out of town, and every time she comes into the city, she pays us a visit. From what I hear she's married to a powerful bigwig and has big bucks."

Since Mason was a struggling student on a budget, his ears instantly perked up at the mere mention of cash. She wasn't in his age range, but her body was tight nonetheless. Besides, he thought that if he could get her interested, then she would request him whenever she came to The Black Door. And a request meant that he was in demand, which translated to more hours at the club, which translated to more income coming in. "Between you and me, I bet I can help Mrs. Big Bucks part with some of that discretionary cash," he said half jokingly.

"Go for it, stud," Rock said, egging him on.

Not one to back down from a challenge, Mason casually strolled up to the bar where she and her friend were sitting having a drink. Though he was a newbie, Mason knew that his toned body was perfect and that he could please his partner in more ways than one. Once he was within earshot he deepened his baritone voice into an even lower register and said, "Ladies."

Hearing the sexy voice behind them, they both swiveled around at the same time to see who owned the seductive Barry White voice.

"Well hello," she spoke up first, checking out his exposed six-pack and the silk G-string, which showcased his well-defined manhood.

Mason watched as she surveyed his body. The way her eyes roamed up and down his muscular frame, he knew without a doubt that he had piqued her curiosity and that she was indeed interested. He wasted no time sidling up to her side, and purposefully positioned himself so that his groin lightly touched her outer thigh. "Let me order you another cocktail," he said, noticing that her glass was nearly empty.

"Only if you will have a drink with us," she answered.

"And have him come over to keep me company," her friend added, motioning to Mason's mentor.

"Sure," he said, and waved Rock over.

Once the two men were standing side-by-side, the women sized them both up as if trying to decide who would make a better lover. Mason knew the drill and flexed his pectorals, then tightened his abdominals so that his six-pack instantly transformed into an eight-pack.

His intended prey reached out and touched the ripples punctuating his stomach, gasping slightly at his hard midsection. She turned to her friend and smiled. "This one is mine," she said, running her manicured nails up and down his Herculean arm.

Knowing that he had won the unofficial contest, Mason wasted no time showing her that she had made the right decision. "Come on, let's go to a booth," he said, taking her hand and leading her to the back of the bar where they could have some privacy. The rear of the lounge was extremely dark, which allowed clients the freedom to get wild without an audience.

"So . . ." she slipped her hand in between his legs once they were seated. "Are you padded?"

Mason knew that some of the servers used tube socks as padding to fill out their G-string, but Mother Nature had supplied him with enough "padding" for two men. He took her hand and guided it inside of his waistband. "Does this feel artificial to you?"

A slight gasp escaped her lips as her hand settled on his heated mound of rising flesh. She instinctively began massaging his semi-erect penis until it responded to her touch. "I want to feel all ten inches inside of me," she said when he was fully erect.

Mason lifted her dress to find that she wasn't wearing any underwear. He then slowly rubbed his middle finger against the tip of her clitoris; with her low moans, he could tell that he had hit her sweet spot. Her moans were barely audible, but he wanted to make her scream so that she'd be his personal client. Maybe if he was lucky, she'd forgo coming to the club when in town, and come straight to him instead. Mason pushed the table back slightly so that he could ease down between her legs. Once on his knees, he began sucking on her engorged clit and at the same time fingering her pussy until he heard her breath quicken and her moans get louder. He looked up at her for that knowing look of approval, and sure enough her face told the story—her eyes were closed, her mouth was open, and her tongue was licking her bottom lip—the story of a woman who was on the verge of a climax. "Cum for me baby," he demanded.

She didn't say a word, just grabbed hold of his shaved head and jutted her hips farther out so that his finger went deeper into her pussy.

"I'm going to give you the best finger fuck you ever had." He then put three fingers inside of her hungry vagina and began pumping faster and faster until he could feel her juices oozing out.

"Oh, yeah, that's it, that's it! I'm ... I'm ... cum*ing*!" she screamed.

Damn, that was quick. If she's this easy to please, then I know she'll have me on speed dial once she gets a taste of Mr. Big, Mason thought, and smiled slyly.

That was a few years ago before he stopped working inside The Black Door to concentrate on med school. But he was right, once he laid the soul pole on Mrs. Big Bucks, she was hooked and called him whenever she came to New York. He hadn't seen her in a while and then she'd suddenly stopped calling. He thought that maybe her husband had gotten wind of her secret member-ship to The Black Door and put an end to her scandalous New York outings.

"I HAVEN'T HEARD from you in so long, I thought you had for-gotten about me."

"How could I forget about you and Mr. Big?" she said, with lust in her voice. "I'm in town for the weekend, and would love to get reacquainted with you guys. What are you doing this evening?"

A smile brightened Mason face. He had just emptied his bank account paying for tuition and could surely use one of her generous tips. "I have an appointment earlier this evening, but I should be done by ten at the latest. Where are you staying?"

"At The W Hotel on Lexington, room 916."

"That's perfect. Leave the key card at the front desk with my name on it, and I'll be there as fast as I can."

"Good, because we have a lot of catching up to do," Mrs. Big Bucks purred into the phone.

After his date with Ariel, Mason made a beeline to the hotel and up to her suite. He inserted the key card and let himself inside. He looked around the dimly lit living-room area and could see that she had ordered (and drunk) a bottle of Dom Perignon, which sat empty, upside down in the champagne bucket. Looking at the evidence, he knew that she was liquored up and waiting in the bedroom to get fucked, so he began to get ready for "work." He kicked off his tuxedo loafers, unbuckled his belt, and slipped out of his pants and boxers. He then unfastened the studs on his shirt and removed his Cartier cuff links (a gift from a client). Standing there in the buff, Mason looked down at Mr. Big, who wasn't so big in his sleeping position. "Wake up, man, you got work to do," he whispered into the air. Since she hadn't seen him in a while, he wanted to make sure to rock her world the second he stepped into her lair, so he grabbed his dick and began stroking it until it jetted out like a lightning rod. "Now we're ready." He smiled and strutted down the short hallway to the bedroom.

"It's about time you got here," she said, sounding annoyed once he entered the room. She was lying on the bed, wearing only a necklace.

Mason's eyes zeroed in on the necklace, and he figured that it must have been at least ten carats or more. *Damn, she got it like that?* he thought. He knew that her husband was rich, but he didn't realize how rich until now.

"Nice necklace," he said, commenting on the bling adorning her neck.

She fingered the exquisite piece, and said, "Thanks. It was an anniversary gift from my husband."

"That's nice, but I got an even better gift," he said, stroking Mr. Big.

She spread her legs. "Well get over here and give it to me."

In two steps Mason was across the room and on top of her. He pushed her thighs apart and entered her with such force that she ran her fingernails down his back, puncturing his skin. From past experiences, he knew that she liked it rough. She'd told him on more than one occasion that she liked it hard and fast, and tonight he'd give the lady in the diamond necklace just want she wanted.

MERI RENICK had to be the wealthiest woman that Ariel knew. She not only married well, but also parlayed her first divorce settlement into several lucrative real estate investments. And when her second husband died, leaving her hundreds of millions, that fortune only added to her "Trump" money. Ariel was having lunch at Meri's lavish Park Avenue penthouse for an afternoon of girly chitchat.

The doorman knew Ariel well since she came to visit on a regular basis. "Good afternoon, Ms. Vaughn," he said, tipping the bib of his cap.

"Hi, Frank, how's your family?"

"Fine, thanks. My son is on his way to college and my youngest just finished first grade." He laughed.

"Now that's what I call a wide spread!" She smiled.

"Keeps me young." He grinned. "I'll tell Ms. Renick you're on the way up."

"Thanks, Frank."

Ariel rode to the twenty-first floor, and when the elevator opened, a tall handsome gentleman with a black briefcase was waiting by the doors and startled her. There were only two apartments per floor, and it didn't take a rocket scientist to guess that he had come from Meri's lair.

"Excuse me," he said, as he brushed past her onto the waiting elevator.

Ariel nodded in return and made her way to Meri's apartment. "I think you need a revolving door," she said, once her friend opened the door.

Meri chuckled, knowing exactly what Ariel was alluding to. "Ironic you should mention that. I've already called the contractor and he's starting construction on the new door tomorrow."

"Ha-ha, very funny."

Ariel walked through the opulent marble foyer into the adjoining living room. After her husband died, Meri had the masculine wood-paneled living area completely gutted. The result was a feminine, ultramodern, stark-white palace with crystal accents throughout. "What did Jacques whip up today? I'm starving." Like most wealthy New Yorkers, Meri had a complete staff that included a chef, a housekeeper, and a driver.

"Grilled ahi tuna over field greens, and—"

Before Meri could finish, Ariel turned up her nose at the ultrahealthy Atkins-like fare. She was a big girl and loved to eat, and couldn't understand all the hoopla over a few simple high-calorie pleasures like potatoes, pasta, and bread. Growing up with a house full of foster siblings, Ariel had to fight for every morsel, and she vowed that once she grew up, she'd never deprive herself of a meal, no matter how many calories she consumed.

"You can get that silly look off of your face. I know how you love your carbs, so I had Jacques mash up a few potatoes with fresh garlic and tons of butter just like you like them. But I'm sticking to the tuna and a salad." She smoothed her stomach. "I've got to keep my girly figure, so the boys won't stray."

"And I take it that was one of your 'boys' I saw at the elevator?"

Meri walked over to the cocktail buffet. "No, it wasn't." She poured them each a dirty martini. "Actually, he was from Harry Winston; he came by to pick up my jewelry from last night. And speaking of last night . . ." She turned around and gave Ariel a devilish look.

"What about last night?" Ariel smirked. She knew exactly what Meri was getting at, but remained coy.

"How was your 'date'?" she asked, handing Ariel a chilled martini with three blue-cheese-stuffed olives.

She took a sip of her drink and said over the edge of the glass, "Oh, you mean Dr. Anthony?"

"Doctor my ass! But I like the cover; I've got to use that one. Didn't I tell you that that escort service was the best?" She sat on the sofa with drink in hand. "They have some of the hottest men I've ever seen." She bit down on her bottom lip for emphasis. "And that 'doctor' of yours was a hottie."

"And smart too," Ariel added. "He's actually a medical student, and is just working as an escort part-time to pay for school."

"Aren't they all?" Meri smirked. "That's nice, but I want some juicy details. How did the night end? Did he try to seduce you? Or better yet, did you try to seduce him?" she asked, relaxing back on the overstuffed cushions, readying herself for a blow-by-blow recap of the evening.

"Not everybody kisses and tells," Ariel teased.

"You live vicariously though me all the time—"

Ariel cut her off. "That's only because you eagerly volunteer to tell me *all* of the intimate details about your dates."

"Well, be that as it may, now it's finally my turn to sit back and

listen since you had a hot date for once, instead of spending another boring evening with boring Preston."

"Preston is not boring. He's just busy, that's all." Ariel had had
her share of young, good-looking men, and they always seemed to
disappoint her in one way or another, but Preston was her rock.
Even though he was preoccupied with his career, she could count
on him to always be there. And growing up without a father, she
wanted and needed the constant stability that he provided.

"Busy? Boring? What's the difference?" She reached over and
nudged Ariel on the knee. "Come on, tell me, did you kiss those
luscious lips and feel him up?"

Ariel laughed slightly. "Meri, you're one old horny broad."

"What can I say? Sex keeps me young. You should try it sometimes; now stop stalling and give up the details."

"He kissed me, but only on the cheek," she reached inside her
purse, "and then gave me this, and said to call if I wanted more
than an escort." She handed Meri the card.

At the sight of the glossy black business card, a wide, devilish
grin spread across Meri's face. "Oh, yes, The Black Door."

Ariel watched Meri's expression and was now more curious
than ever. "What's The Black Door?"

"The question should be, What isn't The Black Door?" Meri
answered, raising her perfectly arched brow.

Ariel looked confused. "What do you mean?"

"Hold on to your platinum and pearls, because what I'm about
to tell you will probably send you into shock."

"Stop the dramatics and just tell me."

"It's a club," she said mysteriously.

The suspense was killing Ariel. "What type of club?"

"An adults-only club for women."

"You mean a strip club, like Chippendales?"

Meri drained the last of her drink, as if she needed the alcohol to help her explain the uniqueness of the club. "Chippendales is child's play compared to The Black Door. First of all, it's for members only, but not everyone is accepted. You have to be referred. They do a thorough background check, to make sure you're not an undercover policewoman, and then they give every member a blood test, to ensure that everyone is healthy and disease free."

"Why all the precautions?" Ariel wondered.

"So the members can be free to walk on the wild side. And to ensure anonymity, everyone is fitted with a custom-designed mask."

Ariel was now perched on the edge of the sofa, her interest totally piqued, wanting to know more. "Why wear a mask, if they do such a thorough background check?"

"You see, my dear, some of wealthiest, most high-powered women in the world are members of this exclusive club, women who can afford anything under the sun, except a scandal spread across the front page of the *Post*. And with the security of a mask, they feel free to indulge in all of the various activities that the club has to offer."

"What kind of activities?" she asked, like an inquisitive schoolgirl yearning for knowledge. Ariel wasn't a prude, but had only had a handful of lovers in her lifetime, and none of them were very creative under the covers. Preston was her most passionate lover and had taught her positions that she'd never seen before, but she still felt that there was a whole world of activities and positions that she knew nothing about, and she was curious to hear all about it.

Meri hesitated for a moment. "How would I know?" she said slyly.

"Because if I had to bet, I'd say that you are a member in good standing. Now tell me what goes on at The Black Door," she said, scooting even closer to the edge of the sofa.

"Let's just say that the club offers everything from ménage à trois to lesbian liaison." She fanned her hand across her face. "To *whatever* your wildest dreams may be."

Meri's explanation knocked Ariel from her perch on the edge of the couch and sent her reeling back onto the plump cushions. "Wow," she exhaled. "I thought places like that only existed in triple-X movies."

"Well, I'm here to tell you that The Black Door is as real as it gets." She returned the card. "Keep this in a safe place, in case of a sexual emergency."

Ariel put the card on the table. "I don't need it. Preston will be home tonight to answer my nine-one-one," she said, proudly. During their lengthy relationship, Ariel had never cheated on Preston, and she didn't intend to start now.

Meri picked up the card and slid it back into Ariel's purse. "Don't be so hasty; only a few select people are offered this card. And if you're in possession of one, trust me, it's like gold."

"I'll take your word for it. Now let's eat. I'm starving."

After leaving Meri's apartment two hours later, Ariel stopped by La Perla to buy some sexy lingerie for that night. She'd planned an intimate dinner at her condo, followed by "dessert." On her way home, she ordered two meals from Table for Two, a gourmet take-out service, instead of slaving in the kitchen over a hot stove. Her next call was to Preston.

"Hey, honey, how did your meeting go yesterday with the senator?" she asked.

"Everything went fine. I'll tell you all about it tonight. I don't want to go into the details over the phone. Where do you want to go for dinner?" he asked, changing the subject.

"I thought we'd *eat* in tonight," she said with a devilish tone.

"Good idea; I'm really tired," he responded, not picking up on the double entendre.

"Not too tired, I hope," she said suggestively. "I'll see you around seven."

"Sounds good," he said, and hung up.

Once she returned home, Ariel took a long hot bath and then slipped into her new teddy. The lavender lace one-piece with spaghetti straps barely left anything to the imagination. She purposely bought the lingerie a size too small, so it tightly hugged her breasts with her nipples protruding through the thin silk fabric. Her naked, round rear end pushed through the thonged teddy; she looked in the mirror and slapped her butt.

"This big ass should reenergize him." She smiled.

The buzzer rang as she stepped into a pair of Ostrich mules and sauntered to the door.

"Wow, you look good enough to eat," he greeted her.

She did a slow pivot, so he could get the full effect. "Glad you approve."

He dropped his briefcase and grabbed her fleshy ass, pulling her in close and giving her a deep French kiss. Preston missed Ariel's kisses and the touch of her. Unlike his ex-wife, who was frigid and used sex as a manipulation tool, Ariel was just the opposite. She was always ready to please him, and he adored her spontaneity. Preston hadn't been devoting much time to their relationship as of late, because of his career, but tonight he'd planned on making up for lost time.

Ariel hungrily kissed him back, while grinding into his rising penis. She could feel him getting harder with each thrust of her tongue. She began to unbuckle his belt, ready for a night of long overdue passion. But the doorbell rang, stopping them in their tracks.

"It must be dinner." She panted. "Open the door for them; I'm going to the bathroom," she said, giving Preston one last kiss.

He straightened up his clothes. "Okay," he said, and slapped her naked butt.

When Ariel returned to the living room a few minutes later, Preston was sitting on the sofa, eating directly from the black plastic container. "I was going to serve the food on a plate," she said, tersely.

"Sorry, honey, but I'm starving. I haven't eaten since early this morning," he said, taking a large bite of filet mignon.

The last thing on Ariel's mind was food; she wanted to start where they had left off. Her juices were still flowing and the beef she wanted was between his legs, not in some plastic container. She leaned down in front of him so that her breast fell out of the teddy and swung free. "Come on, baby, nibble on these instead," she said, rubbing her nipples.

Preston looked at her and said, "I will in a minute. Now come over here and eat before the food gets cold."

Ariel tucked herself back into her teddy and plopped herself down on the couch out of frustration. She picked over her dinner, while Preston devoured his meal. He looked over at her and noticed her change in attitude. "Why aren't you eating?"

"Because I'm not hungry anymore, I'm *horny*!" she exclaimed.

"Trust me, I am too, and I promise that we'll make love all night, just let me get some nourishment in me, so that I can rock your world." He smiled and pecked her on the lips.

"Well, all right, since you put it that way," she said, and picked up her fork and began nibbling.

Preston finished eating first, and laid his head on the back of the sofa to rest his eyes for just a second, but a second turned into a minute, and before long he had nodded off into a light snore.

"I don't believe this shit!" she fumed, and marched into the bedroom, leaving him sprawled out on the couch.

Ariel reached for her purse on the nightstand to get out her pillbox. Preston had given her a headache, and she needed a Motrin to quell the throbbing. She reached into the purse and her hand brushed across a piece of paper. She took out the paper and it was the card for The Black Door. She turned it over and stared at the telephone number on the back. Suddenly, Meri's words, "for a sexual emergency," rang in her ears. Ariel clicked on her cell phone and carefully dialed each scarlet number.

5

"THESE JUST came in, boss," Joe said, standing in the doorway cradling a large cardboard box in his muscular arms. "Where you want 'em?"

Trey looked up from the mound of paperwork on his desk and pointed to an empty chair in front of him. "You can put it right there. Thanks, Joe."

The buff workman nodded. "No problem, boss," he said, and then made a swift exit, leaving Trey to his work.

TREY CURTIS WAS the founder and sole owner of The Black Door. Had someone told him five years ago that he'd be running the most successful private club in the Tri-State area, he would have outright laughed in their face. At the time he had been reluctantly entering the family business. Ever since he could recognize the human voice, it was drilled into him that he would one day work side-by-side with his father. Creative at his very core, Trey had no interest in running a boring business. In high school his studio art teacher sent his portfolio of unique jewelry designs to Pratt Institute for scholarship consideration. And with a 4.0 grade-point average and a creative edge, Trey was offered a four-year scholarship to the alma mater of some of the world's leading fashion designers. He had visions of blazing his own entrepreneurial trail by opening a design house on trendy Fifth Avenue after graduation.

Once Trey announced his plans to change career paths, his father quickly snuffed out those dreams by reminding him of his family obligations. His father was the typical patriarch—domineering and overbearing—and ran a tight household. Most of the time it was either his way or no way. Trey's mother had tried to intervene on his behalf and persuade her husband to let their son follow his own dreams, but his father just wouldn't hear of it. "Since we have no other children, who's going to inherit the business?" his father would say in response.

So to keep the peace, Trey put his dreams of designing ice, on ice, declined the scholarship, and majored in marketing at Yale. He then entered Georgetown, his father's alma mater, for graduate school. Armed with a bevy of impressive degrees, Trey entered the workforce with as much gusto as he could muster under the circumstances. Every day walking into the solemn offices felt like walking toward the guillotine, toward a life where he was cut off from his creative soul. On the one hand, Trey felt as if he weren't being true to himself by abandoning his dreams. But on the other hand, he wanted to honor his family's legacy, so he endured the mundane drudgery. But in the back of his mind he was always working on an exit strategy to leave and pursue a more creative career path.

The days quickly turned into months, and as the months melted into years, Trey found joy wherever he could, which was usually at the upscale gentleman's clubs throughout the city. Over the years he noticed the clientele of the clubs change from male executives with fat expense accounts to female execs wielding platinum cards of their own. The women seemed to enjoy the strippers just as much as the men—if not more—especially the private lap dances.

Trey sat on the sidelines one evening at Scores, watching a scrumptious-looking young woman maneuver her body across the stage. Dressed in a white teeny-tiny nurse's uniform, the dancer poked out her round, naked rear from underneath the hem of her skirt and individually wiggled each cheek at a rapid pace. She then bent over, allowing her enormous breasts to spill out of the deep plunging neckline, all the while mesmerizing the entire audience as she seductively stripped. She slowly peeled off every stitch of clothing until she was clad only in a sizzling red latex G-string and a pair of seven-inch Lucite platforms. She then wrapped her long legs around a highly polished silver pole in the middle of the stage and flipped her body upside down. As her silicone-free, mouthwatering breasts brushed her chin, she stuck out her tongue and began to lick her own nipples, causing the room to go wild. Tens, twenties, and hundred-dollar bills sailed through the air as if it were raining money, littering the stage as she teased the crowd.

Once the song was over, all the men lobbied to get her attention for a lap dance, but she ignored their desperate calls, and sauntered over to a group of women sitting in a corner booth sipping Moët & Chandon. She stopped in front of an attractive woman fanning a black AmEx card back and forth across her face. The stripper leaned over and whispered something into the woman's ear and the woman smiled and nodded yes. As another song began to play, the stripper danced slowly, rotating her pelvis and rubbing her hands up and down her body. The woman's eyes were transfixed on the stripper's movements. The stripper cupped her full breasts with both hands and massaged her nipples between her thumb and index finger until they firmed to her touch. The woman licked her lips as if she wanted to taste the forbidden fruit. Sensing the woman's arousal, the stripper brushed her titties back and forth against the woman's face, positioning her erect nipples directly on the woman's bottom lip. She stared deep into the woman's eyes, silently inviting her to feast on her 38-Ds. Unable to resist the temptation any longer, the woman slowly parted her lips and seductively trailed the outline of the stripper's areolas with the tip of her tongue. Feeling prying eyes on her, the woman suddenly stopped, as if embarrassed.

With a massive hard-on, Trey watched in amazement as the patron flipped the script and teased the stripper. A kernel of an idea began to sprout as he observed the other women in the booth discreetly vie for the stripper's attention. There were plenty of strip clubs that catered to men, but not one that solely focused on women. Taking in the scene before him, Trey realized that women were just as freaky as men were. This was the first time he had witnessed a bisexual interaction between two women and his mind began to click with ideas. What if he opened a private club for women only, where they were free to indulge in carnal pleasures without judgment?

The following day Trey did some research and found that no high-end clubs of that nature existed in the city. Now he was totally psyched, and felt as if he had a new lease on life. With a business of his own, he'd no longer have to live in the shadow of his father. He'd finally be his own man! But in a sense he was still living a lie, because he couldn't come right out and tell his father that he was opening an erotica club for women. Though strips clubs were totally legal, he knew without a doubt that his family would strongly disapprove and order him to abandon the idea altogether, so Trey decided to keep his mouth shut until the timing was right.

He'd been saving money to invest in real estate and had a siz-
able sum tucked away. He called his broker and told him that he
was in the market for a three-story building, preferably in Washington Heights, the neighborhood located above Harlem that was
still primarily uninhabited by the yuppies who were moving north
in droves. He wanted the club to slide under the radar (since more
than stripping would be going on), and thought that if it was located in a low-key area it wouldn't draw any unwanted attention.
Within weeks the agent had found the perfect property, a nondescript brownstone on a quiet block. Trey emptied his savings account for the renovations and within a few months, what was a
shell of a building was now a majestic den of iniquity. The only
change he made to the facade was to add an oak door painted a
glossy black, but he spared no expense on the interior. The foyer
was papered in exquisite gold leaf imported from Florence, with an
eight-tier crystal chandelier overhead. Instead of the usual bright
white bulbs, however, the light fixture was equipped with cobalt-
blue lights, casting a seductive glow over the entry, setting the tone
for what lay ahead. There were two parlors on the main level; one
for older women who just wanted to sip sherry in the presence of
handsome, scantily clad young men who kept their glasses filled
to the brim. The second room served as entry into the land of decadence. Equipped with a secret staircase that led upstairs to the
serious activities, this room—with its champagne and caviar bar,
and ornate gold vodka fountain that spewed ice-cold Belvedere—
prepared members for an unforgettable evening of carnal pleasures.

Initially Trey operated the club at night while he kept his day
job, but all that changed when his father decided to sell the business to a huge conglomerate, saying that the timing and the money
were right. Trey was shocked but pleased because he'd get a chunk
of the proceeds.

With his days of boring office work behind him, he was now free to devote his full attention to The Black Door. To ensure members' anonymity, Trey came up with the brilliant idea to design an elaborate mask for each member. He met with each new member personally to get a sense of her character, and then designed a mask based on her hidden personality. Some women portrayed a delicate flower to the world, while deep inside there was a tigress waiting to be unleashed. For that type he designed a mask with dramatic gold plumage trimmed with sparkling rhinestones and twinkling tiger-eye. Trey also designed a black leather mask with faceted onyx gemstones for himself for nights when he strolled through the club looking for a little excitement. He had finally found a way to combine his creative talents with his business acumen.

HE ABANDONED THE paperwork, walked over to the box sitting across from his desk, and peeked within the open flap. Inside were replacement masks for existing members, as well as masks for the new members. While Trey made the prototype, the masks were actually handmade in Chinatown by a group of Asian grandmothers. He picked up a patent-leather scarlet mask—belonging to a member in good standing—removed the plastic covering and fluffed out the crimson ostrich feathers that adorned the sides.

"Man, that's an interesting one."

Trey turned around, and standing in the doorway was one of his key employees. "Hey, man, what's up?"

Mason walked into the office and gave Trey a high-five. "Just trying to make a dollar out of fifteen cents." He laughed.

"Well, anytime you want to come back inside The Black Door, let me know. I'm still getting requests for your services. I don't know what you laid on these women, but whatever it was, they can't get enough."

"I got the magic touch." He wiggled his fingers in the air. "What can I say?"

"Say you'll come back as a server."

"Man, as much as I love the ladies." He beamed an ultrabright smile. "They were killing me. I mean, some of those old babes were worse than the younger ones. Man, they could go all night." He shook his head, thinking about his tryst the other night. "There must be some kind of female Viagra on the market that men don't know about."

"Well, it's not like you couldn't deal with the pressure. From what I've been told you more than lived up to their fantasies. I know without a doubt that the ladies would be thrilled to have you serve up more of your magic."

Mason blushed at the compliment. "Thanks for the offer, but I like being an escort; it's so much easier. I take them out, listen to their stories, provide a little innocent flirtation, end the night with a sensuous peck on the cheek, and then I'm on my merry way. Besides, being an escort gives me more time to study."

"That's right, it won't be long until I'm addressing you as Dr. Anthony."

"Trust me, it won't be soon enough. I can't wait to start making some serious dollars. This tuition is digging deep into my pockets." He wanted to add, "But I got that covered, because I have a sure thing on the side who's generous with the paper." Mason didn't want to take the chance and piss off his boss, so he kept his mouth shut. It wasn't like he was stealing from the company, but he knew that Trey wouldn't like him sexing up a client outside of the club. It really wasn't Trey's call, since clients were free to spend time with whomever they pleased.

"I bet," Trey said sympathetically. "Well, don't forget that you get a commission for any of your escorts who join The Black Door, and from the sound of it you could use the extra ends."

"Actually, that's why I dropped by. I had a client the other night who fit The Black Door specs to a tee. She's professional, sexy as hell, but more important, I sensed that she could use a good fuck. Man, this chick was wound so tight I though she was going to burst a vessel or two. When I got into the car, she had me memorize a phony background for the evening. Of course, I was the perfect gentleman in front of her perfect friends. I could tell that she enjoyed my company, and at the end of the date I gave her a card for The Black Door. And I was wondering if she called." Though Mason had his side hustle, he still wanted the referral commission. If she joined, he was entitled to his cut.

"I did have a few calls last night. What's her name?"

"Renée Vaughn."

Trey thought for a second. "No, I didn't get a call from her, but don't worry. If she's as sexually frustrated as you say, I'm sure it's just a matter of time before she crosses The Black Door's threshold."

RUSHING FROM room to room, Ariel flitted about the apartment on pure adrenaline. She had taken the afternoon off at Preston's insistence, and was trying frantically to pack for a weekend getaway to Washington. He was picking her up in twenty minutes and she still hadn't decided what to bring for their two-day tryst. She should have been upset by his last-minute invitation, but she was too excited. Preston called earlier that morning trying to redeem himself after falling asleep on Ariel a few nights ago, saying he wanted to make it up to her with a weekend filled with candlelight dinners and plenty of lovemaking. This would be a chance for them to spend some much-needed quality time together. So Ariel eagerly grabbed his olive branch with both hands, wanting desperately to revive their stalled love life. Preston had an eight o'clock breakfast meeting with Senator Oglesby on Saturday, but the afternoons and nights were all hers. And she planned to make the most of their forty-eight-hour rendezvous, so she decided to pack two of Preston's favorites, a fuchsia silk teddy with a French cut and matching ostrich feather high-heeled slippers.

As she continued to pack, a sense of relief washed over her because she hadn't actually gone through with her call to The Black Door. Once she dialed the number and the phone began to ring, she panicked and quickly hung up before anyone answered. She realized that call was just a knee-jerk reaction to Preston's lack of attention. Now that she was back on the front page of his agenda, she could toss out the number to the club and dismiss her fleeting fantasy of becoming a member.

Ariel's cell phone rang just as she tucked a pair of black stilettos into her overnight bag. "Hey, honey, where are you?" she sang into the receiver after checking the caller ID.

"Downstairs. Are you ready?" Preston huffed into the phone, as if in a serious rush.

"Ready as I'll ever be," she responded with a smile in her voice, hoping that this time he would catch the double entendre.

"Well, hurry up," he said gruffly, her suggestive remark going right over his head. "And don't bring a trunk full of clothes; we're only going to be there two days," he said, knowing that she was prone to overpack.

"Okay, okay," she said, and hung up.

Ariel zipped the oversized Prada duffel, spritzed her neck with ENJOY to arouse Preston's senses, and headed out the door. Feeling as if helium were flowing through her veins, Ariel floated to the lobby on cloud ninety-nine. She was finally going to have her man all to herself, without any unnecessary distractions, and she was beyond thrilled.

Preston's black stretch limo with its tinted windows sat curbside in front of her building. Ariel felt like Cinderella waiting to board her golden carriage. The driver promptly jumped out and greeted her with a smile, took her bag, and opened the back passenger door.

"Hey, bab—" Ariel's words caught in her throat at the sight before her. In the backseat with Preston was a young, attractive, unidentified woman, sitting dangerously close to *her man*!

"There you are. What took you so long?" Preston asked, annoyed and barely looking in her direction.

Ariel was stunned into silence. She had a million and two questions: Who the hell is this *woman*? What is *she* doing here? What about *our* romantic weekend *alone*!? But the words just wouldn't come out; they were caught somewhere between her brain and her larynx. Speechless, Ariel slipped into the backseat opposite them and watched in horror as Preston continued talking as if she weren't there.

"The senator wants to get the ball rolling posthaste, so I'll need you to compile my complete dossier." He handed the woman a yellow legal pad. "Here are a few of the milestone cases from my years on the bench, and some high-profile cases from my private practice."

The mystery woman didn't answer right away; she just shifted her eyes between Ariel and Preston, as if questioning Ariel's role.

Preston looked at her darting eyes and instantly picked up on her hesitance. He spoke up, "Michele, let me introduce Ariel Vaughn, my—"

Michele interrupted, "Your attorney, of course." Recognizing Ariel's name from the Law Review at Columbia, she smiled warmly. "I read about your appointment to partner at Yates Gilcrest; very impressive! Yates is such an old-world firm, I'm surprised that they—"

"I'm not his attorney," Ariel blurted out. "I'm Preston's girlfriend," she said in no uncertain terms, then glared at Preston for confirmation.

When Preston saw the vein sprout in the middle of Ariel's forehead—which only appeared when she was incensed—he knew she was beyond upset, and on the verge of rupturing an artery. He began to backpedal at warp speed, talking a mile a minute to avoid a confrontation. "Ariel, let me introduce Michele Richards, my new PA. She's a recent graduate of Columbia and I hired her last week to assist me with my impending Supreme Court nomination."

Ariel sat with a blank look on her face and didn't say a word; she just stared at Preston with the vein growing ever more prominent. She couldn't believe that he had hired a personal assistant without telling her beforehand. Lately it felt as if Preston was growing distant. Earlier in their relationship he discussed everything with her, from his court cases to his ex-wife; his openness was one of the qualities she loved about him. Ariel was pissed, but she didn't want to make a federal case out of his blatant omission. So she sat quietly and let her facial expression speak volumes.

Preston continued. "Ariel, you remember Judge Richards?"

She smiled slightly in agreement. Ariel had known Michael Richards since her days as a law clerk. She'd followed his career in the law journals and admired him immensely.

"Well, when Mike called and said that his little girl was looking for a job, I thought why not hire Michele as my personal assistant. Since my nomination isn't official as of yet, I have to keep things under wraps; therefore, I can't ask my secretary at the office to oversee the tedious details that precede the confirmation process, now can I?" He nodded at Ariel for her to concur, and when she didn't, he continued. "And Michele fit the bill perfectly." He grinned.

Ariel looked at the young woman's perky nipples peeking from underneath her too-tight sweater and thought, *I just bet she does!*

"Ariel knows everything there is to know about me. We have no hidden agendas between us, so please speak candidly," he instructed his new assistant.

Michele smiled halfheartedly at Ariel, glanced down at her legal pad, and began speaking as if Ariel were invisible. "After your breakfast meeting with the senator, I've scheduled a luncheon at the Ritz-Carlton in Georgetown with a few key members of the Senate Judiciary Committee. They know of your reputation, but haven't met you personally, and I thought that it would be a good idea to have an unofficial face-to-face before the games begin. It's crucial for you to befriend them and make a good impression."

Lunch meeting? Preston didn't say anything to me about a lunch meeting, Ariel thought and bit her bottom lip. She wanted Preston all to herself, and started to speak up and protest, but she didn't want to sound like some love-smitten schoolgirl. Instead, she focused her attention on the moving scenery outside the window in an attempt to block them out until they reached the airport. She assumed that Michele was only going as far as LaGuardia; then the driver would take the overly efficient assistant back to the city. Ariel put her chin in her hand and watched the cars dart back and forth in a futile attempt to jockey for position. *This isn't the way to LaGuardia,* she thought, as the driver paid a toll on the upper level of the George Washington Bridge and headed west toward New Jersey. *We must be flying out of Newark.* As the car drove farther from the city, the scenery changed from tall buildings to gray utility poles and ominous smokestacks. Ariel watched the signs whiz by, until there were only two exits before the airport, where she could escape the rattling of Preston's eager-beaver assistant. The woman had not stopped running her mouth since they left the city. She was dropping names like pebbles on a sandy beach, obviously trying to impress her new boss. Ariel crossed her legs and swung the top one back and forth in anticipation of reaching the terminal. "Newark International Airport, next exit," she read. Ariel exhaled a sigh of relief, knowing her salvation was only a few scant miles away. But before she could exhale, the limo swiftly bypassed their exit.

"Driver . . . Driver . . ." Ariel pecked repeatedly on the glass partition that separated the chauffeur from the passengers to get his attention. "You missed the exit."

He rolled down the privacy window. "Excuse me, ma'am?" the driver asked nonchalantly, in a thick southern accent.

Ariel twisted the upper half of her body toward the driver, and blurted through the partition. "You passed the exit for the airport!"

Ignoring her urgent tone, he responded, "Excuse me, ma'am, but we're not going to the airport."

"What are you talking about?" She spun around to face Preston. "Aren't we going to Washington?"

"Yes. We should be there in about three and a half hours, depending on traffic," answered the overefficient assistant.

"Three and a half hours?!" Ariel shrieked.

"Yes, barring traffic," Preston repeated calmly.

"Barring traffic?" Ariel still didn't get it. "I thought we were *flying* to D.C.?"

"We were, but Michele thought we could get more work done in the car."

"That's correct," Michele chimed in. "By the time we would've checked in and gone through security, which is extremely tight going into the nation's capital, we could've fleshed out Preston's entire agenda for his nomination."

Preston? Did she just call him Preston? Ariel was livid, and could feel the vein in the center of her forehead begin to pulsate again. *How dare this young know-it-all barge into* our *weekend, acting like she's on a first-name basis with* my man!

Ariel knew she had to set Ms. Personal Assistant straight, so there would be no misunderstanding going forward. She looked Michele dead in the eyes without blinking a lash and said in no uncertain terms, "I'm sure you meant to address *Preston* as Judge Hendricks. After all, he's going to be a justice. And first names are strictly reserved for close friends and family, of which you are neither."

Michele blinked twice, like a wide-eyed doe. "Oh . . . oh," she stammered. "I didn't mean any disrespect. It's just that we've been on a first-name basis from day one," she said, trying to explain.

Ariel flashed Preston a disapproving look, and then continued. "Well, let me clue you in on a well-known fact. Washington is all about protocol, and I suggest you become accustomed to addressing *Preston* as Judge Hendricks from here on out."

Michele didn't know what to say; she felt like her mother had just given her a tongue lashing, so she just nodded her head in agreement.

"Lighten up, Ariel. I don't mind being addressed by my first name," he said, coming to Michele's defense.

"Well, I mind." Ariel crossed her arms in front of her chest, a clear indication that she wasn't about to waver from her position.

"No problem; I totally understand," Michele cheerfully interrupted, breaking the tension. "Now where were we?" she asked, ready to continue with their strategy session.

Ariel was so mad that she wanted to stop the car and get out, but that was totally out of the question. Instead, she leaned back into the plush leather seat and closed her eyes in an attempt to block them out. Before long, she had drifted off into a deep sleep.

Her short dreams were a series of lewd sexcapades. In one dream, she was being serviced by two men, an older gentleman who licked her close to climax with his extremely long tongue, and then his partner, a younger man with a ten-inch dick, penetrated her, riding her like a thoroughbred in the Preakness until she exploded into ecstasy. In the next dream, she and Preston were naked in the back of the limo, and he was fucking her hard from behind, while a topless Michele watched from the sidelines and masturbated, waiting her turn to be fucked by Preston. That dream jolted Ariel awake and her eyes popped wide open.

"Hey, Sleeping Beauty." Preston smiled. "Are you okay?"

She looked at him oddly. "What do you mean?"

"You were moaning in your sleep like you were in pain."

The thought of her erotic dreams made her blush. "I'm fine, thanks." Ariel looked out of the window. "Are we almost there?"

"Yep, we should be pulling up to the Georgetown Hilton shortly," Michele said.

Ariel was moist and couldn't wait to get Preston alone so she could make her dreams a reality. Within fifteen minutes, the car was parking in front of the hotel.

"Wait here a few minutes while I check you guys in," Michele announced and bounced out of the car, eager to be of service.

Finally, she's making herself useful, Ariel thought and moved next to Preston. "Hey, baby." She kissed him smack on the lips. "I can't wait to get upstairs."

"Me too; I'm exhausted." He stretched his long arms and yawned.

She put her hand between his legs, found his limp manhood, and began a gentle massage. "Not too exhausted, I hope."

Preston felt a charge of electricity, but pulled away. "Stop before Michele comes back."

Ariel didn't stop; instead, she increased the pressure until she felt him grow under her touch. She clicked the automatic locks on the car door in the event Michele returned sooner than expected. She then unzipped Preston's pants, unleashing his erect penis.

"What are you doing?" Preston asked, trying in vain to protest, even though her touch felt good.

She didn't say a word, just leaned over and covered his rod with her mouth. Ariel sucked hard, while teasing the tip of his penis with her tongue.

Preston gasped, "Oh, yeah, baby." He quickly gave in to the pleasure and rotated his hips so that she could get his entire dick down her throat.

Ariel increased the pace until her head was bobbing up and down like a chicken. Just as she was close to bringing Preston to climax, Michele pulled the door handle, trying to get back into the car.

"Oh shit!" Preston jerked his cock out of Ariel's mouth. "Stop before she sees us."

"She can't see into the car; the windows are tinted, remember?" Ariel said, reaching for his still erect member. "Let her wait; I'm not finished."

Preston moved farther away and quickly tucked his dick back into his pants, straightened his tie, and unlocked the door.

Michele poked her head into the backseat and looked at them strangely, wondering why they had locked her out. She noticed that Preston looked nervous and Ariel looked frustrated, but didn't comment on whatever was going on and just said, "You're all set." She handed Preston a key card. "You're in room 25C," she told them before walking ahead.

"Thanks, Michele. See you in the morning." Preston got out of the car and then helped Ariel out.

Once they were in the room, Preston went directly over to the oak desk, opened his briefcase, and began to take out various papers. "I need to fax this over to the senator's office so he can preview it before our meeting," he explained.

"Can't Michele do that?" Ariel asked in a low tone as she unbuttoned her blouse.

"I forgot to give it to her; besides, since I have the information here I might as well do it myself," he said, inserting the first of many papers into the fax machine.

Ariel took off her blouse and slipped out of her skirt. Clad only in a thong and see-through bra she sauntered over to Preston. "Come on, baby, can't that wait for a few minutes?" She unhooked her bra, allowing her boobs to spill out. She caressed both breasts. "You haven't nibbled on these in such a long time, and they're starting to feel neglected."

Preston looked at her stiff nipples and felt his erection returning. He reached out, pulled her close, and began sucking on her nipples. He sat the sack of papers on the desk and unzipped his pants. It had been weeks since they made love and he longed to be inside of her. But the phone rang, interrupting their groove.

"Let it ring; whoever it is will call back," Ariel said into his ear.

He was tempted to let the answering service pick up the call, but he just couldn't. "I need to answer it, it might be the senator."

"Calling this late?" Ariel asked, wrinkling her brow.

"I'm sorry, honey, but I need to pick it up just in case," he said, pushing her slightly away. "Hello? Yes, I have them right here," he said, turning around and picking up the document. "No . . . that's okay, I'll fax them myself. Okay, see you in the morning." He turned back to Ariel, who was standing with her arms crossed in front of her chest. "That was Michelle, she—"

"I heard," she said, cutting him off.

"Don't get mad, honey, but I really do need to fax this document over. The senator needs it for our meeting in the morning," he said, returning his attention to the task at hand.

Ariel was trying to be patient, but the document was at least twenty-five pages long, and it was taking forever, and the fact that the fax machine was outdated didn't help either. After fifteen minutes, he was finally done, and Ariel assumed that they were going to pick up where they had left off, but Preston reached for the phone and began dialing.

"Who are you calling, now?"

"Michele, to ask her how to print out a confirmation receipt. I want to make sure the document was received on the other end."

Ariel walked over to the machine and looked at the various buttons. This fax machine was different from the one in her office, and she had no idea how to get the report. She began pressing one button after the other, but nothing happened, then suddenly the thing began beeping loudly.

"What did you do?" Preston asked, seemingly annoyed.

"I was trying to get the confirmation report, but I must have hit the wrong button," she said, still jabbing at the machine.

"Michele, can you come up here? We have a problem," he yelled into the receiver over the noise.

"We don't need her, I'll just turn the thing off," Ariel said, looking for the power switch. The last person she wanted to see was Preston's new assistant.

"You better put some clothes on, she'll be here in a few minutes," he said, hanging up the phone and zipping up his pants.

Watching Preston regain his composure, Ariel suddenly felt dirty, standing there looking like a naked hooker, like Eve trying to entice Adam with the forbidden apple. She covered her exposed breasts with both arms. "Maybe I should just go back home, and let you concentrate on your work. I feel like I'm in the way."

"You're not in the way, honey. I just need to focus on the meetings Michele has set up for this weekend. I know I promised you a romantic getaway, and initially I was only meeting with the senator, but Michele was able to set up a few lunch meetings," he said apologetically.

"Had I known you were going to be busy twenty-four/seven I would have stayed home." This was new territory for Ariel. Throughout their relationship Preston had treated her like a princess, doting on her and giving her his undivided attention. Now his "princess" seemed to be impeding his work. Even though she knew how important sitting on the bench was to Preston, she was still a little envious of all the attention he was giving to the process.

A feeling of neglect washed over Ariel, and suddenly she felt like a little girl again. She would get this same feeling whenever her foster mother spent more time with the latest addition to the family instead of her. Ariel picked her clothes off of the floor and went into the bedroom. She decided to go back to New York and scheduled a flight for the following morning. Part of her—the mature professional—understood Preston's ambition, but another part of her—the insecure kid—wanted his undivided attention. Since she couldn't have it both ways, she thought it best to leave so that he could concentrate on the true reason for his visit.

THE PHONE WAS ringing as Ariel stepped through her front door back in New York. Thinking that it was Preston, she quickly snatched the receiver off of its base.

"Hello?"

"Where's the fire?" Meri asked, picking up on her overanxious tone.

"Oh, hi, Meri," she said despondently, disappointed that it wasn't Preston.

"Oh, hi, Meri? Is that any way to greet your old friend? What's wrong?" Meri asked, instinctively detecting trouble in paradise.

"Nothing much," she responded lamely.

"Oh, don't give me that. Something's wrong. I can hear it in your voice."

"It's just that Preston is so busy that he doesn't have much time for me anymore." Ariel went on the tell Meri the details of the previous day and about his new assistant."

"Darling, you need to release the sexual pressure that's been building up for months and join The Black Door. That way you'll give Preston the space he wants, while satisfying your needs at the same time."

Ariel thought about it for a moment. "I can't cheat on Preston, it's just not right."

"Well, at least go and see a little eye candy. Sounds like Preston is getting an eyeful with his sex-kitten assistant strutting around."

"You have a point, but I can't go through that rigorous screening process, especially now that Preston is trying to get on the Supreme Court. The last thing I need is for the investigators to uncover my membership in a sex club. First there was Nanny-Gate, and I would hate for there to be a Sex-Gate because of me. That little discovery would surely destroy his chances."

"Hmmm," Meri said while thinking. "I have the perfect idea. Since all of the members wear masks to conceal their faces, why don't you borrow mine and go to the club disguised as me?"

"Are you sure?"

"Of course I'm sure. That's the perfect solution. Right now, you need the services of the club more than I do. I'm going to have my mask messengered over to you today, along with my password and the address of the club. All you have to do is give the password at the door and you're in like Flynn."

Ariel was a bit reluctant, but too horny to decline her friend's generous offer. Seeing a room full of sexy men was probably all she needed to cool her jets until Preston returned his focus to her. "Thanks, Meri."

"Don't thank me now. Thank me after your first visit."

Ariel was filled with nervous energy and began to pace the floor as she waited for her special delivery.

ARIEL COULDN'T believe she was standing in the dimly lit foyer of The Black Door. She had crossed the infamous threshold and was on the verge of entering the main parlor. Meri had tucked a note inside the box along with her patent leather, scarlet mask, explaining the club's layout. She wrote that the entry to the second floor, where carnal festivities took place, was located in the parlor on the left, behind a pair of ruby-colored velvet drapes.

Her nerves were racing a mile a minute, and the beefy doorman, sensing her trepidation, tried to relax her with a little digital stimulation before she entered the main room. He walked up close from behind and gently ran his hand up and down her exposed thigh. At first Ariel flinched from his unexpected touch, but the more he rubbed the more she began to enjoy the feel of his warm hand on her skin. Once she was totally comfortable with his stroking, he moved his hand from her thigh to her thong, but he didn't stop there. Before she could protest his thick fingers were inside of her underwear, playing with her clit. She wanted to yell *Stop*, but his touch felt too good—it wasn't too rough or too gentle, it was just right. She closed her eyes and enjoyed the sensation. Once she was near orgasm, he whispered in her ear, "Now you're ready for The Black Door."

Once he released her, Ariel felt lightheaded from the surprise greeting and staggered toward the door to the inner sanctum. Realizing that she was about to enter a world she knew nothing about, her nerves returned. Ariel put her trembling hand on the handsomely carved mahogany pocket door, exhaled, and slowly slid it open. She was stunned by the opulence of the room. She had expected to see a modern decadent decor, but there were plush sofas upholstered in scarlet and gold raw silk, with an assortment of decorative throw pillows lining the perimeter of the room. A six-tiered crystal chandelier with faint ocher lighting hung overhead, casting a sexy glow throughout the room. There was a group of masked, scantily dressed women milling around an ornate fountain in the center of the parlor, drinking and socializing with a few hot male servers. She could only see the bottom half of their faces, but based on the cellulite thighs, sagging breasts, and curved spine of one woman, Ariel assumed that she was probably close to sixty. The woman seemed comfortable in her see-through negligee as she sipped champagne and flirted shamelessly with a tall, muscular masked man, dressed only in a half-mask and a pair of tight black leather shorts that emphasized the outline of his penis. Ariel's face registered a shocked expression underneath her mask as she watched the woman brazenly reach inside the man's waistband and massage his manhood. After bringing him close to an erection, the woman removed her hand, licked her fingertips, and then led her subject away by the hand.

I bet they're going upstairs to get it on, Ariel thought, as she watched them disappear behind the heavy crimson drape.

She couldn't believe the sexual energy flowing through the air; everyone seemed to be tweaked but her. Walking toward the fountain, she thought, *I need some liquid courage.* She picked up a glass from a silver tray and filled it from one of the spigots. She took a sip and was surprised to taste ice-cold vodka. She had assumed that it was a typical champagne fountain, but she should've known otherwise, because nothing in this club was typical. The moment she stepped through the club's black door, everything was completely skewed. Though Meri had given her the inside scoop, she wasn't prepared for this world of eroticism. Ariel hadn't expected the doorman to get her moist without a simple hello—even though she enjoyed his touch—nor had she expected to witness an overt display of foreplay. She wasn't a prude, but her standards were sub-standard in comparison to The Black Door's.

Ariel let the clear, cool liquor slip past her lips and tickle her tongue; the smooth, imported, distilled Polish vodka slid down her throat and to her head. As she polished off the first drink, she felt a slight buzz, but was still nervous. She filled her glass again, hoping to drown the remaining butterflies in her belly.

"Relax. Just relax; no one knows who you are," she whispered underneath the mask. Ariel was grateful for the decorative shield that concealed her identity. She kept reminding herself that her secret was safe, and it was okay to loosen up and enjoy the sights. After all, that's why she was here. The second drink gave her the courage to venture behind the velvet curtain and up a flight of winding stairs to the second floor.

The sound of Miles Davis's trumpet playing a hypnotic jazz rhythm greeted her as she reached the landing. This floor was much darker than the first level, causing her to blink twice, trying to adjust her eyes to the deep indigo lighting. The dense carpeting muffled Ariel's heels as she slowly walked down the long, narrow corridor. Halfway down the hall, she stopped at a large picture window. It struck her as odd that a window would be set inside an interior wall. Ariel's jaw dropped as she peered through the glass. What she saw made her stare in disbelief; on the other side of the window was a naked woman spread eagle on a king-size bed. Her legs were wrapped around the back of a man with a shiny, tight ass, and he was humping and pumping deep into her pussy. Another man was kneeling over her swinging his dick back and forth across her mouth, as she flicked her tongue out, trying to catch the tip of his pendulum. The woman stretched her neck forward, catching his one-eyed snake in her mouth and sucked frantically like she was trying to extract venom. Ariel's nose was pressed so close to the glass that she fogged it up with her hot breath. She had never seen a threesome before, and the two-on-one action was making her horny. She quickly wiped away the condensation with the sleeve of her dress before anyone noticed.

"Don't worry. It's a one-way mirror. You can see them, but they can't see you," said a deep baritone voice.

Not only could Ariel feel his steamy breath in her ear, but she could also feel his thick shaft in her rear. Whoever was standing behind her had cozied up so close that their bodies were locked in a vertical spoon position.

Then he whispered, "That's the Voyeurism Room, but if you're not into peep shows, we could have our own ménage à trois in private." He pressed closer to her.

Ariel had never had a threesome, except in her dreams. Though the invitation was tempting, she wasn't ready to live out her fantasies, at least not yet. She wanted to say no, but was enjoying the moment, and wasn't ready for him to extract his firm body from hers.

He put his arms around her waist. "Come on. I promise you won't be sorry."

"Not this time," she finally said, pulling away from his grip.

Ariel was only there to "get her look on," but as horny as she was feeling, she just might "get her freak on." In any event she wanted to see more of what the club had to offer before she jumped at the first opportunity. She ventured farther down the darkened passage and could hear moans coming from behind the closed doors that dotted the hallway. The hedonistic sounds of lovemaking were making her hornier.

Maybe I should have taken him up on his offer, she thought and looked behind her, but the masked man was long gone.

When Ariel turned around, she bumped smack into a curvaceous woman wearing a silver thong, matching mask, and little else. Her large breasts sat upright and firm, undoubtedly filled with saline. As they stood nipple to nipple, the woman looked down at the silhouette of Ariel's breast through her sheer sheath and licked her lips.

"Nice titties. Who did them?" she asked shamelessly.

Ariel was caught totally off guard. "What?"

"Dr. Braxton, on Fifth, did mine," she said, sensuously massaging her naked breasts with both hands. "They feel so good and natural." She took Ariel's hand and replaced it with hers. "Don't they?"

Ariel didn't know what to do; she had never touched another woman's breasts before, so she just stood there, frozen in shock.

"Don't be shy, touch them," instructed the woman, as she took Ariel's wrist and moved her hand in a circular motion around the circumference of her perfectly shaped nipple. "They feel real, don't they?"

Ariel had to admit that the breast did feel natural, just a little firmer than her own. "Yes they do, but——"

Before she could say another word, the woman started caressing Ariel's breasts with both hands. "Umm, your titties are so supple. I thought mine were natural, but yours feel like the real thing."

Ariel pulled away. "They *are* the real thing."

"I'm sure they are, honey." She winked and stepped in closer to get another feel. "Let's go in the Pink Room. I would love to taste you," she said brazenly.

Ariel blushed underneath her mask; she was flattered by the compliment, but was by no means bisexual. "No, thanks." She cleared her throat. "I'm straight."

"So am I. But there's nothing like ordering a little fresh fish from the menu every now and then." The woman stroked Ariel's forearm. "Trust me, I eat pussy better than any man. Hell, most of them don't even know how to find the clit." She flicked out her tongue from underneath her half-mask. "I'll make you cum so hard, you'll be begging for more," she said, with an edge of cockiness in her voice.

Ariel had to admit that the invitation was making her wet, but a lesbian affair was not on her agenda. "Thanks, but no thanks," she said sternly, and walked away.

She was experiencing sensory overload; there were sexual innuendoes everywhere she turned. It felt like feast or famine—here she could feast on a smorgasbord of sexual activities, but at home with Preston, sex had taken a holiday—and she was overwhelmed. Ariel had never made love to a stranger or indulged in a one-night stand. She was a relationship kind of girl, and didn't know if she could fuck someone without getting to know him first. *Maybe I should just go home and masturbate to take the edge off,* she thought.

Ariel turned around before reaching the end of the long hallway and retreated toward the stairs. As she was walking down the narrow steps, a man wearing a black leather mask with glimmering onyx adorning the temples was slowly approaching her. There was something different about him. The first thing she noticed was his stealthlike presence. He moved quietly and deliberately, like a confident panther on the prowl. Second she noted his attire; he wore black jeans and a black wife-beater, unlike the other men who strutted around topless in tight shorts and G-strings. His pecs were well defined and she detected a six-pack beneath the cotton T-shirt. Her heart began to race as he approached. The steps were too narrow for two people moving in the opposite direction, so she tried to maneuver her body to allow him room to pass. Soon they were standing on the same step, looking mask to mask. It was too dark to see his eyes through the slits, but she felt his body heat as they stood within a quarter of an inch from one another. Though neither spoke a word, their body language was speaking volumes. Her nipples firmed as she noticed the bulge in his jeans. For a few seconds they stood in what seemed like suspended animation, lost in the moment. Then he firmly put his hands just below her waist right on the outline of her thong. The heat from his touch sent an electric charge shooting up her spine.

"Here comes the proposition." She held her breath in anticipation. This time she was ready to submit to her desires and throw caution down the stairs and out the door. But to her surprise and disappointment, he didn't proposition her; he just gently moved her to the side and continued up the stairs.

As goose bumps covered her skin, Ariel shivered; she could still feel his touch. She contemplated going back upstairs to find him; his silent seduction intrigued her, and she wanted more.

"Maybe I'll get to know him next time." Now that she knew what The Black Door had to offer, she would definitely come back as a willing participant and not a frigid bystander.

SLEEP ESCAPED Ariel, and she tossed and turned all night after returning home from The Black Door. Her dreams were a series of sexual vignettes, starring the man in the black mask whom she encountered on the stairs. In one scene, they were on display behind the one-way glass, fucking and sucking for a ravenous crowd. The thrill of being watched was like an enticing aphrodisiac, causing her to shed all of her inhibitions. In the dream, Ariel maneuvered her body in positions only a gymnast could master, her knees stretching behind her ears like a gold medalist during a floor mat exercise. Her nerve endings were like live wires, and his touch was the conduit that grounded her.

In the next sequence, Ariel watched as the masked man privately danced for her, slowly stripping away his clothes until he was cloaked only in a thin layer of sweat. The sight of his muscular naked body made her salivate with an insatiable desire. After his seductive striptease, he strutted over to her while gripping his erect penis, gently opened her mouth with his hand, and eased his hard cock inside. She sucked fast and hard on his thick dick, like a hungry baby feeding on a wet nurse.

Ariel squirmed and twitched until she woke up panting in a heated frenzy. The sheets were moist with perspiration and twisted in a heap around her body. A pillow was wedged between her legs in an attempt to snuff out the fire raging in her loins. She wiped the sweat from her forehead. *Damn. I don't even know this man and he's giving me wet dreams,* she thought.

The thought of fantasizing about a strange man disturbed Ariel. She had been in his presence all of sixty seconds. But in that minute, he had affected her; it was like he had cast some kind of spell on her and she longed to feel his energy again.

"This is crazy!" She angrily tore the sheet from her body with one hard snatch. "I didn't even see his face, and I'm ready to become his love slave." Ariel had a thing for a handsome man, and though she couldn't see his entire face, she could tell by his sexy full lips and sculpted body that he was just the type of man who could melt her panties right off her ass.

The phone rang as Ariel was rehashing the previous night. "Hello?"

"Hey, baby." It was Mrs. Grant, her foster mom. "I just called your office, and JoAnne said that you were taking the morning off. Are you sick?"

"No, Mom. I don't have any pressing business at work, so I decided to go in late," she explained. She hated to lie to her foster mom, but she wouldn't dare tell her the real reason that she was still in bed was because she was out late at a sex club.

"Oh. I didn't want anything. I haven't talked to you in a while and just wanted to know how you've been getting along."

"I'm fine. How have you been?"

"I'm good, but more important, how are you and the judge doing?"

Ariel should have known that her foster mother had ulterior motives for calling. Lately, her sole focus seemed to be Ariel's relationship with Preston.

"We're doing fine," Ariel said, giving her the short answer.

"Just fine?" she asked, still prying.

Ariel was beginning to feel irritated. She didn't feel like talking about her relationship, especially now that her thoughts were preoccupied with another man. "Yes, Mom."

"Look, baby, I know I'm being a meddling old woman, but I want to see you married before I leave this earth. And the judge can give you the family you never had," she said sympathetically.

Hearing her words, Ariel began to feel guilty. Her mom was right. Preston was one of the good guys, and though he was busy, deep down Ariel knew that he loved her. Suddenly she needed to feel Preston's arms around her before she went back to The Black Door and did something she would regret. "You right, Mom. Don't worry, I won't let him get away. Look, I gotta run. I'll talk to you soon."

"Okay, baby, take care of yourself."

After showering, she dressed in a black pantsuit and V-neck sweater, and called Preston's office. "Hi, Anna, its Ariel," she said to his longtime secretary, "how have you been?"

"Oh, hello Ariel, it's so good to hear your voice," said the older woman. She took a liking to Ariel when she was an inquisitive young clerk, and admired how smart she was then *and* now. "I've been doing well, thank you; and let me just say congratulations on your appointment to partner. Judge Hendricks told me all about the good news."

"Thanks so much, Anna."

"I know you didn't call here to talk to me, but the judge is working at home today since he doesn't have any court cases, so try him there," she suggested.

"Thank you, Anna, I will. Take care and I'll talk to you soon."

Ariel threw on a trench coat, grabbed her purse, and headed downstairs. She didn't want to take the time to get her car out of the garage, so she stood curbside and hailed a cab. "University Place and Fifth," she told the taxi driver. She hadn't spoken to him since she left D.C., and wanted to explain the reason for her abrupt departure.

Preston lived in the Gold Coast, an area of Manhattan near historic Washington Square Park, with pricey, pristine, prewar town houses on tree-lined streets.

As the driver pulled in front of Preston's redbrick, four-story house, her heart began to beat faster. *Maybe I should've called first,* she thought.

After paying the driver, she reassured herself. *Preston and I are well beyond the "call before you come over" phase,* she reminded herself, and rang the bell. Though they had been dating for years, she and Preston never exchanged keys to each other's homes. Growing up, Ariel had never truly had a home of her own, and now that she did, she was a bit territorial.

"Ariel?" Preston looked surprised when he opened the door. "What are you doing here?" He sounded annoyed at the interruption.

It wasn't the greeting that she had expected. "Aren't you glad to see me?" she asked.

He reached out and engulfed her in a warm bear hug. "I'm always glad to see you, honey." He released her and quickly looked over his shoulder. "It's just that I wasn't expecting you to drop by today. Why aren't you at work?"

"Because I took the morning off to visit you. Well . . ." She waited a few seconds for him to invite her inside, but he just stood there with a blank expression on his face. Watching his vacant expression made her angry and her sweet tone vanished. "Aren't you going to invite me in? Or are we just going to stand in the doorway and chat?"

"Oh, of course, I'm going to invite you in, don't be silly." He stepped aside.

The interior of Preston's town house was warm and inviting. The decor was a mix of Art Deco, blended perfectly with turn-of-the-century antiques, priceless oil paintings in gilded frames, and exquisite hand-woven Tibetan rugs strewn across high-gloss cherrywood floors. The living-room walls were painted a calming saffron color, which complemented the crystal chandelier that hung overhead.

"So what brings you by?" he asked, quickly getting to the reason for her visit.

"Preston, we need to talk," she said, settling down on the sofa.

"I agree, Ariel, but now's not the right time. I have a conference call with the senator and a former member of the Judiciary Committee in about fifteen minutes, and then I have another meeting after that. Why don't we have dinner one day this week?" he offered, and began to walk toward the front door, indicating that she should leave.

"Wait." She quickly stood up. "What I have to say won't take long. I just want to say that I'm sor—"

"Preston, here are your notes for the conference call." It was Michele, walking out of his private office.

Ariel took one look at Michele's outfit and a knot formed in the pit of her stomach. If she didn't know any better, she would swear that little Ms. Perfect Assistant was trying to seduce her man. Michele was wearing a white sheer blouse with a matching sheer bra, which gave a braless effect. Though she wore an open blazer, Ariel could clearly see her breasts jiggling from side to side as she walked into the room. Her nipples were pronounced and inviting, making Ariel wonder if Preston had been sucking on them. Maybe Michele was the reason why he wasn't interested in making love to her anymore. Suddenly paranoia reared its ugly head. She hadn't felt this paranoid in years.

A few bad relationships in college, coupled with the fact that she was adopted, had made her extremely paranoid. It took years of therapy to convince Ariel that she was good enough to be loved. The therapist drilled into her head over and over that just because her mother put her up for adoption, it didn't mean that she was unlovable. After hundreds of hours on the couch, Ariel finally got the point, but deep in the recesses of her mind, paranoia lurked like a jealous lover waiting for the most inopportune time to attack.

"Are you *fucking* her?" Ariel blurted out, unable to contain her thoughts any longer.

Michele stopped dead in her tracks and Preston's jaw dropped. Both looked stunned and neither said a word.

Ariel approached Preston, shouting, "Well?"

Preston turned to Michele and said calmly, "Can you please give us a moment?" Once Michele was gone from the room, he faced Ariel. "What's gotten into you?" he asked sternly, but didn't wait for an answer. "First you leave me in Washington when I wouldn't drop everything and have sex with you on command." He sighed deeply in frustration. "Now you come here unannounced, accusing me of having an affair with a girl half my age." He threw his hands in the air and raised his voice. "Do you know how ridiculous and paranoid you sound?"

"I may sound paranoid, but you still haven't answered my question," she said between clinched teeth. She was still fuming and could feel the vein bulging in the center of her forehead. "And don't give me that shit about her being half your age. I was her age when we met." She put her hands on her hips. "Remember?"

Preston shook his head in frustration; he didn't know what to say. He exhaled and began to speak in measured tones. "Ariel, that was nearly ten years ago, and we were both younger. Remember?" he asked, tossing the same question back at her. "Besides, how many times do I have to tell you that the nomination is my priority? I barely have time for you, so tell me how can I make time for an affair?"

Ariel wouldn't relent. "Well, it's not like you have to fit *her* into your schedule, since she's always around."

"Obviously there's no reasoning with you, since you're going to believe what you want. And to be quite honest, I don't have the time or energy to try and convince you otherwise. Now, if you'll excuse me, I've got a conference call to make," he said, turning to exit the room.

Ariel snatched her purse from the sofa and stormed toward the door without saying a word. She knew that she was overreacting, but she couldn't help herself. She understood that Preston's political ambitions were important, but hell, he hadn't even gotten the nomination yet. She shuddered to think what would become of their relationship if he actually became a Supreme Court justice. If he didn't have time for her now, he surely wouldn't have time for her in the future. Tears formed in the corner of her eyes and were flowing freely down her cheeks by the time she reached the door.

"Uh, hi," said a strikingly handsome man standing on the other side of the front door, with his finger on the bell.

He looked slightly familiar, but Ariel didn't immediately recognize him. She wiped her tears. "Excuse me," she said, pushing past him.

He touched her elbow as she passed. "Are you okay?" he asked with concern.

"I'm fine," she sniffled, and rushed down the stairs to the street.

PRESTON APPEARED AT the door. "Come on in, son."

"Who was that?" He pointed in Ariel's direction.

"A double shot of Johnny Walker straight," Preston said jokingly.

"What?"

"That was Ariel. I swear that woman's going to drive me to drink *more*." He sighed.

"*That* was Ariel? I didn't even recognize her. I haven't seen her since I was in college. Why was she crying?"

"It's a long story, which I don't have time to get into right now. I have to get on this conference call. It shouldn't take long, and then we'll go over those papers you came to pick up. Make yourself at home." Preston patted the younger man on the shoulder and led him inside. "It's good to see you, son."

Over the years, Preston's relationship with his son had been strained. The divorce drove a wedge between them, with Preston's ex-wife filling their son's head with stories about his alleged affairs, causing him to drop his father's surname and use her maiden name.

Michele appeared in the doorway of the study and checked out the younger man from behind. His wore ripped jeans, a striped shirt, and a tweed blazer, which hugged his broad shoulders. His hair was cut extremely close, giving a five-o'clock-shadow effect. The rear view was enticing and she was dying to see his face. She cleared her throat, and when he turned around, her knees nearly buckled. His skin was as smooth as liquid chocolate, his eyes were narrow, sexy slits, and his lips were full and inviting. He smiled at her, showing off an identical pair of piercing dimples. He looked familiar; then it struck her that he was the spitting image of Preston, minus the gray hair and age lines around the mouth and forehead. "Can I help you?" she asked, finally speaking up.

His eyes zeroed in on her see-through blouse, and his smile broadened as he checked out her delicious-looking tits. "I'm waiting on my father."

Michele watched him stare at her breasts, and was glad she had taken off her blazer. She arched her back and stood up a little straighter, so he could get the full effect. "Hi, I'm Michele." She extended her hand.

He walked over and took her hand into his, holding it for a few seconds. He looked her up and down and said, "My pleasure."

"I see you guys have met," Preston said, walking into the room. "Michele, can you fax these to the senator?" he asked, handing her a stack of papers.

"Sure, no problem," she replied, took her hand away from Preston's son, and sashayed out of the room.

"Who is *that*?" he asked, raising an eyebrow.

"My new assistant."

"She's hot." He whistled under his breath and shook his hand as if it were on fire.

"A little too hot, I'm afraid. Ariel thinks I'm having an affair with her," he said, totally exasperated.

Preston III raised an eyebrow in doubt, and asked, "Well . . . are you?"

Preston looked hurt that his son would question his integrity, but realized that it was all the years of being brainwashed by his paranoid mother. "Of course not. She's young enough to be my daughter, for Christ's sake."

"Well, in that case maybe I'll ask her out. Wouldn't want all that *fineness* to go to waste." He chuckled.

"I think that's an excellent idea." Preston scribbled his assistant's cell-phone number on the back of a business card and handed it to his son. "I'll tell Michele to expect your call. Maybe then I can convince Ariel once and for all that I'm not cheating on her." Preston walked over to his rolltop desk and took out a file. "Enough about women. Here're the trust fund papers for you to sign. So tell me, what have you been up to lately?" Preston asked, knowing his son's penchant for hopping from career to career.

"I've been studying for the Series Seven. I'm going to try my hand at investing. A buddy of mine is a managing director at Deutsche Bank, and he's willing to show me the ropes."

"Well, it sounds like you're keeping your nose to the grindstone and staying out of trouble."

"I am, Dad, and the money from the trust will help tide me over until I'm trading stocks like the big boys," he smiled.

"Son, I have confidence that you'll be wheeling and dealing in no time," he slapped his son on the back. "I hate to rush off, but I've got another call to make. Let's have dinner soon. Love you." And with that Preston was off to attend to his precious agenda.

"DARLING, WHAT'S the matter?" Meri asked, as she opened the door to a disheveled, sobbing Ariel. Her normally coifed hair was in disarray, and her coat hung halfway off of one shoulder.

"I'm ruining things all over again," she said, and fell into Meri's arms like a limp rag doll, sobbing.

Meri put her arm around Ariel's shoulder, slowly ushered her into the living room, and sat her down on the sofa.

"There, there," she said, smoothing her hair behind one ear. "Get it all out." Meri was one of the few people who knew about Ariel's unfortunate childhood and the years of therapy to overcome her insecurities.

After letting the waterworks flow for a few minutes, Ariel raised her head, sniffled, took a tissue out of her purse, and blew her nose twice before telling Meri about her ordeal with Preston and his overtly sexy assistant. "The moment I saw her parading around his house like a stripper at Scores, my paranoia took over and I just lost it."

"You shouldn't let that girl rattle you like this."

"You're right, but you should've seen her, with her perky tits on display for the world to see. And Preston focused on business as usual, like she didn't faze him in the least."

"I know Preston has been emotionally detached lately, but you don't honestly think he's sleeping with her, do you?" Meri asked, trying to be the voice of reason.

Ariel dabbed her eyes with the tissue. "He must be getting it somewhere, because he sure hasn't been making love to me lately."

"Darling, you have to let go of the paranoia and relieve some of that pent-up frustration. I thought that's why you were going to The Black Door." Meri gave her a questioning look. "You did go, didn't you?"

Ariel's mouth began to curve up at the corners until a smile brightened her face, erasing the remnants of her sadness, and her mind drifted from the present to the infamous Black Door. "Yes, I went."

"And?" Meri asked, anxiously awaiting every scintillating detail.

"And . . ." She fanned the damp tissue across her face. "It was amazing. I couldn't believe all of the *activities* going on under one roof," she said excitedly.

"Did I not tell you that it's the ultimate playground?"

"Playground is an understatement! The Black Door is like Disneyland on Ecstasy. Everybody was so touchy-feely."

"So, tell me, missy who did you touch and feel?" she asked sarcastically.

She thought about the woman who felt her up, and though she did touch the woman's boobs, it wasn't by choice. "Nobody," Ariel said quickly, darting her eyes to the floor, preferring not to go into detail.

Meri put her index finger to her chin. "Hmm, you answered that question just a little too fast. I'm sure *somebody* turned you on."

"Well, there was this one guy who—"

Meri cut her off midsentence. "Did he have on a cobalt-blue mask?" She bit her bottom lip. "The last time I was at The Black Door, he took me down to the dungeon, blindfolded me, tied me up between two pillars, and took me from behind like a Mandingo warrior. I'm telling you, it was the most erotic sex of my life."

"Dungeon?" Ariel looked shocked. "There's a dungeon?"

"Oh, yes, darling." Meri grinned, as if recalling the experience. "And it's chockful of all kinds of toys, from sadomasochistic whips and chains, to sex swings, to orgasmic hot wax. I'm surprised you didn't explore the bowels of the club. Didn't you take a tour of the place?"

"I went upstairs, but only ventured halfway down the hall," she admitted.

"Why only halfway? What happened? I thought you were going to get an eyeful, and possibly get a little more." She winked.

Ariel looked sheepish. "That was the plan, but I got nervous. I've never experienced anything like that in my life. Men *and* women were coming on to me right and left. It was a little overwhelming."

"Ah, yes, the women." Meri arched an eyebrow. "They can be aggressive, but all you had to do was say no and move on. That's the beauty of wearing a mask; you're totally anonymous and can do and say whatever's on your mind."

"At times I forgot that my face was concealed."

"Next time you go back, just remember that your identity is totally safe. Besides, you can be as freaky as you want to be; after all, you are wearing *my* mask, and we both know how much I enjoy sex." Meri chuckled.

Meri's words resonated loud and clear, and Ariel knew without a doubt that she would cross The Black Door's threshold again, if for nothing else than to experience the energy she felt with the black-masked server. She needed to get a healthy dose of self-esteem, and he was just what the doctor ordered.

AFTER RUNNING AN important errand, Trey was back at the club, locked away in his office, up to his eardrums in paperwork, poring over vendor invoices. As he sat crunching numbers on the calculator, his mind drifted to the woman he had encountered on the steps the other night. There was something about her body language that turned him on, causing his dick to rise to new heights. He couldn't get the sensation he felt out of his mind. Trey had an advantage over the members; though they didn't know his identity, he had their complete profiles on record.

Recalling the red patent-leather mask she wore, Trey abandoned the boring paperwork, walked over to the file cabinet, and retrieved a thick manila folder labeled "Client/Mask." He opened the folder and scanned the long list of masks that he had designed. Alongside each client name was a picture of her identity-concealing mask.

"Meri Renick," Trey said aloud, reading the name next to the Polaroid of her mask. To refresh his memory, he read her profile, which included a physical description. The file described her as being five five, but the woman he vibed with on the stairs was much taller. "Maybe she had on stilettos," he reasoned. The file also said that she was forty-something, but the woman he encountered was more youthful. Though he couldn't see her entire face, he was an expert on bodies, and her body was that of a younger woman—ripe and voluptuous. Again he tried to reconcile what was on the paper with what he saw with his own eyes. "She's probably had some work done." Though he met with each woman during the initial phase of membership, he couldn't recall his meeting with Meri Renick, which wasn't unusual, since she had joined a few years ago when the club opened and he had met with a ton of women since then.

Trey had a self-imposed "hands-off" policy and didn't get involved with the members, but maybe he'd have to make an exception this once and bend the rules to satisfy his mounting curiosity.
After all, rules were made to be broken.

"I wonder if she's here tonight." Trey paced back and forth, his
brain racing, trying to decide whether or not to walk through the
club to find Ms. Renick or whoever was behind the red mask. Older
women were not his preference, but she was different somehow,
and it made him want to find out what made her tick.

Finally his inquisitive nature and his libido won out over his
common sense. He wasn't dating anyone seriously and hadn't been
laid in about a month. He went to the private bathroom inside his
office, changed from blue denims and a white cotton shirt into his
signature black wife-beater, which accentuated the ripples across
his taunt midsection, and a snug pair of black jeans, which hugged
his thick dick. Trey opened a bureau drawer, took out his onyx-
embellished black leather mask and put it on, and sprayed his neck
with Bvlgari, his favorite scent. After making his transformation
from club owner to club stud, he left his office on the third floor
and ventured downstairs in search of the woman behind the red
patent-leather mask.

The second floor was pulsating with a hedonistic energy that
was contagious, and it made the hairs on the back of his neck stand
at attention. Trey walked into the Game Room, with its purple
leather-paneled walls and floors, and observed two members playing Naked Twister with two house hulks. The women were bent
over with their legs spread wide across a colorful mat with red,
blue, green, and yellow circles, while the men lay flat on their
backs in the buff, strategically close underneath the women's exposed clits. There was also a game of Dominatrix Dominoes being
played, with human dominoes, dressed in spikes and chains, lined
ass-to-ass, posed to topple one another with the slightest touch of

one's opponent. Trey scanned the masks of each member in the room, and when he didn't see his mark, he moved on.

The Tantalizing Toy Room was where members could choose vibrators, heat-sensitive gels, edible panties, butt-plugs, and fur-lined handcuffs to enhance their pleasure. Trey noticed two women wearing only their masks and high heels, bending across the glass counter pointing and oohing and aahing over a flesh-tone, fifteen-inch dildo.

"Hmm, I could take every inch of that fake dick," said the blonde.

"Plastic ain't nothing like the real thing," responded the brunette.

"I could take a plastic cock up my ass, and the real deal in my pussy, all the while sucking you into a frenzy," challenged the blonde in return.

The brunette grabbed the blonde's ass and said, "Come on; let's go into the Pink Room and find a big-dick server; then you can put your tongue on my sweet spot."

On the way out, the two women looked Trey over thoroughly, sizing him up, trying to decide if he fit their requirements. But they brushed past him clinging to each other, leaving him standing in the doorway. Obviously, he wasn't their flavor.

Trey drifted from room to room looking for the woman in the red patent-leather mask, but his search came up empty. Feeling deflated, he sulked down the darkened hallway toward the stairs. As he navigated the narrow steps, his mind flashed back to the heated encounter with Meri Renick. He hesitated, closed his eyes, and relived their brief moment together. His breath became shallow as he gave into the memory. He didn't know her, but she had his senses wide open, and he was more determined now than ever to find out why.

WORK WAS Ariel's antidote for what ailed her. It was the one constant in her life; in school it was homework that kept her preoccupied. She welcomed the distraction from her daydreams. She would sit for hours and fantasize about her birth mother coming to rescue her from foster care. In her dreams her "real" mother was a beautiful Hollywood movie star who had to put Ariel up for adoption until her career took off. Now that she was a megastar, she'd come back for the baby that she abandoned. Only her mother never came. Now Ariel counted on the myriad cases that she presided over to keep her mind preoccupied. Since Preston was absorbed with his career, Ariel thought that she could find solace in hers, instead of focusing on The Black Door. But she couldn't stop thinking about the man that she had met on the steps. Well, it wasn't like they had had a formal introduction; nevertheless he remained a formidable fixture in her mind.

Ariel picked up a file, flipped it open, and read the intimate details. The client was a well-known sportscaster who was being sued for divorce. New York was one of the toughest states in which to dissolve a marriage, since no-fault grievances existed; you couldn't claim irreconcilable differences. The case before her cited adultery for the breakup, and went on to describe how, during their two-year marriage, the wife had cheated over six times with six different men. She had cleverly hid her infidelity by making calls to her lovers on a second cell phone that her husband was unaware of, since the bills went to a secret post office box. Five of her lovers were athletes; she would interview them in the locker room and after seeing their "equipment," she knew exactly what they were working with, and if well hung, she'd schedule a horizontal interview in her hotel suite. The sixth man was a coworker, whom she had dated for several years before she was married. After the honeymoon years faded and the marriage had lost its lust, she got antsy and rekindled the relationship with her ex-boyfriend, with whom she had always had sizzling hot sex. They fucked in the control room of the station after hours; she sucked him off in her office, and even humped him in one of the stalls in the men's room. Ready to take their relationship out of the shadows of deception and come clean about their affair, her lover insisted that she make a choice—him or her husband. When she didn't choose him, he became enraged and sent a series of anonymous notes to her house. She adamantly denied the allegations to the point of tears, and would've gotten away with the extramarital affairs, until her lover overnighted incriminating pictures directly into the hands of her husband. In the eight-by-ten glossies, she was on her knees giving her lover a good old-fashioned blow job at the *job*. With the mounting evidence, her husband hired a private investigator, who gathered enough dirt to bury her in divorce court and walk away with a hefty settlement.

Ariel closed the manila folder and sighed. "This is a tough

one." She leaned back in her chair and shook her head in distress. "How am I supposed to countersue with all the evidence in his favor?" Ariel repeatedly drummed her pencil on her desk, trying to think of a solution. She had never lost a case, and didn't plan on losing this one, even though the evidence against her client was incriminating. "I need to follow suit and hire a private investigator of my own to find something damaging against the husband. I'm sure he's been creeping around with someone since his wife hasn't been sexing him up; that's the only chance I'll have to keep him from getting half of her assets.

"JoAnne, can you ring Tim Anderson's office?" Ariel asked her assistant.

After a few minutes, JoAnne spoke through the intercom. "Ms. Vaughn, he's in the conference room."

"Okay, thanks. I'll walk down there and speak to him in person." Tim Anderson was a criminal attorney who had a roster of the best PIs in town.

As Ariel approached the conference room, the door was ajar. She could hear voices coming from inside.

"I just love going to Baltimore for depositions." It was Bob, one of the managing partners.

"You mean, you love 'The Block.' " Tim chuckled.

The Block was a strip of triple-X clubs near the harbor catering to men of all classes and ages. After a long day's work, out-of-town businessmen ate a hardy meal of Maryland crab cakes at some of the finest restaurants along the harbor, and then got their freak on with some of the raunchiest dancers in the state.

"Yes indeed, I do love The Block!" She heard the smile in Bob's voice. "You should've seen the redhead who took me into the VIP room." He whistled. "She had the biggest tits *and* ass I've ever seen. I slipped the bouncer a hundred-dollar bill to turn his head while I sucked her nipples and played with her pussy, as she grinded that big ass on my cock."

Ariel couldn't believe buttoned-up Bob was talking T&A instead of billable hours. Then again, thinking back to the Lancaster benefit, she remembered how he ogled her boobs. *He's just a big old freak,* she thought.

"Well, she must've had a twin sister, because the stripper I played with all night had the same *assets*." Tim laughed.

Ariel could hear them slapping five and enjoying the camaraderie that men shared while discussing the female gender. *Men,* she huffed and rolled her eyes. *Why is it that they get kudos for fucking as many women as they can slip their dicks into, while we get judged for enjoying the same pleasures?*

"Excuse me," she huffed loudly, while pushing the door wide open, purposely disrupting their bonding session. She gave them both the evil eye, letting them know that she had heard every single word. "Am I interrupting an important meeting or *something*?"

Bob cleared his throat and changed his tone from that of freaky frat boy to high-powered attorney, and asked with an air of superiority, "What can I do for you, Ariel?"

She couldn't believe his arrogance; she wanted to call him on the carpet and ask, "So did you bill your little outing to the company?" But she knew the truth, and the truth was that the receipts from "The Block" would get billed to the client as a simple travel and entertainment expense, and no one would be the wiser. Ariel ignored Bob's question, refusing to be talked down to, and turned toward Tim. "What's the name of the PI you used on the Collins case?"

"Mac Davis," Tim answered sheepishly.

"What's his number?"

"His card is in my Rolodex. Can I e-mail it to you in about five minutes? Is that okay?" he asked, trying to accommodate her.

"Sure," Ariel said, and walked out, leaving them to their fantasies.

Back in her office, she couldn't help but think about the interchange between Bob and Tim, and how comfortable they were sharing their exploits at the strip club. "Why am I being such a prude? If they can get their freak on, and then boast about it later, why can't I?" With that thought in mind, she knew exactly what her plans were for the evening.

ARIEL RAIDED THE liquor cabinet as soon as she got home, mixed an extra-dry martini, and tossed it back within seconds, then poured another. She planned to arrive at The Black Door free of any inhibitions, and vodka was the lubricant she needed to loosen her self-imposed restraints. Tonight she planned on doing more than just looking.

After showering and smoothing a rich cream all over her body, she browsed through her lingerie drawer trying to decide what to wear. She wanted to make a statement with a bold outfit so there would be no mistaking her intentions.

"Perfect," she said, holding up a red corset with garters, matching thong, and a pair of silk stockings.

Ariel gingerly slipped into the delicate ensemble, looked into the mirror, and smiled at her reflection. Gone was the conservatively clad attorney in a navy-blue suit and white blouse, replaced by a vampishly dressed vixen all decked out in red. The bustier portion of the corset pushed her large boobs so tightly together that they nearly spilled out of the top. She turned around to get a back view and gasped; her butt cheeks were totally exposed with only the thin strip of the thong peeking out from her crack. "I need another drink," she mused, after looking at her nearly naked body.

After draining the last of the cocktail from the V-shaped glass, she put on a nondescript tan trench coat and tied the belt snuggly around her waist. She put the mask in her briefcase and headed downstairs.

The doorman greeted her with a smile and a tip of his hat, "Good evening, Ms. Vaughn."

"Hello, Pete."

"Heading back to the office?" he asked, looking down at her briefcase.

The plain coat concealed her secret perfectly. "You know me, Pete." She almost snickered. "Always burning the midnight oil."

"I'll hail a taxi for you," he offered, holding open the door.

"Thanks."

Inside the cab, she removed the mask and put it on. Since it ended just below her nose, she took out her compact and gloss, and applied a thick layer of Mac's ruby Lipglass. Her lips were now inviting and matched the mask to a tee. A vision in red from head to toe, Ariel felt extremely sexy and totally relaxed, thanks to the cocktails.

Pulling up in front of the club, the driver turned around and said, "That'll be twenty-two fifty." At first a look of shock registered on his face when he saw Ariel's mask-clad face, but the expression quickly faded. This was New York, after all, and you were bound to see any- and everything in the course of a day.

She paid the fare and got out of the cab. From the outside, the club resembled the other brownstones on the block; there were no overt signs to give away its true identity.

Unlike before, Ariel knew what to expect and eagerly awaited the doorman's greeting, and he didn't disappoint as he "juiced" her up after she had given him the secret password. She stopped by the vodka fountain for another drink before heading upstairs to find her intended target.

A bald, bare-chested, vanilla-colored man wearing a red-leather codpiece and fire-engine-red mask strutted toward Ariel as she walked down the long hallway. Once he was within two inches of her, he stopped and slowly circled her like a tiger inspecting his prey. He rubbed the hard codpiece against her butt before whispering in her ear, "I love red." He fingered the ribbing of her thong. "I could bend you over right now and fuck you without taking this off," he said, snapping the elastic waistband.

Ariel flinched slightly. She was wet and ready, and tempted to comply with his demand, but the only dick she wanted inside of her belonged to the man in the black leather mask. She shook her head. "No."

He rubbed his massive hand over her ass. "Come on, baby, let me make you cum."

His hot breath tickling her ear and his hand massaging her butt made her tingle all over. She was close to taking him up on his offer, but walked away instead. She was on a mission and refused to be sidetracked.

Ariel walked by the Voyeurism Room and glanced through the glass. Inside were three couples having group sex. Limbs were intertwined; she couldn't tell where one body part started and where one ended. Instead of lingering at the window, she kept walking down the darkened corridor in search of Mr. Black Mask.

Fuchsia lighting spilled out into the hallway from the Pink Room. Ariel peeked her head inside looking for *the* man, but he wasn't there. Inside were a group of nude women all wearing various tones of pink masks, from hot pink to Pepto-Bismol pink to cotton-candy pink; they were lounging on salmon-colored sofas, drinking pink Cosmos and playing with one another's pink clits. With one look, Ariel knew why it was called the Pink Room; everything from the drinks to the lighting, to the furniture, to the exposed sexual organs was *pink*! Ariel kept walking before she was lured into the sordid soiree.

She roamed through room after room, and saw everything from human board games to a boutique stocked with a cornucopia of sex toys. She saw everything but what she was looking for. Frustrated, Ariel entered a quaint, dimly lit bar area. The walls were draped in leopard skin, as were the bar stools and booths. The bartender wore a black and brown leopard-print mask complete with long whiskers.

"What can I get for you, lovely?" he growled in a husky, animal-like voice.

Ariel didn't want anymore vodka; she was in the mood for something stronger. Her spirits were fading and she needed a jolt of adrenaline to keep up her pursuit. "Hmm." She bit her bottom lip. "Do you have a drink menu?"

He handed her a rectangular card with leopard print on one side and a list of cocktails on the other. She scanned the menu and couldn't believe some of the names and descriptions:

Cumtini Fresh cum, shaken with gin and a splash of grapefruit juice, served on the rocks.
Pussimo Vodka, cranberry juice, essence of pussy juice, and triple-sec, shaken and served straight up.
The Black Door, champagne with a splash of iced-cold vodka, garnished with a black Chilean grape, served chilled in a handblown flute.

Though Ariel wanted a pick-me-up, her taste buds were not up to experimenting, so she chose something a bit more familiar. "I'll have The Black Door."

"A classy drink, for a classy lady," the bartender responded.

Ariel sat on the stool and sipped her drink. Everyone in the room was getting her groove on, except her. There was a woman in one of the back booths sitting on the table with her legs spread wide open with a buffed hunk buried between her thighs. The way her head was thrown back, and the way she was moaning, it wasn't hard to guess that he was noshing on her pussy.

Ariel felt left out. *I guess he isn't here tonight. I might as well go home and masturbate.* She finished her drink and moseyed out.

As she was walking down the hallway toward the stairs, someone grabbed her arm from behind, forcefully pulled her into an empty, closet-sized room, and locked the door. Ariel nearly stumbled, but the firm grip held her upright. She couldn't see her abductor because he had her pressed face-first against the wall, but she could smell his cologne and it was intoxicating. Her body broke out in goose bumps the moment his hand rubbed her ass. He didn't say a word as he ripped off her thong and fingered her clit. Ariel gasped as his fingers plunged deep into her vagina. Once she was dripping wet, he spread her cheeks, bent her over, and then filled her void with his throbbing cock.

"Oh, yes, yes . . ." she moaned, as he moved his dick in and out rapidly.

He grabbed her by the waist and nearly lifted her off the ground with each thrust. Ariel bucked back until they were both on the verge of climax. He quickly removed his dick and came all over her back, then massaged the creamy hot cum into her skin. She shivered with excitement. She had never been fucked so hard before, and it felt good.

Ariel straightened up and turned around to face her seducer. Her knees buckled when she saw the black leather and onyx mask staring back at her. Neither one uttered a sound, just gazed into each other's eyes through the slits of their mask. They were caught in a trance and seemed to be reading each other's minds. She had no idea who this man was, but whoever he was, he not only had her body, but was capturing her mind with his intense stare.

Ariel opened her mouth to speak, but he touched her lips with his index finger to stop any unnecessary dialogue that might ruin the mood. Her inner thighs quivered; she closed her eyes, took a deep breath, and got lost in the smell of sex and his cologne. When she opened her eyes a few seconds later—ready for more—he was gone. Ariel wanted to go after him, but she was paralyzed from the alcohol and the fuck of her life.

11

PRESTON'S SECRETARY poked her head through the door and said in a low whisper so as not to disturb his telephone conversation, "Senator Oglesby is on line two."

Preston held up an index finger and mouthed, "Have him hold for a second."

Anna nodded her head okay, and backed out of the office, leaving her boss to finish his call.

"Son, I hate to end our conversation so abruptly, but I have to take this call. But before I hang up, tell me, have you made a date with Michele yet?"

"I've been so busy studying that I haven't had a chance to call."

"The only reason I'm asking is that I've got to make amends with Ariel. She has it in her mind that I'm having an affair with Michele and if I can tell her that you're dating my assistant, she'll probably let me out of the doghouse." He chuckled slightly, but was serious nonetheless.

"Taking Michele out will be my pleasure. Consider it done. Who knows, maybe we can double date," he joked.

"I don't think Ariel would be thrilled with that idea. Anyway, let me run. I'll talk to you soon," he said, and hung up.

Preston clicked over to his second line. "Senator, sorry to keep you waiting. Did you have a chance to look over my fax?"

"Yes, I read all thirty-two pages, and your dossier reads like a John Grisham novel, minus the murders and espionage, of course. Your legal career is stellar, and you should have no problem securing the nomination. There's only one issue," he said mysteriously.

Preston thought for a minute, and mentally scanned the last twenty years of his professional life, but he could think of no embarrassing blemishes, no payola for favorable judgments, and no turning a blind eye in the face of corruption. "Sorry, Senator, but there isn't one case that I've presided over, or any of my private cases, that would jeopardize my chances to sit on the Supreme Court," Preston said with conviction.

"Yes, that's correct, but I'm not speaking of your years on the bench, or your years in private practice," he said.

"Well, what else is there?" Preston asked, totally baffled.

"Your personal life."

Preston was shocked at his response. "My personal life?" he asked, not quite sure where this conversation was heading.

"Yes, your personal life. The Judicial Committee not only scrutinizes your career, but they're also interested in your life off the bench. They want a well-rounded candidate with a stable household."

"Excuse me, Senator, but my household is more than stable. I own a multimillion-dollar town house in one of the most expensive areas in Manhattan where I've lived for years. If that's not stable, then I don't know what is," he said defensively.

"I'm not talking real estate, Preston. I'm talking family. I know from your file and the society pages that you've been dating Ariel Vaughn of Yates Gilcrest for a number of years."

"Yes, that's true. Ms. Vaughn is not only an attorney, but a senior partner with the firm and a fine woman," Preston said proudly.

"I'm well aware of her background. Can I speak frankly?" he asked rhetorically, not waiting for an answer. "The committee is looking for a family man, someone who is settled in a stable relationship, not a single man with a string of girlfriends."

"Senator, I may be single, but I'm no playboy. Ariel and I have been committed to each other for years," he explained.

"Committed, but not married," he said curtly.

Preston was taken aback. "Excuse me?"

"Of course, I can't tell you how to live your life . . . but if you want to be a serious contender, you have to play the game according to their rules. And character is at the top of that short list of qualifications. We both know that character can make or break your chances. Remember the Thomas confirmation hearings, and how that alleged harassment incident in his past almost cost him the judgeship."

"That's apples and oranges. You can't possibly compare my martial status to an accusation of sexual harassment." Preston was stunned. He had spent years building a career that would one day lead him to the Supreme Court, only to be told that that might not be enough to land the nomination. As a child he watched helplessly on television as grown men and women were attacked by dogs, beaten unmercifully, and jailed all in the name of equal rights. And he vowed that one day, he'd be in a position to make a difference, that he'd use the law as a weapon against discrimination. To Preston there was no better position to be in to institute change than sitting on the Supreme Court.

"Of course there's no comparison; all I'm saying is that marriage bodes well for a nominee's character. It demonstrates stability. Your background will be dissected underneath a keen microscope and one possible red flag will be your long-term relationship; having a 'girlfriend' at your age, instead of a 'wife' shows fear of commitment," the senator said, carefully spelling out what was expected of a viable candidate.

"This should be a moot point since I've been married before," Preston shot back.

"That's the past; we're talking about the future, and to be quite honest, it's high time you made an honest woman out of Ms. Vaughn," he said candidly.

Preston had planned on spending more time with Ariel, not proposing, but now he'd have to rethink his strategy. "Senator, I appreciate your candor and will take your suggestion under advisement."

"Trust me, Preston, I know what the committee is looking for, and that's the complete package." After making his point he quickly shifted gears. "I have to go into a meeting now, but I'll speak with you soon."

"Thanks for your advice, Senator," he said, and hung up.

Marriage was the furthest thing from Preston's mind. His first marriage had been a nightmare. His ex-wife turned out to be a psychotic, self-centered, money-grubbing witch. Preston worked day and night to pay the bills for her outrageous spending habits. And to make matters worst, she brainwashed their son into believing that his father was a lowlife adulterer. She would tell the boy that Preston was never at home because he lived across town with his other family. Preston spent years convincing his young impressionable son that his mother had made up the entire story, but it was too late. The damage had already been done. Preston had asked her why she would tell their son lies, and she simply said, "You have your precious career, and I have nothing but our son. I'll be damned if you'll have him too." At that point Preston realized that she was unstable, and that he really didn't know her at all. He was tempted to leave but he didn't want to abandon his child, so he endured the torturous marriage until his son went off to college, then he promptly filed for divorce.

Though he truly loved Ariel, he had not planned on getting hitched anytime soon, if ever. During his first marriage, Preston had sacrificed his happiness in order to stay under the same roof as his son; now was he willing to sacrifice his freedom in order to nail the nomination? The senator made a strong argument; having a high-powered attorney as a wife would definitely strengthen his chances of securing the nomination. The more he thought about the idea, the more appealing it became; he was willing to give marriage another shot, especially if having a Mrs. on his arm presented a stronger image. The only problem he could foresee would be convincing Ariel to accept his proposal. He had been holding her at arm's length lately, while he focused on his career, and the divide between them was growing wider with each passing day. He would have to do some serious backpedaling to convince her that his proposal was sincere.

No time like the present, Preston thought, as he picked up the phone and dialed her office. "Hi, JoAnne, may I speak with Ariel?"

"I'm sorry, Judge Hendricks," she said, instantly recognizing his distinctive voice, "but she's not in today."

"Is she in court?"

"No, she's out sick."

"Oh, okay. Thanks, JoAnne. I'll call her at home."

In all the years he'd known Ariel, Preston could rarely remember her calling in sick, and he began to worry. He quickly dialed her number. After four rings, she picked up.

"Hello . . ." Ariel answered, sounding foggy and far away.

He softened his normally loud booming tone and asked in a low, caring voice, "Hey, honey, what's the matter?"

"Who is this?" she asked, not recognizing the compassionate voice on the other end of the phone.

"It's me, honey. I just called your office and JoAnne said you were sick. What's the matter?" he asked again.

"I have a slight cold." She coughed. "Nothing serious," she lied. Ariel didn't have a cold; she had a serious hangover. She had staggered home from The Black Door at three in the morning and passed out across her bed. When she awoke that morning, she still had on her red, come-hither outfit and her head was pounding like a giant tom-tom. She popped two Tylenols, called in sick, took off the incriminating negligee, and crawled under the covers.

"Can I bring you a bowl of soup from the store?" he asked, totally out of character. In all of the years that they had been dating, he had never brought her anything from the grocery store.

"No, I wouldn't want to take you away from your busy schedule," she responded, getting in a little dig.

Preston was silent for a few seconds, noting her sarcastic comment. "Ariel, I know I've been preoccupied lately, but I want to make it up to you. I promise that from here on out, things are going to be different," he said, using his most convincing tone.

Reflecting back on her tryst at The Black Door, Ariel thought, *Things are already different.* Her confidence was back, and now she didn't need Preston to satisfy her sexual desires; it felt liberating. "Whatever you say, Preston," she muttered nonchalantly.

"This isn't some empty promise." He raised his voice a decibel. "Ariel, you mean more to me than you'll ever know."

"Yeah, I just bet I do," she said casually.

Preston was baffled. For weeks Ariel had been practically begging him for attention, and now that he was pouring his heart out to her, she sounded like she could care less. If he didn't know better, he'd swear there was someone else in the picture, but he knew that she would never cheat on him. "Why don't I come over tonight and bring you soup, a big box of Kleenex, and some Thera-Flu."

"No, thanks. I'm really not feeling up to company," she said, putting him off.

Preston was offended. "Company? Since when did I become company?"

"Preston, don't be silly. You know what I mean. I'm feeling lousy, and just want to veg out in front of the television; besides, I don't want you to catch my bug."

"Oh, okay," he relented, knowing that he couldn't afford to be ill now that he was embarking on such an important venture. "But, I'm taking you to dinner as soon as you feel better. We haven't been on a date in weeks and . . ." He paused for a second, waiting for her to express her delight; when she didn't, he continued. "I miss you, Ariel."

She fake coughed again. "I'm going to take another dose of NyQuil and go back to sleep. I'll talk to you later," she said, dismissing his sentimentality.

"Feel better, honey."

After Preston hung up, he put his head in his hands and sighed. Their relationship was in worse shape than he had thought, and it was going to take more than a romantic dinner and a few sweet words to win Ariel over. But he wasn't going to let her attitude dissuade him from his mission. Being a Supreme Court justice had been Preston's dream for as long as he could remember, and one minor issue—being single—was not going ruin his well-planned agenda.

12

TREY'S EMOTIONS were all over the place. He was conflicted. On the one hand, he was still enjoying the afterglow of having explosive sex with Meri Renick, but on the other hand, he had broken house rule *numero uno*. When the club opened, Trey promised himself that he wouldn't get involved with any of the members. He felt that if he was going to have a successful business, then he would have to conduct himself like a businessman, not a gigolo.

But nature had called the shots that night when he saw Meri sauntering through the club dressed in that red, seductive, "come-fuck-me" outfit, and that's exactly what he did. His libido was in overdrive as he pulled her into a utility closet without saying a single word, because his body did all the talking. He had sensed from that first night on the steps that she wanted him as much as he wanted her. The space that he pulled her into was as tight as a pod, with just enough room for them to find utopia. Trey came so hard that he saw stars. He always thought that cliché was a misnomer, but he actually saw a few celestial beings as cum rushed out of the head of his penis. Just thinking about being inside of her was making him hard, and he began to crave her body, like a dope fiend craving a crack pipe. His attraction to her was disconcerting. He wasn't into older women, yet he was irresistably drawn to her and couldn't get the feel of her smooth ass off of his mind.

I have the perfect antidote to cure this craving, he thought, as he looked at the cell-phone number scribbled on the back of a crumpled-up business card. He dialed the seven digits. The only thing better than pussy was *new* pussy.

"Hello," cooed a sweet voice on the other end of the line.

"It's Trey," he said, as if his first name were enough of an introduction.

"I've been waiting for your call. What took you so long?" she asked.

"I didn't know there was a time restriction," he teased.

"You're so fine that I'd wait forever and then some."

That was the response Trey had gotten all of his life from women—young and old—and the compliment fed his soul. He never had a problem getting a girlfriend; his problem was staying interested in one woman long enough to make a commitment. He was the consummate bachelor, always staying one step ahead of the C-word.

"You want to get together tonight?" he asked, knowing fully well that she wouldn't be able to resist his invitation.

"Sure," she said eagerly. "What did you have in mind?"

Trey had only one thing on his mind at the moment, and that was sex. "Why don't you come over for dinner and *dessert?*" he said suggestively.

"Okay," she answered readily, not skipping a beat.

"I'm at 128 East Thirty-eighth, right off Park. See you around nine."

"I can't wait," she said, and hung up.

Contrary to his character, Trey's apartment wasn't the typical bachelor pad. He lived in a tony co-op on the East Side in a beautifully restored, prewar Art Deco building. His unit was a spacious duplex with blond hardwood floors throughout; three balconies—two on the main floor, and one off of the master bedroom; two guest suites; and maid's quarters. Since he worked in a sex-laden environment, he didn't want that same look at home, so for the decor, he chose a soothing monochromatic theme of earth tones with a smattering of color. Trey's Italian furniture was sleek, with clean lines, as were his electronics, and his artwork consisted of original gouaches by Dalí, Erté, and Pollock.

After a quick shower, Trey put on a pair of silk drawstring pants and a ribbed tank, splashed his face with his signature Bvlgari cologne, and headed downstairs to the kitchen. Trey was an amateur chef and took pride in his unique pasta creations. He looked in the fridge to find something to whip up, but there was only a head of wilted butter lettuce, a wedge of brie speckled with mold, a half-empty can of whipped cream—that he used between the legs of his last dinner guest—and a bottle of Moët & Chandon Nectar.

"Guess I'll have to order in," he said, taking the champagne out of the refrigerator. Trey took the menu for Table for Two out of his kitchen drawer and read over the entrées. Not knowing if his dinner guest was a carnivore, vegan, or vegetarian, he ordered surf, turf, and a spinach soufflé.

After ordering dinner, Trey lit votive candles throughout the apartment. The glow from the flickering flames, reflected off of the alabaster walls, creating a cozy, romantic feeling in the cavernous space. Once the ambience was set, he brought a silver bucket filled with ice, the champagne, and two crystal flutes from the kitchen into the living room and set them on the cocktail table.

The doorman rang just has as he popped the cork. "Perfect timing," he mused. Trey gave the okay to let his guest enter, and cracked the front door slightly before walking back into the living room. He sat on the sofa, poured two glasses of champagne, and casually took a sip.

"Hello . . . ? Trey . . . ?" she called out from the foyer.

"I'm in here."

She followed the sound of his voice, and within seconds was standing in front of him. He handed her a glass of champagne.

"Welcome to my humble abode." He smiled.

"Nice place," she said, looking around the dimly lit room, put the flute on the cocktail table and then took off her coat.

Trey's dick pulsated and began to rise the moment he saw her outfit. She wore a black satin minidress with shoestring laces running down each side, exposing her thighs, with the glossy fabric accentuating her firm nipples. She looked good enough to eat, and he wanted a taste, but he played it cool. Trey knew if he appeared unaffected by her seductive outfit, then she would work harder to get his attention. And sure enough, when he didn't comment on her sexy number, she bent over, picking up her glass directly in front of him, so he could peek at her cleavage. He swallowed hard, but didn't say a word as he watched her juicy titties hanging loose underneath the dress. He could see her nipples brushing against the fabric, and wanted to suck them so bad that his mouth began to water, but he ignored the urge. "Hope you're hungry," he said suggestively.

Her eyes zeroed in on his crotch, and though the room was only lit by candlelight, she could see his semierection. She put the glass to her lips, drained the contents in one fast gulp, licked her lips, and then said, "I'm starving."

It took all of Trey's willpower not to pull her down on top of him, but he had to maintain his composure; otherwise, he'd lose his control and appear desperate. Trey had lost his cool with Meri, and that was enough to snap him back to reality. And in his reality, he would never become pussy-whipped—though he loved sex—and be controlled by one woman. "Good. I ordered dinner from Table for Two. It should be here soon," he said nonchalantly.

She looked confused and didn't know quite how to read him. One minute he seemed to be flirting, and the next he seemed indifferent. She assumed he'd be all hands the second she removed her coat, but he wasn't. Normally, she didn't have sex with a man until they'd known each other for at least thirty days, but she'd make an exception for Trey. She walked over to him, spread her legs, and sat directly on top of his growing rod.

"I want an appetizer before dinner," she whispered in his ear.

"What did you have in mind?" he asked casually, as if she weren't sitting on his cock.

She reached down and massaged his dick through the thin silk fabric. "I have a taste for beef sausage."

"Is that right?" Trey was trying desperately to maintain his cool, but his dick was as hard as a copper pipe and he was dying to bust a nut.

"Yep, that's right." She slipped between his legs onto her knees, released his penis through the pants' opening, and began to lick the shaft. She trailed her tongue around the circumference of his head, and then slid his dick into her mouth.

Trey grabbed her hair as she sucked him off. "Yeah, baby, that's it. Don't stop."

She bobbed her head up and down frantically until she brought him close to climax, then replaced her mouth with her hand and jerked him off.

"Now that's what I call an appetizer," she panted, wiping her mouth with the back of her hand.

After he came, Trey was satisfied and ready to toss her out, but he had to tread carefully since they traveled in the same circles. "Yeah, baby, that was good."

She got off her knees and cuddled next to him on the sofa. "I wanted to do that the first time I laid eyes on you," she confessed.

"Good things come to those who wait," he teased.

"Like I told you before, I'd wait for you forever," she said, dreamy-eyed.

When he heard the sincerity in her voice, Trey knew he had to make his intentions clear, otherwise, she'd get hurt and he'd have to deal with the backlash. "Listen." He moved away slightly. "I'm not looking for a relationship."

"Neither am I," she lied. "I just want to hang out."

"That's cool. We can hang, as long as we're on the same page." Just as he made his statement, the doorbell rang. "There's dinner," he said, and excused himself to answer the door.

They ate in silence. Trey's mind was still on Meri. He felt as if he was under some kind of hypnotic spell, and his attempt at breaking free had proven futile. He hated to admit it, but what he needed was more hair of the dog, and that hair belonged to Meri.

13

ARIEL GATHERED an armload of case files and put them in the out-box for JoAnne to file; her workday had come to a close, and none too soon. She'd been dragging around for a few days. She still felt drunk from too much vodka and hedonistic anonymous sex and just couldn't seem to pull herself together. The B-complex vitamin she'd taken that morning had long worn off, and all she wanted to do was go home, take a bath, and get into bed. But to her chagrin, Preston insisted on taking her to dinner. Normally, she would have jumped at the chance to have a night out with him, but her feelings were beginning to shift. Ariel hadn't expected to make a connection at The Black Door; she was just supposed to be an innocent bystander, but she had become a willing participant instead. Now the connection she made had her questioning her feelings for Preston. She dictated one more letter for her assistant to transcribe, then gathered her belongings and headed out the door.

"JoAnne, can I have this in the morning?" she asked, giving her assistant the microcassette.

"Sure, no problem. Have a good night, Ms. Vaughn."

"Thanks, JoAnne, and don't stay too late." JoAnne, a single mom, had been with Ariel since she started with the firm, and was a hard worker who clocked serious overtime to keep her daughter in private school.

Ariel didn't feel up to tackling the subway. Instead, she hailed a cab outside of the office. In the back of the taxi, she leaned her head back and closed her eyes. She instantly flashed back to the encounter with Mr. Black Mask. No one had ever manhandled her like that before; it was both frightening and exhilarating at the same time. Frightening because he snuck up from behind, caught her off guard, and pulled her into a pitch-black room; exhilarating because excitement surged through Ariel's body the moment she realized that it was the man she'd been hunting for all night. But she was also perplexed by his sudden disappearance. The other male servers she encountered at the club were verbally aggressive— practically begging her for sex—but he didn't say one word, just fucked her and walked out. She should've been offended by his abruptness, but Ariel found herself drawn to his mystique, and wanted to know more about the man behind the mask. His body was perfect, as if Michelangelo had carefully sculpted him out of marble. She could feel the hard muscles of his arms when he grabbed her by the waist. And the smell of his cologne was like an aromatic aphrodisiac that made her horny with lust. Just the thought of him was making her wet. Ariel pressed her legs together in an effort to quell her mounting desire.

The muffled sound of ringing disturbed her lustful reverie. She rolled her eyes at the interruption, dug the tiny cell phone out of her purse, looked at the caller ID, and sighed. "Hello, Preston," she said, with about as much enthusiasm as a sluggish mollusk.

"Hey, honey, where are you?" he asked excitedly.

Ariel was still upset at the way Preston had dismissed her accusations when she had confronted him at his town house. He practically laughed in her face when she quizzed him about Michele. "On my way home."

"We have an eight o'clock reservation at Spice Market. I'll pick you up at seven-thirty, so be ready. I can't wait to see you, honey," he said.

The Invasion of the Body Snatchers quickly flashed through Ariel's mind. Did someone replace the real Preston with a replica? It wasn't too long ago that he was pushing her away, focusing on his precious career. His attitude had suddenly shifted, and he was practically hunting her down for a date. She didn't know whether to be thrilled or suspicious. "Okay. I'll be downstairs at seven-thirty."

"I'll see you then, honey." Then totally out of character, he made a kissy sound into the receiver before hanging up.

Ariel looked strangely at her cell phone. *What's gotten into him?*

Traffic was snarled in midtown, as usual, and the taxi sat motionless for what seemed like fifteen minutes, before inching at a snail's pace toward Ariel's building. Three-quarters of an hour later, she was finally home.

Once inside her apartment, Ariel went into the bedroom and threw herself across the bed for a catnap. She'd planned on sleeping for twenty minutes, take a shower, and get dressed, but when the phone rang, she looked at the clock on the nightstand; it was ten minutes after seven. She'd been asleep for almost an hour.

"Hello," she said frantically.

"Where's the fire, darling?" Meri asked, picking up on her panicked tone.

"Hi. Can't talk. Running late," she blurted out. Preston was a stickler for time, and though she was still miffed at him, she didn't want to start the evening off on a negative note.

"Oh." Meri sounded offended.

"Listen, I'll call you later," Ariel said, rushing her off of the phone.

"Okay, darling," Meri said, and hung up.

Ariel didn't have time to shower, so she quickly refreshed her key areas by sponging off with a washcloth and soap. She then rushed to the closet and snatched a black jersey dress off of its wooden hanger, then put on a pair of black sling-backs, sans hose, and a strand of pearls. She brushed her hair in a neat chignon, patted her face with translucent power, and applied a layer of Russian Red to her lips. She threw her ID, cell phone, credit card, and the tube of lipstick into an evening bag, spritzed her neck with ENJOY and flew out of the door in record time.

Preston's Towncar was waiting curbside as she exited the building. Ariel slowed her gait and exhaled. She didn't want to appear eager, even though part of her was thrilled that her man had taken the initiative and actually planned a date. Nevertheless, she remained cool as she got into the car.

"Wow, you look great!" he exclaimed, as he took her hand and helped her settle into the backseat. He took a deep whiff. "And you smell great too!"

"Aren't you full of compliments this evening."

"And you're deserving of every single one and *more*." He smiled.

Unable to withstand the pleasantries any longer, Ariel blurted out, "Look, Preston, we need to talk."

He lightly touched her knee. "I know, honey, but let's wait until we get to the restaurant. We'll have a great dinner, wine, and a wonderful conversation that's long overdue."

Ariel reluctantly relented. "Okay, Preston, whatever you say."

In an effort to ease the mounting tension, he pressed one of three buttons on the armrest and instantly, soft jazz filled the air as they focused their attention on the passing scenery instead of on the pink elephant that sat awkwardly between them. The limo floated south on Fifth Avenue toward downtown, while they remained silent, listening to sound of vintage Billie Holiday singing softly in the background.

Twenty minutes later, the car was pulling in front of one of Jean George's acclaimed restaurants. The Spice Market was located in the Meatpacking District, Manhattan's newly crowned trendy area. It was formerly a desolate commercial zone populated by butchers and bloody carcasses hanging from meat hooks in the day and cat-size rats prowling the streets at night. Over the years, the neighborhood made a drastic change, converting abandoned warehouses into million-dollar lofts with art galleries and avant-garde cafés drawing the "beautiful" people by the masses. Now the once barren area was swarming with uptown types splurging at overpriced boutiques and dining at some of the finest restaurants in the city.

"Hendricks, table for two," Preston said to the hostess.

Ariel stood back and marveled at the cavernous, bilevel space. Though grand in scale, the room had a romantic, slightly erotic feel. The decor was Malaysia meets Manhattan, Zen-like with a flair of urban chic.

The hostess seemed to immediately recognize his name without referring to her reservation list. "Right this way, sir." She led them up an elongated staircase into a cozy, softly lit private chamber. "Your server will be with you momentarily."

Ariel positioned herself on the russet cushions, and Preston followed suit. The waiter appeared in the doorway looking like a genie fresh out of the bottle, dressed in a smock and harem pants. "May I bring you cocktails?"

Knowing exactly how Ariel liked her martini, Preston took the liberty and answered for them both, "We'll have two ice-cold, extremely dry Belvedere martinis. I'd also like to see your wine list."

The waiter returned shortly with their drinks and went on to explain the specials. "For starters, we have a succulent crabmeat salad with vermicelli; Thai fried fish cakes; and spring rolls. And for the main course, there's the onion-and-chile-crusted short ribs, or grilled snapper served whole on a bed of lime and sesame noodles. And just so you know, the dishes are meant to be shared and are brought out when ready, not necessarily in any particular order," he informed them.

"Everything sounds good, so I'll leave the selections to you," Preston told the waiter.

"As you wish, sir." He nodded genie-style.

Once the waiter was gone, Preston raised his glass and clinked it with Ariel's. "To us."

She took a sip and, as the icy cold vodka slid down her throat, she began to finally relax. Ariel couldn't remember the last time that she and Preston had had a romantic dinner, and it felt good to be pampered.

Preston slid closer and softly kissed her neck. "I've missed you, Ariel," he whispered into her ear.

"You've been so pre—"

He kissed her lips to stop her talking, and instinctively finished her sentence. "I know I've been preoccupied lately, but I promise, things are going to change. You are the most important person in my life, and I—"

"That's funny, I thought Senator Oglesby was the most important person in your life," she said, cutting him off.

Preston looked wounded, as if her words had cut him to the quick, but he immediately recovered. "I'll admit that sitting on the Supreme Court has been a dream of mine for a long time, and the senator has been an inescapable part of this tedious process, but—"

Ariel cut him off again. "What are you trying to tell me, Preston?

That our relationship has to simmer on the back burner until you're confirmed?" she asked, raising her voice half a decibel. She could feel the vein in the middle of her forehead start to sprout, and downed her martini in one swift gulp in an effort to cool her jets.

"What I'm trying to tell you," he reached into his breast pocket, and pulled out a small aqua box, "is that I love you." Preston opened the tiny lid. "And I want you to be my wife."

Ariel looked into the plush little box, and looking back at her was a four-carat, princess-cut diamond engagement ring. Her jaw dropped in complete shock. A proposal was the last thing she had expected. Even though they had been dating for years, he never once alluded to marriage, and she never pushed the envelope. The way Preston had been acting lately, she assumed that the last thing he wanted was a permanent commitment. "I . . . I . . . don't know what to say," she stammered.

He took the ring out of the box and placed it on her finger. "Just say yes."

She stared at the ring and admired the way it glistened in the candlelight. The rainbow-colored rays were mesmerizing, rendering her speechless.

"Ariel, will you marry me?" he asked, anxiously awaiting her answer.

"Preston, don't you think we need to have a serious discussion about what's been going on lately, before we dive headfirst into a situation that neither one of us is ready for?" she asked.

"If you're talking about Michele, I'm going to tell you once and for all that nothing is going on between us. It's strictly professional. Besides, she's dating my son."

She looked surprised. "Little Preston?"

"He's not so little anymore. He's a grown man now. And he and Michele are dating," he said again to bring the point home.

"Wow, I haven't seen him since . . ." she hesitated, trying to recall their last visit, ". . . since, I don't know when."

"Actually you did see him, the other day at the town house. He was coming in when you were going out."

Once again, she looked surprised. "That was Little Preston?"

"Yes, in the flesh." He took her hand and looked deep into her eyes. "Now do you believe me when I tell you that I'm not sleeping with Michele?"

She nodded her head yes. "But . . ."

"No buts, honey. Just say yes."

"Preston, you've been pushing me away so much. Now you do a complete about-face and propose marriage. This has taken me totally by surprise, so I'm going to need some time to think about this unexpected turn of events." In the back of her mind, she could hear her foster mom's voice telling her to say yes, but after her encounter at The Black Door, she wasn't sure what she wanted.

He slumped back in his seat, as if the oxygen had been sucked out of his lungs. Preston knew Ariel was upset with him for being preoccupied, but he didn't think that she would actually mull over his proposal. "Take all the time you need," he said, trying to sound sympathetic to her feelings.

"Thanks for understanding."

But Preston didn't understand. He knew most women wanted nothing more than white lace and promises, but Ariel had practically turned him down cold. Well, he wouldn't pressure her tonight, but he wasn't about to let her slip through his fingers either. He had too much riding on her decision, so one way or another she was going to be Mrs. Preston Hendricks.

14

ARIEL SAT with her back to the closed door, gazing out of the floor-to-ceiling windows of her office. The cerulean sky was cloudless and crystal clear, and she saw a jetliner streak through the picture-perfect sky and wondered where it was headed. She imagined traveling on that plane and being whisked away to a tropical island where her days consisted of eating, drinking, and fucking. Daydreams had consumed her entire day, and she found it difficult to concentrate on anything other than the massive rock that occupied her finger. She held her hand out and admired how the sun caught each exquisite facet, causing the diamond to cast off a kaleidoscope of brilliant colors. Even though she hadn't accepted Preston's proposal, Ariel couldn't bring herself to take off the engagement ring; it was stunning and she was captivated by its beauty.

All morning and half of the afternoon, Ariel was racking her brain trying to figure out why Preston had made a complete 180.

The only plausible reason was that he was trying to make amends for putting his impending nomination before their relationship, but his gesture of devotion couldn't have come at a worse time. Though she loved Preston, sex with her secret lover was so explosive that it made her question if she was indeed ready to sleep with one man for the rest of her life.

Conflicting thoughts were swirling inside her head at warp speed and it was making her dizzy. Ariel needed a sounding board to help her sort through her tangled feelings. She thought about calling her foster mother, but Mrs. Grant would be anything but diplomatic; she'd probably called Preston herself and accept his proposal on Ariel's behalf. She swiveled the chair around to the front of the desk, picked up the phone, and called Meri instead.

"Hey there," Ariel said, trying to sound calm.

"Darling, I take it you finally have time to talk. You rushed me off the phone so fast last night that I didn't have time to tell you about Stanton," Meri said, wasting no time steering the conversation to her favorite topic—men.

"Who?"

"Only the most delicious man I've ever tasted," Meri said, using one of her standard lines.

"Didn't you say that about, uh, what's his name?"

"Paul," Meri answered, knowing exactly whom she was referring to. "Well, he was on last week's menu. *Stanton* is the dish du jour, and I'm feasting on a daily basis. You should see the head on his dick; it's so big and smooth that I can't keep his schlong out of my mouth. And the way he eats pussy is mind blowing. I haven't had a sixty-nine this good since 1969." She laughed heartily.

Meri never ceased to amaze Ariel. She was the most sexual being that Ariel had ever met. Her libido was in perpetual overdrive, and she consumed men like a black widow devouring her unsuspecting prey. "How long are you going to keep this one around?" Ariel asked, knowing that Meri didn't keep her boy toys around for too long. Once their newness wore off, she'd discard them and go to her well-stocked shelf for a new toy.

Meri let out a deep belly laugh, then said, "As long as he keeps my clit happy and his dick hard, I suspect he might stay around for a few weeks before I trade him in."

"Oh my! That long? You must really like him," Ariel teased.

"As a matter of fact, I do," Meri answered seriously, dropping her cavalier tone. "He's more than just a pretty body. Believe it or not, he actually has a great mind. We have meaningful conversations about politics, social issues, and even religion."

Not quite buying Meri's change in attitude, Ariel joked. "Before, during, or after sex, of course."

"Touché," Meri said dryly. "Anyway, enough about me. What's going on in your world?" she asked, ready to change the subject.

"My world has been rocked and is spinning wildly on its axis," Ariel said, staring at the engagement ring.

"Do tell, darling."

Trying to collect her thoughts, Ariel hesitated. "I don't even know where to start." She sighed.

"Start with the juicy stuff first."

"Of course, you'd want the dirt first." Ariel chuckled. "I went back to The Black Door and—"

"And did you finally get your brains fucked out, or did you just stand around and take in the sights?" Meri interrupted.

"Meri, Meri, Meri," she repeated, unable to fully verbalize the sensational experience. "The sex was so good, I saw stars."

"Stars? Which one of the hunks turned you out?" Meri, asked knowing that The Black Door was brimming with sexy young studs willing and able to please at a moment's notice.

"Who said I was turned out, missy?"

"You didn't have to say a word; your tone says it all. So tell me, which one of the masked men tickled your fancy?"

Ariel's mind quickly drifted back to her erotic encounter, causing her temperature to rise a few degrees. And even though Meri couldn't see the gesture, she fanned her hand in front of her face at the memory. "Well, I didn't see his mask until after the dirty deed was done."

For once it was Meri who was shocked. "What do you mean?"

"He caught me totally off guard from behind, and practically dragged me into a small room. My face was pressed so close to the wall that I couldn't see too much of anything, and when I finally turned around, *he* was standing right in front of me."

"He? Who are you talking about?"

"Didn't I tell you about the guy in the black mask?"

Meri thought for a second, recalling their last conversation about The Black Door. "No, you never mentioned anyone in a black mask."

"I met him that first night in the stairwell and the chemistry between us was . . ." She hesitated, trying to find the right word. "Electric. I've never been drawn to a man like that before, not ever. My libido perked up the moment I laid eyes on him, and I wanted to wrap my arms around his neck and tongue him right on the stairs."

Meri was surprised to hear Ariel speak so candidly about desiring a man; usually she was the one who shared every single detail of her sexual exploits. "What stopped you?"

"I didn't respond quickly enough; you have to remember this entire experience is new to me and I froze, but I was totally thawed out the other night. Whew!" She sighed. "Just thinking about him makes me hot all over."

"So, when are you going back for more?"

"I'm not," Ariel said flatly.

"Why? Now I'm confused. You just had the sex of your life, so why wouldn't you go back for a double dose?"

"Because Preston proposed last night," she said, finally getting to the real reason for the phone call.

"What?" Meri nearly dropped the receiver. "How did you guys go from barely seeing each other to getting engaged?"

"We're not actually engaged, because I haven't given him an answer yet. I told him I needed some time to think. His proposal came totally out of the blue, and I'm still trying to get my mind around his complete change in attitude." Ariel went on to tell Meri the details of Preston's proposal, and his admission of undying love.

"Sounds like you're being paranoid, darling. All I can say is that it's about time. You guys have been dating longer than most couples have been married. So when's the big day?"

Ariel was surprised by her response. She expected Meri to shoot holes in Preston's heartfelt story, since she had told Ariel numerous times that she needed to dump him for a younger man. "Maybe I am being a little paranoid, but I'd expect you of all people to understand."

"I do understand, but I think you're overreacting. Isn't this what you've always wanted?"

"Frankly, I'm not sure what I want." Ariel exhaled loudly, obviously frustrated. "Growing up I dreamt of the perfect house, with the perfect husband and the perfect kids, but now I realize that nothing's perfect. Least of all me and Preston. I'm having decadent sex with a stranger, and he's blinded by a political career that will take him to Washington. I'm well established in New York, and not sure if I'm ready to pull up stakes and follow Preston to D.C."

"Darling, don't sound so glum. You can always transfer to Yates Gilcrest's Washington office. Besides, I think every woman should have at least one extravagant wedding in her lifetime, and you, my

dear, have yet to jump the old broom," she said lightheartedly, trying to lift her friend's spirits.

Contrary to popular belief, Meri was a proponent of marriage.
Having been married twice, she'd experienced the good and the
bad. Her first husband was a cheap tyrant who monitored every
single penny she spent, and when she went over his ridiculously
low budget, he cut up her credit cards and removed her name from
his bank account. Unable to live underneath a microscope, she divorced him and walked away with more money than she had ever
spent during their marriage. Her second husband, on the other
hand, was the love of her life. He was a generous man who showered her with love and lavish gifts on a regular basis. When he
died, she was devastated, and began dating younger men to dull
her pain.

Ariel chuckled nervously. "It's not about the pomp and circum-
stance; it's about a lifelong commitment, and I'm just not so sure
I'm ready to devote the rest of my existence to one man."

"Hmm, does this have anything to do with your Black Door
lover?" Meri asked knowingly.

Ariel didn't say a word because she didn't want to admit the
truth. And the truth was that she couldn't stop thinking about the
masked man, and what he was like outside of the club. In the recesses of her mind, she fantasized about waking up each morning
with him in her bed, how they would make love before heading off
to work, and end every evening wrapped in each other's arms.

Having been around the block more than once, Meri instinctively picked up on Ariel's hesitancy to commit. "Listen, I know
you're probably romanticizing what it would be like to have a relationship with a handsome hunk, but trust me, the sex quickly fiz-
zles out once you try to convert a 'working' man into an honest
man. Darling, believe me, I know what I'm talking about; save
yourself some heartache and marry Preston. He may not be the

hottest bun in the bakery, but he's a man you can depend on, someone who'll be there when times get tough."

Meri made a good argument. How could she possibly build a
life with a gigolo? "You're absolutely right. I've been living on Fantasy Island for the past few days and haven't been thinking
straight."

"Good sex will do that to you. Just remember that The Black
Door is not reality. It's an adult playground, somewhere to go to get
your brains fucked out, and nothing more. Besides, you can always
go back on those nights when Preston is burning the midnight
oil," Meri teased.

"Get serious. Once I get married, I'm giving you back your red
mask."

"Oh, so you've made a decision?" Meri asked, noting her slip.

Not realizing what she had said, Ariel hesitated a moment to
let her mind catch up with her mouth. "So it seems. The more I
think about marrying Preston, the more sense it makes. He loves
me, and will no doubt be a good husband. Besides, it's not like I'm
getting any younger. If I don't get hitched now, it'll probably never
happen."

"Spoken like a true middle-aged woman."

"Hey, hey, speak for yourself. I'm not middle-aged yet."

"Don't tell anybody, but I'll never admit to being a day over
thirty-eight," Meri whispered, as if she didn't want to be overheard.

They both let out a hardy howl. And when the laughter subsided, Meri said, "I insist on giving you an engagement soiree. You
can invite anybody you like. It'll be fabulous."

"Can I invite my friend in the black mask?" Ariel joked halfheartedly.

"We'll save *him* for the bachelorette party."

The women chatted for an hour, discussing plans for the engagement party and wedding. The more they talked, the more ex-

cited Ariel became. Even if Preston was not the Prince Charming of her fantasies, she would make the marriage work; after all, she still had memories of The Black Door to keep her warm on those lonely nights when Preston was preoccupied with his work.

When Ariel hung up from talking with Meri, she was totally elated. Her apprehensions about getting married had quickly dissipated as they hashed out plans for an extravagant black-tie engagement party. With talks of champagne, caviar, and walking down the aisle, Ariel could feel herself being drawn into a world of caterers, engraved invitations, and florists. She wanted a quaint ceremony with close friends and family, not an over-the-top wedding like Meri had suggested. But before any plans could be finalized, she needed to formally accept Preston's proposal.

No time like the present, she thought. Ariel looked at her watch. It was late afternoon and Preston was probably in his chambers. Instead of calling, she decided it best to tell him in person. She gathered her belongings and headed out the door.

LOWER MANHATTAN WAS a world within itself. The imposing municipal buildings with their Roman and Grecian columns and ivory steps seemed centuries away from the modern glass-and-steel skyscrapers dominating midtown. The taxi stopped in front of the federal court building, where Preston reigned, and let Ariel out. The hallways were bustling with people hurrying to hear their fate in front of a judge. She passed through security, pushed her way onto a crowded elevator, and rode up to the sixth floor to Preston's chambers.

"Hi, Anna, is Judge Hendricks available?" she asked his secretary.

"Ariel, I haven't seen you around these parts in a long time. What brings you by?"

"I thought I'd surprise the judge." She smiled.

The older woman smiled back. "Isn't that sweet? He just returned from court and doesn't have anything else on his calendar for the rest of the afternoon, so go right on in. I'm sure he'll be happy to see you."

Ariel lightly tapped on the door, then walked in and flipped the lock behind her. Preston looked up from his legal pad and when he saw Ariel, a huge grin spread across his face.

"Hey, honey, what did I do to deserve this visit?"

She raised her left hand and wiggled her ring finger. "Proposed, that's what." Ariel took off her blazer, tossed it in a chair near the door, and sauntered toward him. If this relationship was going to work, Ariel realized that they needed to reignite their sex life. Besides, the sooner she forgot about her tryst at The Black Door and put the entire experience behind her, the better.

"So, Ms. Vaughn, have you come to deliver your answer in person?" He grinned hopefully.

Ariel parked herself on the edge of his oak desk and crossed her long legs so that the split on her skirt exposed her upper thigh. "Yes, I have, Judge," she answered using her pet name for him.

Based on her body language and glib tone, Preston assumed that Ariel was no longer upset with him, and he couldn't be happier. If she accepted his proposal, that would be one less item on his plate to worry about. "Well . . ." He ran his hand up and down her exposed thigh. "Don't keep me in suspense any longer."

"I've given your proposal a lot of thought, and . . . yes, I'll marry you!" The moment she said it aloud, Ariel knew that her future was meant to be spent with Preston, and not with some no-name gigolo.

Preston stood up, grabbed her by the waist, and pulled her close to him. "You've made me so happy," he whispered in her ear, and then kissed her passionately.

Ariel wrapped her arms around his neck and greeted his tongue with hers. She pressed her hips into him, and could feel his penis getting hard. She began grinding into his growing erection.

"Wait," he stepped back, "we can't; Anna is still here."

"Yes, we can." She moved toward him. "I locked the door. Come on, baby, it'll be like old times." Ariel turned around, flipped up her skirt, took off her pantyhose, and leaned over the desk. "Don't you want me?" she asked over her shoulder.

Preston looked down at her exposed ass and licked his lips. Unable to contain his desire any longer, he unzipped his pants and unleashed his throbbing dick. He spread her cheeks apart and fingered her pussy. She was as wet as a river, and her moistness made him grow an extra inch. Over the past few weeks, Preston had put sex out of his mind, but with Ariel spread-eagled across his desk, all he could think about was fucking her until they both came. He entered her and began to frantically pump back and forth, but before she could get her rhythm, he ejaculated prematurely.

Ariel couldn't believe that Preston had come so quickly; she didn't even have time to get into the groove before the groove was over.

"Sorry, honey, it's been so long since we made love that I just couldn't control myself," he said, apologizing for climaxing too soon. He turned her around so that her body was facing him. "Don't worry, I promise I won't leave you hanging," he said, kneeling down. Preston spread her lips and began sucking her engorged clit.

She threw her head back and moaned, "Oh, baby, that feels so good."

As Ariel was on the verge of finding ecstasy, the phone rang. Initially, Preston ignored the insistent ringing, but after the forth ring, he stopped midlick, looked over at his desk, and noticed that a red light was blinking on his phone.

He stood up immediately and wiped her juices from his mouth. "That's my private line. I've got to get that; it might be the senator," he said, abandoning her needs to attend to his business.

Ariel was livid! Preston had just promised to satisfy her; now he was breaking that promise to satisfy the senator, and she couldn't help but wonder how many times she would be tossed aside for his precious agenda. Still horny, she wanted desperately to cum. Ariel closed her eyes, tuned out Preston's conversation, and envisioned the only thing that would quickly satisfy her lust: The Black Door.

15

TREY RETURNED to the scene of the crime. Well, actually the scene had changed, but the crime was still the same. He was going to his new friend's apartment for a home-cooked meal, instead of gourmet takeout and *dessert*. She had called earlier in the day and invited him over for dinner. His first inclination was to decline, but Trey still had Meri on the brain, and he needed a serious distraction. Since he had broken cardinal rule number one and fucked a client, he was trying to erase that experience from his memory, but the erotic visions wouldn't go away; they were etched in his mind and played like a continuous loop.

"Aren't you a sight for sore eyes?" she said, opening the door and admiring Trey from his Prada loafers to the top of his closely cropped hair.

He licked his full lips. "And you look good enough to eat." The last time they were together, she had given him a hair-raising blow job. And tonight he'd return the favor.

"Let's have dinner first, before *dessert*," she said, trying to slow down the momentum to prolong their date. She didn't want an abbreviated evening like before. "Come on in." She stepped aside, inviting him into her apartment.

As Trey followed her into the living room, he could see her long legs, slim waist, and tight ass through the ultrasheer flowing caftan that she wore. She had a svelte dancer's body that seemed made for fucking, and he was going to do his best to give her a serious workout tonight.

"Have a seat." She pointed to an armless, midnight-blue, ultrasuede sofa. "What can I get you to drink?"

"I'll have vodka on the rocks with a twist."

"Is Belvedere okay?"

He winked. "It's perfect."

She handed him a slim Bang & Olufsen remote. "Put on some music. I'll be right back."

Trey looked around her cozy, contemporarily furnished apartment and saw a wall-mounted stereo system with a stack of CDs on each side. He walked over, thumbed through the music selection, and chose Jill Scott's new album, as well as the latest from Sade and James Blunt. After he put the CDs in the carousel, he lit the votive candles that were sitting on the mantel. He turned off the bright lamps on the side tables, so that the room was bathed only in candlelight, creating a romantic scene. Once the mood was set, Trey stood in place and grooved to the soft jazz.

Walking into the room carrying their cocktails, she stopped short as she noticed the change. Before she could respond, Trey took the drinks out of her hands, set them on the mantel, and swept her up in a tight embrace.

He could feel the soft mound of her breasts pressing against his chest and the closeness turned him on. Swaying back and forth in a seductive slow dance, Trey nuzzled his nose into her neck, then gently rubbed his hands up and down her lower back, until they stopped and rested on the round of her butt. He pressed his groin into hers as he massaged her cheeks. "Baby, you feel so good," he whispered in her ear.

"Listen, Trey." She stopped dancing. "Let's get one thing clear. I want a relationship," she blurted out.

He didn't say a word; just stood there looking shocked. Her announcement came straight with no chaser, and he didn't know what to say. He had assumed, based on their last visit, that all she wanted was a hard dick and a good fuck.

She continued, "I didn't plan on going down on you the other night, but you looked so damn sexy in those silk drawstring pants that I couldn't help myself. But I want you to know that I'm not looking to be your fuck-buddy. I know I told you that I didn't want a relationship, but I was lying to myself and to you."

"So what are you looking for?" he asked, taking the bait.

"I'm looking for someone to fall in love with, someone to share my life with," she said without hesitation.

In all his life, no woman had ever said point-blank what she wanted. Usually they hinted around and waited for him to add two and two together, but of course he chose not to do the math. Trey had drifted in and out of dead-end relationships most of his life and never desired a serious commitment. Looking at her beautiful body, he thought, *Why not?* Besides, the short-lived affair with his Black Door lover was a one-time occurrence with no future. "Baby, I appreciate your honesty, but I'm not ready to stand at the altar just—"

She cut him off. "I'm not asking you to marry me. All I'm saying is that I want more than dinner and a quick fuck. I've done the casual sex thing, and quite frankly it doesn't work for me. I want to spend quality time with you outside of the bedroom. I think we have a lot in common. Besides, we do have mutual acquaintances," she said, selling him on the idea of them becoming a couple.

Trey reached out and stroked her face. "Spoken like a woman who knows exactly what she wants."

She stepped closer and hugged him tight. "I do know what I want, and that's a relationship with you," she reiterated.

"Okay, let's take it one day at a time," he agreed noncommittally.

She reached up, wrapped her arms around his neck, and kissed him deeply. "Trey, you've made me so happy. We're going to make one hell of a power couple."

"Let's start with some power sex," he suggested, rubbing the small of her back.

"Well . . . I was thinking that we should start over." She took her arms from around his neck and slightly stepped back.

"What do you mean start over?" He furrowed his brow in confusion.

"Since I usually don't have sex on the first *or* second date, I want to forget about the other night and pretend like it didn't happen. I don't want to be the girl who went down on you the instant we hooked up."

Trey was mystified and squinted his eyes, trying to make sense of what she was saying. "What are you talking about? Why would I want to erase what happened? It was fabulous." He slowly moved his hand from her back around to her crotch. "Now it's my turn to reciprocate."

She pulled away. "I'm serious, Trey. Let's get to know each other better before we make love."

He wouldn't relent. "Don't be silly, baby. We're both consenting adults." He pressed his hard cock into her, so she could feel his erection. "And, I know you're not going to let all of this go to waste."

His dick felt good against her pulsating vagina, and she hungered for him, but she had to stay strong. She wanted to be more than just his late-night booty call, and was trying desperately to backpedal in order to redeem her self-respect. She had always wanted to be a wife and mother, and Trey was husband material. If she played her cards right, and rationed the pussy, they would be engaged before the end of the year. "You have such a healthy appetite, and I promise I'm all the woman you'll ever need."

Trey was getting hornier and hornier by the second. "And I need *all* of you right now."

"Come on. Let's have dinner first, and then we'll talk about *dessert*," she said, trying to pacify him.

Trey couldn't believe the drastic turn of events. The moment he agreed to a relationship, she began denying him sexual pleasures. Suddenly, he was beginning to doubt his decision. Trey wasn't used to working this hard to get laid. He was surrounded by gorgeous women on a daily basis, and could have any one of them at his discretion. His first thought was to say *fuck this* and go to the club, but he didn't. He hated to admit it, but he also wanted more than just a one-night stand. He had devoted the past few years to making The Black Door a success, and now that the business was thriving, it was time for him to devote that same energy into developing a successful personal life. And since his first choice—the woman in the red mask—was off-limits, he was going to give this "relationship" a try—at least for the time being.

MERI WAS the consummate socialite. Having graced the guest list of lavish soirees around the globe, she was well versed in the art of entertaining, and spared no expense on Ariel and Preston's black-tie engagement party. Only the best would do for her dear friend. Cases of vintage Dom Perignon were stacked in the pantry, waiting to replenish the chilled bottles already in the fridge. Beluga caviar on toast points, smoked salmon with capers, tuna ceviche, and filet mignon medallions sautéed in garlic and mushrooms and drizzled with black truffle oil were on tonight's menu, as well as an assortment of mini exotic fruit tarts and chocolate ganache tortes. Johnnie Walker Blue Label and hand-rolled cigars would serve as the perfect accoutrement to cap off the festive evening.

Meri's penthouse was swarming with an army of uniformed caterers, waiters, and assorted workers scurrying around carrying out their final instructions hours before the main event began. A stickler for detail, she barked out orders like a strict drill sergeant. With clipboard in hand, she marched from room to room checking off completed tasks from her to-do list. Tonight had to be perfect, so she left nothing to chance. She walked into the powder room to make sure that the housekeeper had changed the normally white guest towels to the silver-trimmed black ones. Meri had decided to infuse her stark-white decor with splashes of black to coordinate with tonight's black-tie affair.

"Perfect," she commented upon seeing the black towels and a black Diptique candle in place.

Next she strutted into the library to check on the cigar roller that she had flown in from Miami's Little Havana.

"Hola. Como está?" she asked, using the little bit of Spanish that she knew.

"Muy bien, gracias." He smiled in response.

"Habla inglés?"

"Yes, a little," he answered, with a thick Cuban accent.

"Good, because that's about all the Spanish I know." She walked closer to examine his inventory.

Displayed across a six-foot-long Biedermeier desk was an array of paraphernalia—tobacco leaves, loose tobacco, cutters, elongated matches, and an enormous hand-carved humidor filled with pre-rolled cigars. She lightly fingered each item, gave a nod of approval, and checked off "cigar purveyor" from her list.

"Everything appears to be in order."

He didn't say a word, just grinned and nodded his head up and down.

"Once people meander in and begin smoking, I'll need you to keep the pocket doors shut." She pointed to the doorway. "I want to try and keep the smoke contained to this room as much as possible. Understand?"

"Sí, sí, miss." He nodded again.

"Very well," she said, and walked out.

The next stop on her reconnaissance mission was the kitchen to check on dinner, but the instant the enticing aroma of sautéed mushrooms and garlic tickled her nose, she knew everything was under control.

The last item on the list was for her to take a relaxing bath and get dressed. Meri went into her bedroom suite to bathe and make the transformation from delegator to diva. An hour later she reemerged, donned in a floor-length black jersey gown with deep slits running up each leg. Her ten-thousand-dollar 38-Cs didn't need a brassiere to create cleavage and fill out the generous neckline; they stood erect on their own. She put on a diamond-and-onyx pendant that rested between the two mounds of mouthwatering flesh. She slipped on a pair of black bejeweled Jimmy Choos, walked over to the mirror, and inspected her reflection.

"You're one hot babe," she said, smoothing the thin fabric over her oversized breasts. "Not bad for an old broad." She winked at herself.

Just as she stepped out of her boudoir, the bell rang. She sauntered over to the foyer and opened the door.

"Wow! You look fabulous," Ariel exclaimed, taking in Meri's surgically enhanced body. "A little too fabulous, I might add. Tonight's supposed to be all about *me*, so why are you trying to upstage moi?" she teased.

"Daarliing, I paid good money to display this body," she said, striking a pose in the snug-fitting Roberto Cavalli dress. "And besides, you already have a man. I'm still trying to find one."

"Last time I checked you had more than one." Ariel laughed and walked inside.

"Touché." Meri closed the door. "But to be honest, I'm tiring of the boy-toys and ready to settle down with an M-A-N. Besides, if my best friend is getting hitched, I might as well rejoin the club."

"I don't believe my ears. Could it be that the infamous Meri Renick is retiring from the game?" Ariel put her hands to her cheeks in mock shock.

"Only if I find Mr. Right. Who knows, he could be here tonight. Since Preston has invited some of his colleagues, I just might snag a husband."

"Just make sure he's not already married to someone else," Ariel said knowingly.

"Don't worry, my days of being the 'other woman' are over. The only husband I want is my own. Anyway, enough about me. Look at you," she said, taking her friend's hand and twirling her around to get a 360-degree view.

Ariel wore a pearlized white Ralph Lauren gown with an empire waist and boatneck, which covered her rose tattoo. The dress was conservative at first glance, but the back was extremely sexy with a deep V-shape that started at the shoulders and tapered down into a point, stopping at the small of her back. "Thanks it's new. Thought I'd wear white tonight, since I won't be walking down the aisle in the proverbial virginal color."

"You can wear whatever you want these days, from black to white and every hue in between. Besides, white is a symbol of the purity of your love, not the purity of your vagina," Meri said boldly.

"That's true, but I'd feel like such a hypocrite wearing white, especially after my Black Door escapades." She blushed.

"Speaking of The Black Door, I think you should go back one more time before getting hitched."

Ariel had a brief flashback of her tryst and exhaled deeply at the memory of her masked lover. "No, I don't think so. Last time was too intense. It was so hot that I could see myself craving that man on a daily basis," she confessed.

"Well, just think of it as your bachelorette party, your one last hurrah," Meri said convincingly.

"Since Preston has been the attentive fiancé lately, and has made me his number-one priority, I don't need the services of the club anymore," she responded, trying to convince her friend as well as herself.

Meri raised an eyebrow, as if doubting Ariel's words. "Spoken like a true bride-to-be. On that note, I think we need a drink." Meri stopped one of the servers milling about and asked him to bring them a chilled bottle of champagne.

They settled in the living room and toasted before the party began. Meri raised her flute. "To the new Mrs. Hendricks, may you and Preston have a long, healthy, happy life together."

Ariel clinked her glass with Meri's. "I'll drink to that."

"Where's Mrs. Grant? I thought she'd be with you tonight."

"She wanted to come so badly, but she has a new set of three-year-old twins and didn't want to leave them with a babysitter. She's so happy that I'm getting married; you'd swear she was the one engaged," Ariel mused.

"She just wants the best for you. After all, she's never had children of her own, and having raised you, I'm sure she considers you her natural daughter."

"Yes, she does, and I love her like my natural mother. I made her promise that she'd leave those kids long enough to come to the wedding, and she said that's one event she wouldn't miss for the world," Ariel said.

"And she's not the only one; I myself will definitely have a front-row seat to witness the nuptials," Meri said, taking a sip of her champagne.

Ariel looked down at her engagement ring. "Wow, this is really happening, isn't it?" she asked rhetorically. "To be honest, I didn't think Preston would ever propose. His last marriage was a disaster, and I resigned myself to the fact that he probably never wanted to get married again. Sometimes I think he's going to get spooked and change his mind."

"Ariel," Meri said, "stop being paranoid, and accept the fact that Preston loves you and wants you to be his wife," she said sternly. "Darling, you've got to let go of that 'I'm not worthy' baggage."

"I know, I know, but I've carried it around so long that it's hard to put down. But I promise I'm going to make a concerted effort to let go of the past."

Meri raised her glass. "I'll most definitely drink to that."

BY THE TIME the first guest arrived, the two women had polished off one bottle of Dom, and were onto their second. The bubbly elixir had put them in a festive mood and they were feeling no pain.

"Anna, so good of you to come," Ariel said, greeting Preston's longtime secretary and giving her a warm hug.

"I wouldn't have missed this occasion for anything." She kissed Ariel on the cheek. "I've been hoping for a long time that you and the judge would tie the knot," she gushed, like an overprotective aunt. "Oh, by the way the judge wanted me to tell you that he'll be here shortly. He had a last-minute conference call."

So much for being his number-one priority, Ariel thought. "Thanks, Anna."

The party was nearly in full swing with colleagues and close friends mingling, munching on delectable hors d'oeuvres, sipping champagne, and chatting—but still no Preston. Ariel was fuming and could feel the vein protruding in the middle of her forehead. She couldn't believe his audacity. How could he be late for his own engagement party? She excused herself from a conversation with coworkers, slipped into Meri's bedroom, and called his cell.

"Where the hell are you?" she asked in a hushed tone, when he picked up, careful not to be overheard by the guests. "I can't believe you're late to *our* engagement party. I hope this—"

He cut her off midsentence. "Calm down, honey. I'm downstairs with my son and his date," Preston said casually, as if his tardiness was a nonissue.

"Well, it's about time," she responded.

Ariel rejoined the party and watched Meri work the room. She was chatting up a distinguished-looking gentleman wearing a Brooks Brothers suit, with graying temples, a protruding belly, and tortoiseshell spectacles. He was the polar opposite of her type, which was the young, hard-body GQ model type. "Looks like she found a victim," Ariel mused.

"Sorry I'm late," Preston apologized, walking up and giving Ariel a light kiss on the lips. "Look who I bumped into in the lobby?" he said, gesturing to the handsome couple standing beside him.

Ariel exhaled deeply, looked at the pair, and said unenthusiastically, "Hello, Michele." She wasn't exactly happy to see Preston's overtly sexy assistant. She took one look at Michele's spaghetti-strap slip dress and slightly rolled her eyes. The outfit would have been suitable for a black-tie affair if she had chosen to wear a strapless bra, but in true vamp form, her hard nipples were pressed against the thin silk fabric for all to see. *This girl has no shame*, she thought and rolled her eyes. Disgusted, Ariel turned her attention to the man standing next to Michele. "Hi, I'm Ariel Vaughn." She extended her hand.

He shook her hand in his. "I know," said the handsome stranger.

"What?" She looked confused.

"Don't you remember Preston III?" her fiancé asked.

She gave him a long hard look, and suddenly felt a familiarity that she couldn't explain. "I haven't seen you in . . ." She paused trying to think of their last encounter.

"I saw you at the town house a few weeks ago. You were rushing out as I was coming in," he interjected in a rich baritone voice.

"That was you?" Now she understood why he seemed familiar. "And I was thinking that I hadn't seen you since your graduation from college. So, what are you doing now?"

Preston affectionately slapped his son on the back. "He's a businessman.".

"Oh, really? What type of business are you in?" Ariel asked, wanting to know more about her future stepson.

Michele possessively looped her arm through his and beamed proudly. "He's an investment banker and a real-estate mogul."

He blushed. "I'm not an investment banker yet. I just passed the Series Seven. And as for real estate, I only own one property," he said, correcting her.

"Stop being so modest. It's only a matter of time before you're a mogul, and I'm going to be right by your side." She was clinging onto him like an insecure girlfriend afraid of loosing her man to another woman. Then, as if on cue, the man-eater of the evening approached, brandishing two lethal weapons perched high on her chest.

"Weell, heelloo, daarliing," Meri purred, seductively stretching out each syllable, looking directly at Preston's handsome son and ignoring everyone else. She extended the back of her hand in his direction as if she expected him to fall down on one knee and kiss it. "I'm Meri Renick, the hostess of this fabulous soiree." She beamed.

Preston III slowly scanned her from head to toe, and back again, took her hand in his, held it for a few seconds, and then asked with a questioning look on his face, "You're Meri Renick?"

"The one and only." She smiled proudly.

"Oh," he simply said, and let go of her hand.

"And I'm Michele Richards, his girlfriend and Preston's personal assistant," she interrupted, breaking the vibe between her man and Meri.

"I'm sure," Meri commented, barely glancing in the girl's direction.

Sensing a catfight brewing, Ariel said, "Come on, let's get you guys a glass of champagne. This is a celebration after all."

Once everyone had a flute of bubbly, Preston III raised his glass. "To my father and Ariel. May you guys have a life filled with much happiness!"

"To happiness," they all sang in unison.

After the toast, Michele wasted no time ushering her date away from Meri's clutches. Preston and Ariel mingled and were all smiles as they strolled through the party hand-in-hand greeting their guests, which were an intimate combination of relatives, co-workers, and a few former colleagues.

Now that Preston was by her side, Ariel relaxed and began to enjoy the party. She was drifting on cloud ninety-nine as Preston affectionately clenched her hand and proudly introduced her to the judges who laid down the law in New York and beyond. Ariel knew most of the Manhattan clergy, but the ones from the outer boroughs, she had only read about in the trades. Preston, however, was on a first-name basis with every attorney in the room. She watched as he engaged each of them with personal stories; he even knew the names of their spouses and children. Preston was in the zone, schmoozing and shaking hands as if he were campaigning for office. He was a natural politician. Watching him in action, she finally understood why being a Supreme Court justice was so important to him. It was in his blood. Ariel vowed right then and there that she would support him in achieving his dream, as long as he didn't spend every waking moment obsessing over his impending appointment. Though she hated to admit the truth, she'd come to the realization that she was the type of woman who needed daily affection (something she seldom received as a child). And when Preston threw himself into his work, she felt like a neglected afterthought.

"Mike, you remember Ariel?" he asked Michele's father.

"Of course, how could I forget the smartest *and* prettiest clerk that ever roamed our halls?" he replied, kissing her on the cheek.

Ariel couldn't believe how much she admired Judge Richards and at the same time despised his daughter. The admiration she felt for Mike certainly hadn't spilled over to Michele. He was a hardworking dedicated judge, while she on the other hand only seemed to be dedicated to finding a man. Initially Ariel thought the young vixen had her sights set on Preston, but the way she was fawning all over his son, Ariel rightfully assumed that Michele had zeroed in on his offspring instead.

"So, Preston tells me my little girl is doing a great job." He smiled proudly, directing his comment to Ariel.

If you call prancing around in see-through tops and skintight dresses doing a great job, then I guess you could say that she's work-ing overtime! Ariel thought, as she eyed Michele pressing her boobs against her date's arm.

Knowing how Ariel felt about Michele, Preston knew that she wasn't about to give the girl any kudos, so he quickly spoke up. "Yes, she's efficient and extremely resourceful to say the least, and I'm sure you know that she and my son have started dating." He looked over at them, drinking champagne. "Who knows, Mike, we might be in-laws one day." Preston chuckled.

"Now wouldn't that be ironic; after all the years we've known each other, we might actually become family," he said, warming up to the idea.

"Well, let's mingle," Preston said, grabbing Ariel's hand.

"Oh, sure. I'm happy for you two, and let me just say congratu-lations again."

As they walked away, Preston stopped a passing waiter and took two flutes. He handed one to Ariel, looked deeply into her eyes, and said, "I feel like the luckiest man alive to have you in my life." He lifted her hand and kissed it. "Thank you for agreeing to be my wife. I promise you a life of happiness, and——"

His declaration of love was cut short by the nagging ring of his cell phone. He tried to ignore the interruption coming from his breast pocket, but the phone just kept ringing, and when it stopped and went into voice mail, the incessant ringing would start all over again. He finally took the ringing phone out of his pocket and looked at the caller ID.

"I'm sorry, honey. I have to get this. It's the senator."

Ariel was livid. "This is *our* night, Preston. Can't he wait until tomorrow?" she said, fuming.

"I know, but it might be important." Just then the phone stopped. "I need to call him back. I won't be long, I promise." He leaned in to kiss her, but she pulled back in anger.

As she watched him retreat into the library, she could feel her body temperature rise and the vein sprout again in the middle of her forehead. Preston was making and breaking promises in the same breath and his wavering enraged her. She wanted to believe that things were going to be different, but her instincts and his actions were telling her that she would always play second string to his demanding career. Ariel dejectedly walked over to the picture window, and with her back to the party, she gazed down at the passing cars and began to silently weep for the life that she would never have. Yes, she would have a husband, but not an attentive lover who doted on her constantly.

"Hey there. Why are you standing here all alone?" asked a voice from behind.

Ariel quickly wiped her eyes in an effort to hide her pain and then slowly turned around. "Oh, hi," she said to Preston III, trying to sound cheerful.

He took one look at her tear-stained face, reached into his breast pocket, removed a freshly starched handkerchief, gingerly dabbed the remaining tears from her cheeks, and said, "I surely hope those are tears of joy."

She looked into his eyes and could feel his genuine concern as they held each other's gaze. His eyes were familiar, as if she'd known him in another life; the warm brown sent a chill up her spine. The familiarity she felt probably had to do with the fact that he was the spitting image of his dad.

"Here take this." He gave her the starched white handkerchief. "I think you could use it more than me." He smiled.

His kindness touched her. Unlike his father, he was caring and concerned. "Thanks." She wiped her face with the cotton cloth, switched gears, and asked, "So how long have you and Michele been going out?"

But before he could answer, the lady in question came rushing up to him. "There you are, baby. I've been looking all over for you. I want to introduce you to my father," she said, possessively looping her arm through his.

He looked at Ariel as if to say, *sorry for rushing off,* before being led away by his needy girlfriend.

As Ariel watched them walk away, she admired how he tenderly put his arm around Michele's shoulder. He seemed to be an attentive partner, and she longed for the same type of relationship.

With Preston still behind closed doors, she drifted aimlessly from one conversation to the next. Her spirits were dissipating as fast as the bubbles in her champagne. Then, out of the blue, she had an epiphany. Her happiness was dependant on one person and one person only: Ariel. She knew instantly what she was going to do to reenergize her soul.

ARIEL FLIPPED through the fifty-page deposition in her hands, trying to make sense of the transcript. She stared at the paper as if it were written in Japanese; she was having difficulty deciphering the words. Her lack of focus had nothing to do with the language, but with her preoccupation with Preston. She was still seething from his behavior at the engagement party. By the time he finished his conference call with the senator and reemerged from the library, most of the guests were gone and the party was winding down. He tried to smooth things over with Ariel by promising her a long, uninterrupted weekend, but she wasn't buying any more of his false promises. She was tempted right then and there to break off the engagement, since he seemed to already be married—to the senator—but a cooler head prevailed. She realized that once the nomination process was over, she would have more of Preston's undivided attention.

"Ms. Vaughn, Mrs. Renick is on line one," her assistant said through the intercom, interrupting her reverie.

"Thanks, JoAnne," Ariel answered, and then clicked over to Meri. "I was just thinking about the party. Thanks so much for throwing us such a fabulous affair; everyone seemed to have a good time . . ."

"Everyone except for you," Meri said, wasting no time getting right to the point.

"I-I . . ." Meri's directness caught Ariel off guard, causing her to stutter. "I did too have a good time."

"If having a good time means crying and being consoled by your fiancé's son, then I guess you had an absolute ball!" Meri said sarcastically.

"I didn't know you were playing I Spy last night," she shot back. Ariel thought that she had been discreet, and didn't think that anyone noticed her sobbing over by the window.

"Ha-ha, not so funny. One minute you and Preston were strolling hand-in-hand, the epitome of happiness, and the next minute he had disappeared and you were near the picture window crying your eyes out. Before I could come over and ask why you were so upset, Preston III was there giving you his white hanky."

With so many people milling about, Ariel couldn't believe that Meri had witnessed the entire incident, and recited every single detail even down to the color of the handkerchief. "You don't miss a thing, do you?"

"Well, if you must know, I wasn't watching you per se, I was eyeing Preston III." She did a low whistle. "He is one fine young man!"

Ariel rolled her eyes and shook her head at Meri's comment. "*Young* being the operative word. Besides—"

"Young and *grown*. He must be in his late twenties, nearly thirty, which is old enough for me."

"Wait a minute, missy. I thought you were tried of the boy toys and were ready to settle down and get married," Ariel reminded Meri.

"Oh, I could *so* marry young Preston; he's just my type—tall, muscular, and handsome. And the way he was checking me out when we met, I'd say that I'm his type as well," Meri said confidently.

Ariel laughed at Meri's chutzpa. She was nearly twice his age, and based on his choice in girlfriends (a twenty-something bombshell with real boobs), Meri was nowhere near his type, but that didn't stop her from lusting after him. "Tell me you're not serious."

"And why wouldn't I be?" she asked, sounding slightly offended. "Didn't you see the way he was looking at me? If I didn't know any better, I'd say he wanted a piece of Meri," she said, regaining her confidence.

With all of the available men at the party, Ariel couldn't believe Meri had set her sights on Ariel's future stepson, and tried to dissuade her from pursuing Preston's only child. "Even if that was true, there's no way Michele is going to let him out of her sight long enough for anyone to get their claws into him."

"Darling, don't you know that when a man wants to wander, he'll find a way out of no way to cheat," Meri said like a woman who spoke from experience.

"Well, from what I've seen of him and Michele, they're smitten with each other, so you might as well redirect your crosshairs and set your sights on another victim," Ariel suggested. She then steered the conversation in another direction and asked, "What about that guy in the tortoiseshell glasses that you were talking to at the party? He looked like a nice man."

Refusing to let the topic die, Meri responded. "Nice, yes, and I might even have dinner with him once or twice, but he's nowhere near hot!"

"I thought you were through with the hot young guys and were ready to settle down with a M-A-N," Ariel said, reiterating Meri's own words.

"That was before I saw Preston's fine-ass son. Now he's some-one that I'd like to sink my teeth into. I bet he's just yummy." She smiled through the phone.

Ariel shook her head in frustration, then said, "Meri you know I love you like a sister, but I'm not ready to have you as a daughter-in-law."

"Aw, Mom, don't say that." She laughed.

"Stop teasing, Meri; this isn't funny. I know how you like *entertaining* beefy studs, but I'd appreciate it if you wouldn't sleep with Preston's son. Since you and I are so close and he's practically my stepson, it'll seem like incest."

"Darling, don't be so dramatic. I'm not crossing any bloodlines, he and I are both consenting adults, and . . ."

"Meri, *please!*" she shouted in frustration.

"You don't have to get your panties in a bunch." She sighed. "I'll leave your precious stepson alone, but only as a personal favor to you."

"Thank you," Ariel said, relieved that she was finally able to get through to her horny friend.

"But just know that if I had met him in another environment without knowing he was related to Preston, I wouldn't hesitate to make him my lover," she added.

"Okay, I get it. Now can we *please* talk about something else?"

"Of course, darling. Enough about the young Preston. Tell me what happened between you and the older Preston?"

Ariel exhaled hard, and then told the story. "I still can't believe he came late to the party, and then had the nerve to take a call from the senator, leaving me alone for nearly two hours to greet our guests."

"Haven't you realized by now that Preston has an agenda that doesn't include you?" Meri asked point-blank.

"It sunk in at the party, when he spent more time talking with the senator than with me. The reality hurts, but I finally get it," she said, sounding like a wounded puppy.

"Darling, put away the violins and stop feeling sorry for yourself. You don't need a pity-party. Stop trying to lure Preston away from his mission. You need an agenda of your own, and I'm not necessarily talking about work, if you know what I mean."

Meri's words reconfirmed what Ariel had been thinking, but she still felt guilty about contemplating returning to The Black Door. She was practically a married woman and going back to the club just didn't seem right. Her feelings were vacillating faster than an oscillating fan. One minute, she was ready to make a beeline back to her lover and the next minute, she was the devoted fiancée vowing to stand by her man. "I hear what you're saying, and trust me I've thought about going back to The Black Door, but—"

"But nothing," Meri interrupted. "I know you're love starved, because I can hear it in your voice. You should have a little fun before you get married, and stop obsessing about Preston. Trust me; you need to put him on the back burner and focus on your needs instead."

"Excuse me, Ms. Vaughn. Judge Hendricks is on line two," JoAnne interrupted through the intercom.

"Meri, I hate to cut our conversation short, but Preston is on the line. I'll talk to you later."

"Okay. Just remember to put your needs first," Meri said one more time, drilling her point home.

Ariel said good-bye and then clicked over. Preston's unexpected phone call softened her resolve, and the anger she felt toward him began to fade. "So, what did I do to deserve this call?"

"Do I need a reason to talk to the love of my life?" he asked cheerfully.

"You've been so busy lately that I didn't think you had time for idle chitchat."

"I just wanted to apologize again for last night, and to ask if we can reschedule our long weekend. I know I promised you a few days of no interruptions, but the senator wants me to take the shuttle to Washington for an impromptu meeting. I should be back Saturday night, and we can have a late dinner, and a . . ."

Ariel extended her arm and held the phone far away from her ear. She didn't want to hear another word he had to say. Twenty-four hours had not passed and yet again he was going back on his word. She didn't need broken promises. She needed the love of a good man and knew exactly where to find one.

18

FOR THE first time since donning the red leather mask, Ariel finally felt completely comfortable behind the disguise. Her need for sexual stimulation overshadowed her inhibitions, and she no longer felt like the frigid bystander afraid to venture out and try a naughty new experience. Unlike her first visit to The Black Door, she didn't need liquid courage to fuel her desire, so she bypassed the vodka fountain and the members who were casually lounging in the parlor area and made a beeline straight upstairs where the serious players played. She was on a mission to find the black-masked hunk. He had caught her totally off-guard the last time with a sneak attack from behind, but tonight all of her senses were on high alert, and she was primed, ready, and wet for some serious fucking.

Ariel sauntered like a pro on the prowl as she peeked her head into the various rooms that dotted the darkened hallway in search of her lover. He wasn't in the Game Room, the Pink Room, the

Tantalizing Toy Room, the Voyeurism Room, or the Leopard Lounge. She looked to her left and noticed a door that she hadn't seen before; it was painted black, and scribed in white at eye level was the number 8 and two lowercase *m*'s. She slowly turned the knob, opened the door, and slipped inside. The darkened room was set up like a cozy home theater with three rows of oversize black leather seats facing a large projection screen. She stood in the doorway and looked at the screen to see what movie was playing. She expected to see a typical triple-X film, but from the loud clicking noise bouncing off the walls, and the grainy black-and-white images, Ariel assumed it was an 8 mm porno flick. She found an empty chair in the back and made herself comfortable.

Ariel had always assumed that the retro porn movies were watered-down versions of modern-day smut, but watching the activities unfold on the screen, she realized that she was totally mistaken.

A full-figured woman with alabaster skin and jug-sized titties was bent over the side of a brass bed with her big juicy ass pointed toward the ceiling. It appeared as if she was waiting for someone, and sure enough, on cue, in walked a lean man who was buck naked, except for a black Stetson and a pair of black, pointed-toe cowboy boots. He stood with his back to the closed door and licked his lips at the woman's exposed ass. He then slowly walked toward her with his dick in his hands. When he got within touching distance, he took his limp dick and swung it toward her ass. With each point of contact, his cock grew larger and larger. When he walked into the room, his penis was the size of a sweet pickle and as droopy as a wilted rose; but after several smacks against her round ass, his nonthreatening member was now a twelve-inch lethal weapon. He took a jar of lubricant off of the nightstand and rubbed a handful of the slippery gel up and down his thick shaft. Once he was lubed up, he grabbed her cheeks and spread them wide apart, then took his ivory pole and inserted the tip into her anus. She quivered slightly, but didn't shy away as he slid every inch of his thick rod deep into her ass. Once his dick disappeared inside of her anus, he grabbed her by the waist, put one boot-clad foot on the edge of the bed, and rode her like a prized steer. She gritted her teeth, flicked her long blonde hair from side to side and bucked back ferociously like a wild animal.

Ariel could feel herself getting wet as she watched the couple fuck as if their lives depended upon reaching a climax. She had never been butt-fucked before, but watching how much the woman seemed to enjoy the anal stimulation, Ariel was curious and wondered what a dick up the ass felt like. Lusting for some action herself, she unconsciously licked her lips as the couple came simultaneously before collapsing on the bed in sheer exhaustion.

"I bet we could pick up where they left off," said a husky voice from behind.

"Is your dick as big and hard as his?" she asked brazenly. Ariel finally realized that she could say *and* do anything she wanted at The Black Door. Not only did the mask protect her identity, but she also knew that everyone who crossed the threshold of the club was disease free and ready to please.

"Bigger," he replied, with an air of confidence.

"Come around and let me see what you're working with."

Within seconds, a short muscular man was standing in front of her. From the sound of his deep masculine voice, she had assumed that he was at least six feet tall, but he stood all of five two at best. Ariel opened her mouth to ask him what he could possibly do for her, but the words caught in her throat once she glanced at the hefty bulge protruding between his legs.

I bet he has a pair of tube socks stuffed in his G-string. And then, in a bold, uncharacteristic move, she reached out and pulled down the small piece of fabric that held his padding in place. Ariel's jaw dropped at what popped out.

"Now, are you satisfied?"

She was speechless as her eyes traveled down to his nakedness. She expected to see a minute penis, barely big enough to fuck Barbie, but staring back at her was the biggest dick that she had ever seen in her life. The tip of his semierect dick hung halfway down his thigh. The saying "hung like a horse" must have been coined specifically for him.

"Well . . ." He began to stroke his mammoth-sized member. "Is this what you want, baby?"

The miniman stroked harder and harder, and Ariel watched in sheer amazement as his dick grew nearly twice in size. She didn't think that it was possible for someone so little to have such a gargantuan penis, but she was dead wrong. Standing there barely the height of the theater seats with a fully erect dick that was well over twelve inches, he looked like some kind of freak in a traveling sideshow.

"Come on, baby, let me tap that ass," he said seductively, approaching her with his now rock-hard pole of destruction.

"I don't think so." Ariel could just picture him rupturing a vessel with his abnormally large dick. She wanted joy, not excruciating pain; she didn't want to end up in the hospital while trying to have a little fun. She got up and pointed to his groin. "That thing is dangerous."

She towered over him like an Amazon; her titties where in direct alignment to his mouth. He stuck out his tongue and licked the outside of her red bustier; then before she could object, he reached up and slid down the satin fabric. At first he gently kissed her nipples until they became erect; then he began to suck on them like he was breastfeeding. Ariel let out a slight moan at his touch. Enjoying the sensation, she rested her hands on his shoulders and closed her eyes. He may have looked like a troll with an enormous dick, but he sure could suck the hell out of a nipple. For a split second, she thought about letting him fuck her, but the moment he pulled her close and she felt his elephant-sized cock against her thigh, her eyes popped open and she backed away.

"Thanks, but no thanks," she said, and turned to leave.

He reached around her waist, gently pulled her back, and began to grind his erection into her ass. "Come on, baby, don't leave Big Poppa like this."

His dick was so big that it instantly went in between her legs and came out the other side. She looked down and saw at least ten inches sticking out. "Damn, you're just too long for me," she blurted out. Besides, she was looking for someone else.

Before he could respond, Ariel broke loose, pulled her top up, and made a swift exit.

TREY WANDERED THROUGH the club with one thing on his mind: finding his red-masked lover. Their last tryst had left him sexually satisfied *and* confused. On paper her description read one way, but in person she was different somehow and he wanted to know why. He was a man full of questions and she was the only one who could supply the answers. Trey had nonchalantly perused the first-floor parlors, but she wasn't among the ladies who lounged. He then casually (so as not to arouse suspicion) made his way to the second floor. Peeking his head into the various chambers, he kept coming up empty-handed, and then, rushing out of the 8 mm Room, she bumped smack-dab into him, nearly falling into his arms.

Ariel was so busy trying to get away from the Lilliputian with the big dick that she wasn't paying much attention to what, or better yet, *whom* she had run into. And when she finally turned around and realized that she was standing in front of the object of her desire, the shock of his presence took her by surprise, rendering her speechless.

The mask concealed the upper portion of her face, and Trey could only see her mouth, which was agape. Looking at her expression, he assumed that he had startled her. Trey decided to use the situation to his advantage, so he grabbed her by the hand before she had a chance to protest and led her down the corridor. They bypassed room after room, until they were standing at what appeared to be a dead end. He tapped the bottom of the back wall twice with his left foot, and then, as if in a scene from a James Bond movie, the corner of the wall quietly opened.

Once they were inside of Trey's private lair, he pushed the door shut. Ariel couldn't see a thing because the room was as black as pitch, so she stood there a moment waiting for her eyes to adjust to the darkness. She heard his muffled steps cross what she assumed was a carpeted floor, and then heard the turn of a switch; suddenly the room was bathed in soft, sexy, sienna lighting. Ariel glanced around and took in the opulent decor. The walls were painted metallic pewter, which complemented the gray drapes that hung at the floor-to-ceiling windows. In the center of the room was a king-size circular bed covered with a snow-white velvet duvet. Huge silver and white pillows were strewn about the perimeter of the bed, and overhead was an ornate pewter chandelier with tiny shades covering flame-shaped lightbulbs.

They stood at opposite ends of the room, staring at each other. Ariel self-consciously licked her ruby lips as she checked out the definition of his solid pecs and sculpted six-pack through his black T-shirt. Her eyes then traveled south and stopped at his crotch. She could feel the heat emanating from her pulsating clitoris as she stared at the large bulge against his tight jeans. The sexual tension in the room was so thick that you could hack through it with a machete. Every nerve ending in Ariel's body was tweaked, and she was on fire. Unable to contain her raging hormones any longer, she slowly sauntered toward him, and didn't stop until they were standing mask to mask.

He opened his mouth to speak. His intention was to have a conversation with her so he could satisfy his curiosity once and for all. But she put a finger to his lips to silence his words, just as he had done to her the last time.

Ariel ran her hands up and down his chest. Her fingers were like tiny rovers exploring every inch of his muscular physique. Once she had explored the upper regions of his body, her hands ventured below his belt and landed on his groin. She tried to massage his manhood, but the thick denim was proving to be an annoying barrier, so she unbuckled his belt, unbuttoned his jeans, and then unzipped the zipper. His pants dropped to the floor, leaving him standing there in a pair of sexy black boxer shorts. Ariel looked at the tent that his erect penis made out of the cotton fabric and grinned with pleasure. She slid her hands around the waistband of his underwear, and then ripped them off. The last time he had fucked her so fast that she didn't get a chance to see his dick, but this time she wanted to see exactly what he was working with. She looked down and gasped. He had the prettiest penis that she had ever seen in her life. It didn't curve to the right or to the left or droop downward; it pointed perfectly straight. He wasn't enormous like the little freak in the 8 mm Room. He was the ideal size. As she rubbed her hand over the smooth head, her mouth began to water. She wanted him inside of her, but first she needed to taste his juices. Ariel kneeled down, flicked out her tongue, and teased the tip of his penis. She then took him inside of her ready mouth and sucked hard until she heard him moan with pleasure.

"Oh baby! Don't stop!"

And she didn't stop until she tasted his sweet cum oozing out of the tip. She was in heat and wanted him to shoot his hot load down her throat, so she sucked harder and harder trying to get him to climax, but he flipped the script and took control.

He reached down and gently lifted her up by the elbows until she was standing, then gallantly scooped her into his arms and carried her to the bed. He laid her on her back, straddled her, and slowly unlaced her bustier. Her breasts spilled out once the strings were loose. He lightly fingered the edges of the red rose tattooed above her left breast, then leaned in and kissed each flaming petal before reaching underneath her skirt and taking off her thong.

"Damn," he said, looking down at her 38-Cs. He took a titty in each hand and sensually juggled them up and down. He watched her nipples grow with each bounce and when they hardened, he covered them with his hot mouth while digitally stimulating her wet pussy.

"Ohh," she moaned. She wrapped her legs around his back and jutted out her hips until her clit touched his dick.

He knew she was hot for him, as he was hot for her, but he wanted to tease her just a little longer, so he reached around to her ass, and spread her cheeks apart. He applied a little pressure to her anus with his finger until she began to squirm. The feeling of her tight ass made him grow even harder. "I need you," he whispered in her ear.

"I need you too," she said.

Trey removed his finger and embraced her tightly around the waist, then firmly rocked back and forth until he was inside. Her tight pussy hugged his dick like a long-lost friend, and they began humping and panting like two dogs in heat. Sweat dripped off of his body onto hers, until they were both covered in each other's salty juices.

"Harder! Fuck me harder!" she yelled.

Her demand turned him on even more, and his thrusts became

deeper and deeper, until he was bucking like a wild bull at the rodeo. Trey was lost in the moment and fucking so hard that he didn't realize that his mask had fallen off.

"I'm cumming, I'm cumming." He withdrew and ejaculated all over her chest. He then reached down and massaged the hot creamy secretion around her titties.

Ariel's head was reared back in ecstasy, and her eyes were closed, as she enjoyed his touch, "Hmm," she moaned. "You make me feel so good."

As Trey watched his cum glisten on her big luscious breasts, he could feel another erection coming on. "And you make my dick so hard," he said in a deep baritone voice.

She was so caught up in the rapture earlier that she hadn't paid much attention to his voice, but hearing him now, he sounded vaguely familiar. She sat up on her elbows and opened her eyes so she could hear him better. Ariel expected to see his black mask, but the mask had fallen off and she saw his entire face instead. Her body froze and she became as stiff as a corpse when she realized whom she had just fucked.

He felt her tense up. "What's wrong?" He tapped his semierect dick against her thigh. "Don't you want some more of this good loving?"

Ariel was speechless and scrambled around until she was on her feet. She grabbed her bustier, tied it haphazardly around her chest, pulled on her skirt, and ran for the door.

"Hey, where are you going?" he yelled at her fleeing back.

Trey slumped back on the bed totally baffled. "What the hell just happened?" he wondered out loud.

"Oh, shit," he said when he looked down and saw his mask lying on the floor. "Guess she didn't like my mug."

He reached down to pick up the mask and lying next to it was her sexy thong. Trey picked up the delicate piece of fabric and sniffed her essence. He still had questions as to her true identity, but one thing was for sure, whoever she was, she fucked like no other woman he had ever been with. He was determined to have her again, and again, and again, and . . .

SENATOR OGLESBY'S home office in Washington was the epitome of a distinguished politician's habitat. A handsome, brown tufted-leather sofa rested against the back wall, and matching high-back chairs sat in front of a hand-carved maple desk. Original Tiffany lamps adorned the corners of the massive piece of furniture. Of all the well-appointed furnishings, the coup de grâce was his "ego wall." Each in their own matted gold frame were photographs of the senator shaking hands, slapping backs, and cheesing it up with presidents, prime ministers, ambassadors, and an A-list of well-known diplomats from around the globe; there were even some entertainers thrown in for good measure. The pictures were a clear indication that he was well connected and could reach out and touch the who's-who of the country with a mere phone call. Though Preston could hold his own and had an impressive Rolodex himself, he still felt honored to be sitting among the presence of such dignitaries.

"I spoke with the president's aide yesterday, and told him that I'll have my list of potential nominees to him by Monday. And of course your name is first on that short list," the senator reassured Preston.

"Robert, I can't tell you how much I appreciate all of your efforts."

The senator leaned back in his chair and smiled. "What are frat brothers for?"

Preston had met Robert Oglesby at Georgetown Law. He was an incoming freshman and Robert was the upperclassman who was assigned to give him the grand tour. As it turned out, they had both pledged the same fraternity in college, and from that day on, they became fast friends. At the time, Preston had no way of knowing that Robert would play such a pivotal role in his future. The Oglesby family were third-generation politicians and were deeply entrenched in Washington's political inner circle. Robert's grandfather even had close ties with the Kennedy clan, so there were very few who wouldn't gladly do him a favor upon request. And when Robert realized that his good friend wanted to sit on the Supreme Court, he was more than eager to assist.

Preston shifted to the edge of his chair and asked eagerly, "So what's the next step after you submit the list?"

"That's when the fun begins." Senator Oglesby chuckled.

Preston squinted, so that his eyebrows creased toward the bridge of his nose. "What does that mean?"

"It means that an unofficial investigation of the nominees will be conducted to rattle any skeletons that are lurking in the closet. It's damage control to uncover any unsavory scandals before the official investigation begins," he said, pinning Preston with a questioning stare.

"Well, bring on Columbo, Kojak, and the entire *CSI* team, because I have absolutely nothing to hide," Preston replied with total confidence.

The senator raised his eyebrows. "Are you sure? I knew of a case where the nominee appeared blemish free on paper, but had a convenient memory lapse and totally forgot about a former mistress, only to have her resurface five years later when the hearings began. Of course she crawled out of the woodwork brandishing pictures of him in a compromising position. Needless to say, he was tried and condemned once the pictures were published, and he kissed his chances of being a justice good-bye."

"Well, you don't have to worry about some floozy cropping up out of nowhere trying to sabotage my nomination. I was married, *faithfully*, I might add, for fifteen years, and now I'm engaged to an established and well-respected attorney. So I assure you, my personal life is more than intact and up to the scrutiny of an investigation." Preston had been tempted to cheat a number of times. He and his ex-wife basically led two separate lives; when she couldn't rattle his cage by trying to turn his son against him, she moved out of the bedroom into the guestroom, forcing him into celibacy for the last two years of their marriage. Always with his eye on the bigger picture, Preston was smart enough to know that an affair could taint his character, if it was ever exposed. And now sitting here listening to the senator quiz him about his private life, he was overjoyed that he hadn't given in to temptation.

"That's good to hear. So, tell me, when am I going to have the pleasure of meeting the future Mrs. Hendricks? She has a great reputation in the legal community, and will truly be an asset to your nomination." He reached inside his desk drawer, took out a black, leather-bound daybook, and thumbed through the pages. "How does next Tuesday sound? The Mrs. and I will be in New York for a couple of days to see a few Broadway shows. If you're available, you two can join us for dinner one evening."

"That's works just fine. I'm sure Ariel will be delighted to finally meet you," Preston lied. He knew that Ariel was envious of the time that he spent with the senator. But maybe after meeting him and hearing firsthand how involved the entire process is, she would have a better understanding and cut him a little slack.

He penned the date in his book. "Okay, it's settled. Now what about your professional life? Every case that you've ever presided over will be dissected under a very keen microscope. Both sides will read over the decisions you've handed down over the years, trying to decide if you're going to be a top-down justice like Thomas and Scalia, or a bottom-up justice who's sensitive to precedent and the facts of every case. You know the law is actually politics in disguise. It's not an exact science, since laws are basically created to champion one cause or another. And the Judiciary Committee will try to determine if you'll favor the right or the left."

Preston didn't say a word, just nodded his head. The senator then went on. "And what about your religious affiliation? We've known each other for eons, but I don't know if you're Catholic or Protestant or Baptist. Well, whatever denomination you are, you'd better dust off your membership card." He chuckled. "And become active, if you're not already. It'll bode well for you to be closely affiliated with a church. And another thing that'll look good is if you've done some pro bono work."

"I have, as a matter of fact. I'm the lead counsel for the Boys' Theater of Harlem, and have been for years. I negotiate their contracts; it's my way of giving back to the community," Preston said proudly.

"Excellent." The senator reached across his desk, opened a humidor filled with fat hand-rolled cigars, and took two out. "Well, if I was a betting man, I'd say you are the perfect candidate and should have no problems securing the nomination," he said, snipping the tip of each torpedo-shaped cigar, and handed one to Preston.

Preston leaned back in his chair with a huge grin plastered across his face and stuck the stogie in his mouth. He could just picture himself ensconced with the esteemed justices and handing down the law—the final word—which couldn't be disputed. And why shouldn't he? He had built a stellar career over the years without any unsavory blemishes for the sole purpose of sitting on the Supreme Court; his professional and personal lives were above reproach. So let them investigate to their hearts' content, because his life and those around him were absolutely blemish free.

ARIEL WAS GRATEFUL for the weekend and that she had a two-day reprieve to get her head right before going into work on Monday. She lay in bed most of the day drifting in and out of a fitful sleep. Her dreams were a series of turbulent nightmares, jolting her awake the moment she settled into a deep slumber; but they were no comparison to the real-life nightmare that she experienced at The Black Door. Ariel's mind was still reeling at her shocking discovery.

"How could I have been so naïve?" she asked, pounding her fist into one of the down pillows near her head.

Ariel wanted to talk the situation out with someone so she could get an objective point of view. But there wasn't anyone to hash things over with. She thought about calling Meri, but she would be anything but impartial. And Ariel wasn't in the mood for another one of Meri's long-winded speeches about how she should satisfy her needs since Preston was too busy to satisfy them. As a matter of fact, it was Meri's advice that had gotten her into this mess in the first place. If she had never gone to The Black Door in the red mask, disguised as Meri, none of this would have happened. If only she hadn't given in to her carnal desires, she'd be basking in the glow of her impending nuptials, instead of wondering if her indiscretions would ruin her *and* Preston's future.

"Damn it!" she shouted, and jammed the pillow again with another forceful blow. Ariel lit into the plump pillows and beat them ferociously until they were as flat as a pair of two-by-fours. She took her frustration out on the inanimate objects because she couldn't physically beat herself to a pulp. And that's exactly what she wanted to do for being so damn *stupid* and getting herself into an impossible predicament.

Just as she finished her assault on the innocent bed accessories, the phone rang. The noise startled her and she stared at the ringing phone in horror, like it was sent Express Mail directly from Satan. She froze. Ariel didn't know whether to answer it or to throw the annoying thing against the wall. At first she thought it might be her black-masked lover, but then she realized that there was no way that he could possibly have her telephone number. Fortunately, the ringing stopped before she could decide what to do. Ariel slumped back on the headboard, relieved that the voice mail had intercepted whoever was on the other end. But her reprieve was short-lived, because no sooner had the house phone stopped then her cell phone rang. She fished the tiny gadget out of her purse and looked at the caller ID, exhaled, and flipped open the phone.

"Hey there," she panted, slightly out of breath from going postal on the pillows.

"Uh, hi," Preston said, and then paused. "What's wrong with you?" he asked, picking up on the undertones in her voice.

"What do you mean?" she asked defensively.

"You sound breathy, like you just finished running the New York Marathon."

"I . . . uh . . . just rushed in from the bathroom," she lied.

"Oh, I was wondering where you were, because I called the house phone before I called your cell."

"How was your trip?" she asked, steering the conversation into another direction.

"It was great!" He beamed. "The senator and I had a very productive meeting. He basically gave me the rundown of what to expect, and I can't tell you how thrilled I am that the ball is finally rolling."

"That's good news," Ariel said with as much enthusiasm as she could muster, which wasn't much.

Preston was so absorbed in his favorite topic—himself—that he didn't pick up on her lackluster response. "Why don't I come over and tell you all about our meeting?"

Ariel rolled her eyes to the ceiling. She wasn't in the mood to hear Preston droning on and on about his precious nomination. She wanted—no needed—to concentrate on her own problems, and she wouldn't be able to focus on a solution if Preston came over and filled her head with his political agenda.

"Honey." She coughed slightly. "I think I'm coming down with another cold. I'm going to take some NyQuil and turn in early."

"Oh," he said, sounding disappointed. "Well, you get some rest. I need you to feel better before Tuesday."

"Why? What's Tuesday?"

"The senator and his wife are coming to town and they want us to have dinner with them," he explained.

Ariel wanted to scream! The last person she wanted to meet was the senator. He was a constant presence on the phone, interrupting them at the most inopportune times. She was afraid that she'd tell him off to his face, and didn't want to make a scene in public.

"I don't know if I'll be able to make it. I have a partner's meeting Tuesday afternoon, and if I know long-winded Bob, I'm sure he'll talk well pass five o'clock. I probably won't get out of the office until late," she said, trying to get out of what was sure to be a boring evening of political mumbo-jumbo.

"I'm sure they'll understand if you leave a few minutes early. Honey, I really need you there. The senator is anxious to meet you."

"Well," she said with a sigh, "maybe I can join you at the

restaurant instead of you picking me up at my apartment." She conceded, realizing that it was useless trying to escape the inevitable.

"Great. I'm going to make reservations at Town for six. Try and get some rest and I'll talk to you tomorrow."

Ariel said good-bye and hung up. She had accommodated Preston's need (as usual), but her problem was still foremost in her mind. "What the hell am I going to do?" she asked aloud, hoping a voice from above would magically give her the answer she craved. When nothing but silence greeted her, she realized that a genie wasn't going to appear and blink her problems away.

"Well, I know one thing for sure," she said to herself. "I'm never going back to The Black Door."

Once those words left Ariel's lips, she felt better, but she knew that that was just like putting a Band-Aid on a gaping wound. Sooner or later, the flimsy piece of adhesive would give way and expose the ugliness that she was desperately trying to hide.

TOWN WAS a stylish three-star restaurant adjacent to the lobby of the Chambers Hotel on West Fifty-sixth Street. The tony boutique hotel was tucked away on a quiet midtown Manhattan block and was inconspicuous from the outside, except for its enormous wooden lattice door. Unlike the generic exterior, the interior was grandiose, with lofty ceilings and plush seating arrangements, giving the lobby a living room–type feeling. The second-story lounge overlooked the lobby, providing a bird's-eye view for those who perched on stools in the balcony-bar sipping vibrant-colored martinis and people-watching. And with the beautiful citizens of the city styling and profiling, as if on a photo shoot, there was plenty to observe.

Preston, the senator, and his wife arrived first and were immediately seated at a choice table near the back of the restaurant. Usually it took months in advance to secure a reservation, but with

Preston's connections, he was able to lock down a choice table with only a three-day notice.

"What an impressive menu," commented Angelica. Angelica was in culinary school when she and Robert met at a social mixer on the Hill. Her father was a congressman and wanted his daughter to marry a promising young politician, and Robert Oglesby fit the bill perfectly. He was from a well-bred family with heavy political connections and destined to make a name for himself in Washington. Angelica, however, had no interest in politics or politicians; she was a creative type who envisioned her life abroad as a chef in a five-star Parisian restaurant, but the moment she met Robert all of that changed. He was strikingly handsome, smart and witty, and swept her off of her feet the first night they met; twenty-five years later they were still very much in love.

Robert put his arm around the back of her chair and leaned in closer so that he could read from her menu. "What looks good, my love?"

"The terrine of fried beets and goat cheese sounds absolutely delicious; maybe I'll start with that and have the halibut with fresh fennel as an entrée." She looked at her watch. "If we're going to catch the opening of the show, I think we should order shortly," she suggested.

Preston could feel the heat rising up through his collar. *Where the hell is Ariel?* he wondered. "When the waiter brings the Veuve, we can order, and I'll order for Ariel, so you won't miss the beginning of the play." His eyes darted quickly around the cavernous room. "I'm sure she'll be here soon."

They were each on their second glass of champagne by the time Ariel came rushing toward the table. "I'm so sorry I'm late," she huffed, "but the partners' meeting ran over."

Preston stood up and gave her a quick peck on the cheek. "Honey, there you are," he said calmly, trying to hide the angst brewing inside the pit of his stomach. "Ariel, this is Senator Robert Oglesby and his wife, Angelica."

The senator stood up as well. "Ariel, I've heard great things about you." He smiled warmly, extending his hand.

"I'm so glad to finally meet you," she said, giving him a firm shake. *So this is the man who's been interrupting my time with Preston,* she thought. Though she had seen him numerous times on C-SPAN, and in the *Times,* she had never met him in person and was struck by his commanding presence. The distinguished-looking senator was tall with graying temples, and his clean-shaven face was extremely handsome. He resembled a young Clint Eastwood, and could have easily been a movie star instead of a politician.

"The pleasure is all mine." He smiled broadly. "I was hoping to meet you in Washington a couple of weeks ago, but Preston said that you had to rush back to New York unexpectedly."

Ariel cringed at the memory of Michele intruding on *their* weekend and scheduling a series of time-consuming meetings. "Yes, it was quite unexpected." She smiled politely. Switching from that unpleasant memory, she turned to the senator's wife. "And please excuse my tardiness, Mrs. Oglesby."

"Angelica, please." She smiled. "I know how unpredictable meetings can be. Robert's always running late for lunch, brunch, and dinner, so I've learned how to occupy my time." She chuckled, lightening up the mood.

Ariel assumed the senator's wife would be a buttoned-up, pearl-clad, gray-haired, bun-wearing matron, but Angelica was extremely stylish. Her platinum-blonde hair was cut short with wispy bangs swept over to one side, and instead of a single strand of Mikimotos, she wore a necklace of graduated diamonds. Dressed in a multicolored Diane von Furstenberg wrap dress, she reminded Ariel of Meri, older but no less up-to-date with the latest fashion trends. For a second, Ariel wondered if Angelica was a card-carrying member of The Black Door. Ariel shook off the thought, thinking that it was ludicrous. Besides, she lived in Washington and was married to a high-powered politician. Ariel was so preoccupied with The Black Door that she immediately assumed that every woman she saw who had a touch of flair was a closet freak. Ariel's reverie was interrupted by Angelica's necklace, which sparkled in the candle-light like the illustrious Hope Diamond. Ariel blinked, and couldn't help but stare; the "bling" was blinding. "Angelica, your necklace is stunning."

She touched the center diamond, which must have been five carats or better, and said, "Thank you so much. An anniversary gift from Robert."

What an extravagant present, Ariel thought, but didn't dare ut-ter those words.

Robert noticed the look of awe registered on Ariel's face. "Noth-ing's too good for my wife." He beamed, looking longingly at his spouse.

Ariel could clearly see the love that he had for his wife. It was visibly apparent that he absolutely adored her; their love was palpa-ble. Suddenly, Ariel felt a tinge of jealousy creep up her spine. She knew that Preston loved her, but she wondered if he was her soul mate. It was clear that Robert and Angelica were made for each other, but Ariel had her doubts about herself and Preston. They were both preoccupied with their own interests; he had visions of his precious nomination to keep him warm at night and she had vi-sions of her black-masked lover. Their last tryst was so incredibly hedonistic that she was getting wet just thinking about how her body melted into his, and how their rhythm was synchronized as if *they* were soul mates instead of she and Preston. The thought of him sucking her clit until she came made her want to run out of the restaurant, go home, put on her disguise, and rush to The Black

Door for more fucking. But she couldn't, because after seeing his face, she vowed that she would never return to the club again.

Ariel looked around the table and noticed that they were drinking Veuve Clicquot. Though she loved champagne, she wanted something stronger to take the edge off. But before she could order a vodka on the rocks with two limes, the waiter came over and poured her a flute of champagne. Once her glass was filled, Robert lifted his and toasted. "To Preston, the next Supreme Court justice." They followed Robert's lead and raised their flutes. "To Preston," they sang in unison.

"Hey, why didn't anyone invite me to the celebration?" asked a deep baritone voice approaching the table.

Preston turned around in his chair and faced his offspring. "Son." He smiled proudly. "What are you doing here?" he asked, knowing it took months to get a reservation.

"I'm meeting Michele for dinner. The chef is a friend of mine, and I have an open reservation," he said, looking around the table, waiting for an introduction.

Preston stood up and proudly put his arm around his son's shoulder. "Senator and Mrs. Oglesby, this is my one and only son, Preston III."

Preston III was impressed. Senator Oglesby was a heavy-hitter in Washington, and could make or break a career. The mere fact that he was in New York having dinner with his father could only mean that he was helping his father achieve his lifelong dream. Until now, he had always thought that his father's dream of sitting on the Supreme Court was far-fetched, but now he realized that that dream was closer to being realized than he thought.

"Preston III." The senator smiled. He knew that Preston had a son, but had never met him. "It's so nice to meet the chip off of the old man's block," he said, shaking the younger man's hand.

"Please call me Trey," he said, returning the shake. "Preston III sounds too formal."

"Of course you know Ariel." Preston nodded toward his fiancée.

Ariel's heart was palpitating and her palms began to sweat as Trey smiled in her direction.

"Hi there, how are you?" Trey asked Ariel. The last time he had seen her was at the engagement party, and she'd been upset about being neglected by his overambitious father.

She looked at him quickly, then darted her eyes down to the table, and answered in a shy, mousy voice, as if speaking in a low tone would diminish her presence. "Fine, thanks."

He noticed that she was avoiding eye contact with him. *She's probably still embarrassed about sobbing on my shoulder.*

"Well, Trey, why don't you join us for dinner?" the senator asked. "Preston has bragged about you over the years, so now I finally have a chance to talk to his number-one son," he said in jest.

"Well, since you put it that way, how could I possibly resist? I'm sure my date won't mind."

Preston motioned the waiter over and told him to bring two extra chairs and place settings.

Blood immediately rushed to Ariel's head, and she began to feel faint. This was the moment that she had dreaded ever since her lover's mask had fallen off during the fuck of her life, revealing someone she would have never expected in a trillion years—Trey. Her two worlds were colliding, and no one at the table was aware of the catastrophic collision but her. She tried to remain calm, but she was breaking out in a cold sweat. Trying to cool her jets, she picked up the champagne and drank it down in one smooth gulp. When the waiter returned with the extra chairs, she ordered a double Belvedere sans the rocks. She needed the extra shot of vodka to help her deal with the fact that she was about to have dinner with her fiancé and his son—*her lover.*

"So, Trey," the senator said, pinning him with an inquisitive look. "What do you do for a living?"

Trey hesitated for a split second, as if contemplating the question, and then answered, "I just passed the Series Seven, and I'm going to try my hand at equity investing. I'm also into real estate investing."

Listening to Trey speak, and seeing him sitting across the table from her, brought home the reality of what she had actually done. Her one saving grace was that he hadn't seen her face. She tried to take comfort in that thought and remain calm, but after five minutes of watching Trey converse causally with the senator, she was unable to take the pressure any longer. Ariel abruptly said, "Excuse me." She got up from the table and rushed toward the ladies' room. She couldn't bear to sit there another second. On the one hand, she still desired Trey, but on the other hand, she knew fucking him was practically incestuous.

In the ladies' room, Ariel ran cold water and soaked some paper towels for a compress. As she patted her forehead with the cool towels, she silently cursed herself for being so naïve and getting into an impossible situation. But how could she have known that Preston's son was a "server" at The Black Door? Her last memory of Trey was of him as a gangly young man barely out of his teens. She had no way of knowing that he would grow up to be a buffed stud. Besides, she would have never recognized him behind that mask. But one look at his face and she knew immediately that she had been fucking her future stepson. With that thought, she ran into the nearest stall and lost her lunch.

"WELL, HELLO EVERYONE," Michele said, as she approached the table.

Trey immediately stood up and pulled back her chair. "Hey

there," he said casually, as if greeting a platonic buddy. Ever since his last encounter with his mystery woman, he'd been standoffish with Michele. She was beautiful and a great lay, but she wasn't the woman in the red mask.

Michele looked at the senator and his wife and knew exactly who they were. She'd seen enough press clippings to recognize the eminent power couple. But what she couldn't figure out was why were they having dinner with Preston and she didn't know a thing about it. After all, she was his personal assistant and should have set up the meeting in the first place.

"Judge Hendricks," she said to Preston, "I didn't know that Senator Oglesby and his wife were on your calendar this evening."

Robert looked from Preston to Michele. Assuming she was merely Trey's date, he wondered why she would be privy to Preston's schedule.

Preston noticed the puzzled look on Robert's face and knew exactly what he was thinking. "Michele is not only Trey's girlfriend, she's also my personal assistant. She's the person you've been speaking with over the telephone these past few weeks, regarding my Washington itinerary," he said, clarifying the issue.

"Oh, yes. It's so nice to finally put a face with a name."

Michele chimed right in. "I was with Preston in Washington." She put her hand to her mouth. "Oops, I mean, Judge Hendricks," she said, correcting her slip. "But I didn't get a chance to meet you, because I was locked away in a hotel room, shuffling his schedule around to accommodate a few impromptu meetings."

"Yes, Michele has been a lifesaver," Preston said, singing her praises. "She's going to be a tremendous help going forward."

"That's good to know, because my man here"—Robert slapped Preston on the back—"is headed for greatness, and he's going to need a tight crew on board."

"I can assure you, Senator, you don't have to worry about that.

I've got his back." Suddenly Michele had an idea. "If it's okay with you, Judge, I'd like to throw a small cocktail party at the town house while the senator and his wife are in town. That way he can see firsthand that you're surrounded by a tight network of supporters."

"Michele, that's an excellent idea," the senator agreed. "And of course I hope you're going to be there, Trey. I'd love to pick your brain about real estate in New York. I'm thinking about investing."

"Sure, I wouldn't miss it."

"Miss what?" a calmer Ariel asked, returning to the table.

"Michele just suggested that we give a cocktail party while Robert and Angelica are in town," Preston said gleefully. He was pleased that the senator had agreed to spend time in his home.

Upon hearing those words, Ariel nearly broke out in another cold sweat. She wanted to scratch Michele's eyes out for being so damned efficient. Why couldn't she just keep her big mouth shut? Getting through dinner would be touchy enough; now she would have to see Trey again in the same week. She was trying desperately to steer clear of him, but that was proving impossible. Ariel was clinging to the one shred of hope she had left: her mask had stayed intact and he still didn't know her true identity. But the question was, how long could she keep up the charade?

21

LYING AWAKE with the moonlight streaming through the blinds, Michele perched herself up on one elbow and watched "her man" sleep. This was the only time that she could stare at him without him feeling self-conscious. She loved everything about Trey, from the curve of his lips, to the sexy dimples that pierced his cheeks, to his slightly shaved head. He was so fine, and she was proud to be his woman.

Since the age of three, Michele had lived in the shadow of her younger sister. Two years her junior, Janet was prettier and smarter, and their parents never missed an opportunity to sing Janet's praises. "Look at my baby, she's the cutest, most talented girl in the pageant," her mother would say, as she watched Janet take command of the stage and wow the judges. While Michele was chubby and clumsy, Janet was the polar opposite. Her petite frame and graceful mannerisms made her the perfect contestant for the beauty-pageant circuit. Convinced that Janet was a future Miss

America, their mother entered her daughter in as many competitions as possible. She'd drag Michele along as a junior roadie, and Michele would have to carry her sister's gowns and makeup cases like a little flunky. She resented being treated like Cinderella, but never complained, just waited for the day when she'd grow into her own. As a teenager Michele began to shed her baby fat, and her body transformed from a chunky kid into a voluptuous young woman. Armed with a new figure, she threw out her baggy pants and sweatshirts and replaced them with sexy T-shirts and tight jeans. Though she had finally overcome the fat-girl complex, she still didn't win over the cute boys, because they were always attracted to her sister the beauty queen. It wasn't until college that Michele was able to step out of the shadows, and she stepped out in style wearing even more revealing clothes. She used her body to get the attention she never got as a child, and when Trey noticed her titties that day at Preston's town house, she knew it was just a matter of time before she got him into bed. But she wanted more—she wanted to marry him. He was the son of a future Supreme Court justice, and by marrying him, she would finally trump her sister, who was married to a traveling salesman. She knew that her father respected Preston and would be thrilled if she became his daughter-in-law; then maybe she'd finally become the apple of her dad's eye.

Michele's eyes roamed the length of Trey's nude body and beneath the thin top sheet, she noticed that his dick was growing longer and longer until it was fully erect. She assumed that he was having a dream about making love to her, so she leaned over and whispered in his ear, "Is that for me, baby?"

AFTER DINNER AT Town earlier that night, Trey had planned to put Michele in a taxi and send her home, but she insisted on spending the night at his apartment. She had even brought along a small tote bag in anticipation of going home with him. Since they hadn't been spending much time together, he reluctantly agreed. Michele could be aggressive at times; when he first met her at his father's town house, her confidence turned him on, but now it was becoming annoying. She wanted to be with him every waking second of the day, and her constant affection was suffocating. He knew the real reason behind the annoyance was the fact that he wasn't with the woman he truly desired. For the first time in his life, Trey was falling in love—or was it lust? He knew it was crazy to feel strong emotions for a woman he had never formally met; well, he had actually met her at his father's engagement party, but for some reason he hadn't felt a connection then. However, at the club, their chemistry was off the chain—it was cosmic—and he couldn't deny what he felt. Initially it baffled him as to why she fled after seeing his face, but then he realized that she probably recognized him from the engagement party and was embarrassed because she'd been making love to Preston's son. The way she ran out of the room, he knew that she wouldn't return to The Black Door anytime soon. But that was okay. He had her file, which included her name *and* her address. Trey knew that it was totally unprofessional to show up on a client's doorstep, but their relationship had gone far beyond professional and was now personal. He felt it, and he knew that she did too.

"BABY," MICHELE WHISPERED again. "Are you asleep?" She lightly nudged him.

Michele's words were drowning out his thoughts, but he kept his eyes shut, trying to replace her face with Meri's. Preferring to stay in a pseudo dream state, he didn't answer her question, but just remained on his back as if he were comatose. Trey didn't make a sound, hoping that she would take the hint and leave him alone.

"Well, I know somebody who's up," she said, lifting the sheet. Michele reached down and began stroking his dick.

He wanted to yell, "Stop! Get out of my bed! I don't love you." But her touch felt too good, and with his testosterone now in high gear, he craved more.

Trying to elicit a response from him, she replaced her hand with her tongue. She seductively traced the rim of his penis's head, and then trailed her tongue down the shaft. When she got to the end of his erection, she began licking his balls is if they were sugarcoated.

Unable to play possum any longer, he instinctively moved his pelvis up and down in a slow rhythmic motion.

Feeling him come to life, Michele wasted no time going for the gusto. Trey hadn't made love to her in weeks and she was long overdue. Her hormones were raging and she desired him with every fiber of her being. She threw the sheet back all the way and straddled his naked body. She positioned the opening of her moist pussy on top of his shaft and rocked back and forth until his hard dick slipped inside of her.

The warmth of her wet pussy turned him on even more than her wet mouth, and he grabbed her by the waist, pulling her down even harder so that he was deeper inside.

Feeling the full length of his shaft, Michele shouted, "Oooo, baby!!"

Trey stuck three fingers inside of her mouth to muffle her screams, so that she wouldn't wake his neighbors. He lived in a quiet co-op building, and the last thing he needed was for the board to call him on the carpet for disrupting the peace in the middle of the night.

Michele began sucking on each finger like they were cylindrical lollipops, and the sensation made him want to come, but he didn't. Instead he rolled her off of him onto her back. In the missionary position he knew that he would have more control over ejaculating; they had just started fucking and he didn't want to bust a nut so soon.

In an effort to pull him in closer, Michele wrapped her legs around his back and squeezed her thighs tight like a vise locking him in place. She wanted to devour his dick, so that her pussy would be the only one that he craved.

Trey could sense from her aggressiveness that she was trying to dominate the situation and pussy-whip him, but of course he wasn't going to let that happen. Much to his chagrin, he was already "whipped" by one woman, and that was more than enough.

In an effort to loosen the grip of her legs and gain more leverage, Trey pushed up and arched his back until her legs dropped to the side. He then grabbed her wrists with one hand and pinned them to the bed. Michele raised her legs and tried to wrap them around his back again, but he caught her right leg just under the kneecap and bent it to his chest. His thrusting became more intense, but he still wasn't penetrating deep enough, so he released her arms and grabbed her by the ankles. He spread her legs high in the air into a wide V and stretched them as far as they would go. Trey began ramming her pussy forcefully to let her know that he was in control. "What's my name?" he demanded in a harsh voice.

She contorted her face and panted, "T . . . r . . . e . . . y," barely getting out each letter.

Michele winced with a tinge of pain as his dick hit her cervix; this wasn't what she expected. She was in love with Trey, and hoped that he felt the same way. She wanted him to convey his feelings by making tender love, not fucking her like some two-dollar hooker off the street. "Wait . . . Stop!" she pleaded between breaths.

Trey's eyes were tightly shut and he didn't respond; he just kept humping her like a mad dog.

"Trey!" she yelled, trying to bring him out of his lust-induced trance. When he still didn't respond, she kicked her legs wildly until he released his grip. She then rolled from underneath him and onto her side. Tears began streaming down her cheeks; she didn't know why he was treating her so rough, like she was a piece of meat.

Michele's back was to him, but Trey could hear her sniffling and assumed that she was crying. He suddenly began to feel guilty. He knew that he was manhandling her, but he couldn't stop himself. Once his dick was inside of her pussy, his animal instincts took over and he just wanted a good fuck; besides, he didn't love her and it showed. Trying to mend the moment, he touched her back, but she scooted away.

Trey didn't know what to say, so he snuggled up close and spooned her. He knew that most women loved to spoon; it made them feel loved. He made this grand gesture because he didn't want to destroy their relationship in one night. He was no fool; he knew that there was no wrath like a woman scorned, and he didn't want Michele as a vengeful adversary. Besides, he didn't know what was going to happen with Meri, and he knew that a bird in the hand was better than one in the bush.

Though Michele was still upset with Trey, she allowed him to cuddle her. She was conflicted. First he was treating her like a one-night stand, and now he was holding her like a precious doll. If she didn't know any better, she'd swear that he had another woman. She thought about asking him point-blank if he was in love with someone else, but she was afraid to hear the truth. Besides, now was not the right time. She knew the best strategy was to do a little research on her own and find out firsthand if he was cheating on her. Michele wasn't about to lose Trey to another woman. If there was someone else in the picture, she would do whatever it took (and that meant anything) to secure her position as his future wife.

ARIEL'S LIFE seemed like one of those melodramatic soap operas with the glitzy characters and surreal plot, where in one episode the maid seduces the man of the house, breaks up his marriage, and becomes the new lady of the manor. In another bizarre twist of fate a mother reunites with a daughter she gave up for adoption twenty years ago, only to discover that her long-lost daughter is engaged to her son (the younger woman's half brother). As far-fetched as these story lines were, they were no comparison to the sequence of events that Ariel was experiencing in real life. She was still having a hard time wrapping her mind around the fact that she had been fucking her future stepson.

Ariel sat slumped over the vanity with her head in her hands. Instead of applying makeup, she sat with her eyes clenched, thinking about the law of averages. What were the odds that she would go to The Black Door in the first place, and then to top it all off, attract the one man on the planet who was totally off-limits? She willfully lifted her head, opened her eyes, looked in the mirror, and searched her beet-red eyes for some kind of understanding as to why this had happened. If only she were the frigid type who didn't need to be sexually satisfied on a regular basis, then she could have waited until Preston made time for her. But no, she was a horny broad who wasn't satisfied with just the synthetic plastic of a vibrator; she was the type of woman who needed to feel the hardness of a man's penis, and not some poor imitation, thrusting inside of her pussy. If only she had called one of those 800 numbers and hired a beefy stud for sex or, better yet, she should have propositioned Mason, her escort for the Lancaster benefit, instead of going to The Black Door. Then none of this would be happening.

The telephone rang as she was counting up the useless if-onlys. Ariel looked at the caller ID and was tempted to let the call go into voice mail. But she knew that he would just call her cell phone, so she reluctantly picked up.

"Hello," she said dryly.

"Hey, honey." Preston's tone was as bubbly as a glass of Dom. "Instead of seven o'clock, can you be at the town house by six-thirty?" he asked anxiously.

Ariel turned around and looked at the clock on the nightstand. It was already a quarter to six, and she was nowhere near ready. She sighed. She didn't want to come within ten feet of the town house or anyplace where Trey was invited.

"Okay, I'll try," she said, knowing that there was no way she was going make it downtown in forty-five minutes.

"Great. See you then," he said, paying no attention to her sullen tone.

I see he's already riding high, Ariel thought, once she hung up the phone.

Instead of putting on a slinky cocktail dress, she wanted to put on a pair of flannel pajamas, crawl into bed, and hide underneath the covers until the party was over, but that was totally out of the question. Preston would find her absence inexcusable; he was counting on her for support. If she didn't show up, that would only raise suspicions, and the last thing she needed was for him to second-guess her fidelity. Ariel did love Preston. He gave her the type of security that she didn't have growing up; in a sense he was a father figure—which was probably why she was attracted to him in the first place—and the last thing she wanted to do was to hurt him.

Ariel rose lazily from the vanity chair and moped into her walk-in closet to find something to wear. She switched on the light, stood back, and looked at the row of cocktail dresses. She stared at the dresses hanging on their padded hangers hoping that one would spark her interest, but nothing jumped out at her. They all seemed dull and boring. She then walked closer to get a better view. She took an emerald-green dress with tiny ruby buttons off of its hanger, placed it against her body, and looked in the full-length mirror that hung on the back of the door.

"Too Christmassy," she said to herself.

Next, she reached for a lavender dress with a two-tiered flounce hemline. "Too belle of the ball." She frowned, looking at the *Gone with the Wind*–inspired gown.

She then removed a slim-fitting, black Gucci dress with a V neckline and held it up to her body. The dress was perfect—sexy yet conservative—except for the plunging neckline, which exposed a portion of her tattoo.

"I'll just wear a scarf to cover this," she said, running her hand over the detailed rose that was stenciled on her left breast.

Now that she had decided what to wear, Ariel went into the kitchen and made herself a double martini. Though time was of the essence, she didn't rush. She drank a few sips and exhaled slowly. The cool liquid slipped down her throat and eased her frayed nerves. She polished off the first glass and then poured another before making her way into the bathroom.

She filled the large Jacuzzi tub with warm water and several drops of eucalyptus oil for a relaxing soak. A cold drink and a warm bath were just what she needed to calm herself before facing Trey again. Ariel languished in the tub for over thirty minutes before climbing out.

She took her time dressing and applying makeup. Since she was already late, it didn't make much sense to rush at this point. And the less time spent at the party, the better. Just before she left the apartment, the house phone rang. She didn't bother looking at the caller ID because she knew that it was Preston calling to find out what was taking her so long. And sure enough, once the phone stopped ringing, her cell phone rang. She didn't want to hear his barrage of questions, so she turned the phone off without answering the call.

Ariel decided to drive her black convertible Mercedes CLK instead of taking a taxi. She wanted the feel of the cool evening breeze on her face, to help clear her head of the nagging thoughts of doom. She couldn't help but envision Preston taking one look at her and Trey and knowing instinctively that they were lovers. She would just have to try and steer clear of Trey so that Preston wouldn't sense the chemistry between them.

She cruised down Fifth Avenue at a snail's pace, to the dismay of the taxi drivers who honked impatiently at her slow-moving vehicle. Ariel didn't increase her speed; she just ignored their incessant horns and menacing stares as they zoomed past her. Though she took her time, she arrived at Preston's town house sooner than she wanted, and as luck would have it, there was a parking space right in front. She had hoped that she would have to circle the block a few times until she found a parking spot, but not tonight.

She parked and sat in the car glancing up at the bay window, trying to see who was inside, but the only thing that she could see through the curtains were shadows moving back and forth.

Ariel switched the lever that automatically raised the convertible top. Once that was secured, she turned off the engine and maneuvered her weary body out of the luxury two-seater.

As she climbed the front steps, her heart began to beat faster and faster with anticipation. She could hear the low hum of various conversations, and couldn't help but wonder if they were talking about her. Ariel knew that it was ludicrous to think that anyone knew her secret, but that didn't stop her from being overly paranoid.

"Get a grip," she scolded herself before ringing the doorbell.

Opening the front door, Meri sang out, "Daarliing."

Ariel's mouth dropped. The last person she expected to see, let alone open the door, was Meri. Before she could ask her what she was doing at Preston's cocktail party, Meri said, "Preston has been looking all over for you. What took you so long?"

"Well, here *I* am, but the question is . . . what are *you* doing here?" Ariel asked once she was inside of the foyer.

"Remember the distinguished-looking man with the graying temples and glasses that I met at your engagement party?" Meri asked, and then answered without waiting for a response. "Well, we've gone out to dinner a few times since then. He's a colleague of Preston's and was on the guest list to this swank shindig and invited me as his date."

"Oh, I see." Ariel was glad to see a friendly face and was tempted to tell Meri about her impossible predicament, but she didn't want to chance Preston's overhearing the details of the sordid story.

"What's with the scarf?" Meri asked, looking at the silk scarf wrapped around Ariel's neck.

"I drove the convertible and was trying to ward off some of the night air," she explained, instead of saying that she was trying to hide her tattoo. If Ariel had said that she was purposely hiding the red rose, Meri would no doubt ask why, and that would initiate the conversation that she was trying to avoid.

"You can take it off now and show off that rack of yours." Meri chuckled.

"I'm still a bit chilled. I think I'll leave it on for a while," she said, touching the scarf and securing it in place.

"Well, just so you know . . ." She paused. "You look like a mummy all wrapped up like that."

She could tell that Meri wasn't gong to drop the subject, so she said, "If you must know, Ms. Nosy, I'm trying to be conservative to-night and not expose my rose."

"If I had big natural boobs and a beautiful tattoo like yours, I would flaunt them all over the place!"

Ariel rolled her eyes to the ceiling; she wasn't in the mood for another one of Meri's self-indulgent conversations. "You do a good job of flaunting your bought boobs, so what's the difference?"

"Yes, that's true." Meri jiggled her titties, and then smoothed her hands over the low-cut dress that enhanced her silicone cleavage.

Preston rushed up to Ariel and asked, "Where have you been? I've been calling you nonstop, and your cell phone goes right to voice mail. You should have been here hours ago," he said in a hushed tone, so as not to cause a scene.

Ariel wasn't in the mood for explaining so she kept it simple and said, "Sorry I'm late."

"So am I," he sighed. "The senator's wife has been asking for you. She's in the library chatting with some of the other guests. I think you should go in there right now and apologize for being late," Preston suggested strongly.

Ariel didn't like the tone of his voice; he was giving her a direct command as if she worked for him, and she didn't appreciate it one bit. She wanted to support Preston, not be one of his lackeys.

"I'm going to get a drink first," she said in an authoritative voice, defying his order.

"There's sherry in the library," he said, insinuating that she should make a beeline straight to Angelica.

Ariel knew that this was his night, but she couldn't stand being bossed around like a worthless peon. She would greet the senator's wife in her own time, *not* Preston's. "I don't want sherry. I want vodka." She turned to Meri. "Come to the kitchen with me; I'm sure there's an ice-cold bottle of Belvedere in the freezer." She turned back to Preston. "I'll speak to Angelica in a few minutes."

Preston stood with a scowl painted on his face as he watched Meri and Ariel sashay to the back of the house.

"Well, I guess you told him," Meri joked, once they were alone in the kitchen.

"It's not that I don't want to support Preston. It's just that I can't stand it when he gets on his high horse and acts like a pompous jackass." She snatched open the freezer door and took out a chilled fifth of vodka. "I mean, who the hell does he think he is anyway? He hasn't even got the nomination, and he's already acting like an esteemed justice." Ariel was so upset that the vein in the middle of her forehead began to pulsate and her body temperature increased a couple of degrees. She whipped the scarf off of her neck and tossed it on the back of a chair.

"Darling, you must understand that a man's career is *always* going to take precedence over his personal relationships. They're wired differently like that; why do you think the divorce rate is so high in this country?" Meri asked, raising an eyebrow.

"Well, maybe I should forgo the wedding altogether."

"Now, now, don't go getting all emotional." Meri opened the cabinet above the sink. "Where are the glasses? You need a drink to calm your nerves before you go back into the party and tell Preston that you want a divorce before you even have the wedding," she said in jest, trying to lighten her friend's dark mood.

"Ha-ha, very funny," Ariel said dryly. She opened the cabinet above the microwave, took out two shot glasses, and poured them each a shot of vodka.

Meri raised her glass. "Here's to men. Can't live with them, and life would be totally boring without them."

Ariel clicked her tiny glass against Meri's. "Touché."

"So this is where the real party is?"

Meri and Ariel both swung around to the sound of the voice, and standing in the doorway was none other than Trey. In her fit of anger, Ariel had completely forgotten about seeing him tonight.

"Well, hello." Meri smiled broadly and extended her hand to him. "I'm Meri Renick. We met at the engagement party." She shamelessly batted her eyelashes at him.

Trey took her hand in his and held it for a few seconds as he searched her eyes, looking for the spark in them that he saw at the club, but it wasn't there. He felt nothing special, so he shook her hand politely. He didn't know what to make of this; he had been longing to see Meri tonight so that they could talk. He had planned to ask her if she wanted to take their escapades to the next level. He wanted a real relationship with her, not just sex, and hoped that she felt the same. But looking at Meri tonight, he knew that she wasn't the same woman who had fucked him into a heavenly bliss. Trey released her hand and turned to Ariel. "Hey there."

Ariel darted her eyes to the floor; she was afraid to make eye contact—one look deep into his warm brown eyes would cause her knees to buckle. He was the man of her desires and she wanted him more than anyone else in the world, but he was Preston's son, so she had to restrain herself. "Hi," was the only word that she could manage to say.

Trey was beginning to think that Ariel didn't particularly care for him; this was the second time that she had shied away from him. From the way she was acting, he couldn't help but wonder if she had a problem with him, but that didn't make any sense. They barely knew each other, so how could he have made a negative impression? Trey didn't want there to be any bad blood between him and his future stepmother, so he started to strike up a conversation to break the ice. But he stopped short when he looked at Ariel and noticed a rose tattoo peeking out from beneath the neckline of her dress. He blinked several times, thinking that his eyes were playing tricks on him.

It can't be. Though he could only see the outline of the top of the rose, he recognized the tattoo instantly. The blood-red color and intricate details of the petals were exactly the same as the woman behind the red mask. He looked from Meri to Ariel and it suddenly made all the sense in the world. He knew that Ariel wasn't a member of the club, so she must had come to The Black Door wearing Meri's mask. The realization that he had been fucking his father's fiancée was startling, rendering him speechless.

He looked closely at Ariel, whose eyes were still cast to the floor. *That's why she ran out when she saw my face.*

Trey didn't know what to do. Fortunately Ariel didn't see him when he spotted the tattoo, so she obviously still thought he didn't know her true identity. Now was neither the time nor the place to confront her, so he decided to follow her lead and act like everything was status quo.

"If you don't mind, I think I'll join you ladies for a shot or two," he said, retrieving a glass from the cabinet and pouring himself a much-needed shot of vodka.

"By all means, please do." Meri beamed.

Ariel wanted to scream. She couldn't believe that she was standing next to her *secret lover* having a drink. *Just chill; he doesn't know that it was you behind the red mask,* she reminded herself.

"So, ladies, why are you hiding out in the kitchen?" Though Trey directed the question to them both, he was looking straight at Ariel.

"We're not hiding; we just wanted something a little stronger than sherry or champagne," Ariel said, finally looking him in the eye.

Trey felt a tingling sensation in his crotch the moment their eyes connected. There was no denying that Ariel was the woman behind the mask. For a split second, he was transported back to The Black Door, and as he thought about sucking on her luscious titties, his dick began to grow.

Trey turned up his glass and drank the shot of vodka in one smooth swallow. "So, what do you think of the senator?" he asked, trying to take his mind off of his slowly rising erection.

Admiring Trey from head to toe, Meri chimed in, "*He's* not my type."

Ariel also polished off her shot. As she and Trey reached for the bottle at the same time, her upper arm brushed across his chest. The feel of his firm pecs was electric and she staggered slightly from making contact with him.

Trey felt the charge too, and his dick went from a slowly rising erection to a full-blown hard-on. He wanted to pull her dress up and fuck her right there on the table. Instead, he took hold of her arm and steadied her balance.

Ariel stood directly in front of him, so close that she could feel his erection. She longed to release his big hard dick and fuck him.

Unbeknownst to everyone, Michele was standing in the doorway watching the interchange between Trey and Ariel. It wasn't what they said, it was what they didn't say. The way their bodies seemed to gravitate toward each other spoke volumes. Trey was a chick magnet and had that effect on women, young and old. He even had Meri swooning and salivating. Michele thought that if his charisma had his future stepmother and her friend in awe, then there was no telling who else he had under this spell. Her woman's intuition told her that Trey was involved with someone else, and over the years, she'd learned to trust that little voice in the back of her head. And now it was telling her to play it cool until she found out the truth.

TREY SAT at his desk trying to crunch the month-end numbers, but he kept punching the wrong buttons on the calculator. Instead of hitting the plus sign, he'd hit the subtraction key, and was inadvertently subtracting the profits when he should have been adding them to the bottom line. He pushed the spreadsheet aside; his mind was mush and he knew it was useless trying to concentrate on accounting when he was preoccupied with his recent discovery.

He took Ariel's thong out of his desk drawer and held it up to his nose. She had left the underwear behind after rushing out of the club unexpectedly. He took a big whiff, trying to smell her scent, but any traces of her essence were long gone. He wove the silk through his fingers; the feel of the smooth fabric reminded him of her velvety-smooth skin. The thin, flosslike panties were the only memento from their evening together and he cherished them dearly. Just looking at the thong transported him back to their last encounter.

From the moment she put her finger to his lips, he knew that night in his private lair would be spectacular, and it was. The way she ran her hands up and down his chest, like he was her very own prized possession, made the hair on the back of his neck stand at attention. And when she kneeled down and put her mouth around his dick, he wanted to scream like he'd never had a blow job in his life. The sensation of her tongue swirling around the circumference of his penis felt like a sensuous tickle, making him want to cum all over himself like an inexperienced teenager making love for the very first time. Trey had been with many women in his lifetime, from supermodels to housewives to kinky corporate executives. He'd even had a ménage à trois with twin bombshells, but this was the first time that any woman had made him want to cancel his player's membership.

At the cocktail party, the moment that she had brushed up against him in the kitchen and he felt her groin against his dick, he was tempted to throw caution to the wind and kiss her (tongue and all) right in front of Meri. But before he could make his move, Michele walked in and said that his dad wanted everyone to come into the living room pronto.

As Trey followed Ariel out of the kitchen, he watched the way she moved, and was captivated. He was mesmerized by the movement of her butt cheeks as they moved up and down in a syncopated rhythm. He had seen her naked body, but watching her juicy ass bounce smoothly against the fabric of the cocktail dress was just as stimulating as seeing her gyrate her tits and ass in his private lair. Something about seeing her all dressed up turned him on. Unlike Michele, who had no sense of decorum, Ariel was sexy yet classy at the same time, and he liked her sophisticated style.

His father began his speech by thanking everyone for attending, but before he continued, he reached out for Ariel and pulled her close to his side. The way his arm rested comfortably around her shoulders as he spoke, and the way he lovingly gazed at her

told Trey that his dad truly loved Ariel. The sight of them standing there together made Trey realize the severity of his actions.
He'd been fucking his future stepmother. If his father ever found
out, it would devastate him to say the least. Though their relationship had its ups and downs, Trey didn't want to destroy his
old man.

Initially Trey had no clue that Ariel was the woman behind the
mask. But now that the masks were off and their identities were revealed, sleeping with his father's fiancée would not only rock the
boat, it would capsize the entire vessel. Under different circumstances he wouldn't let Ariel slip away so easily. But knowing that
she belonged to his dad, Trey realized that sleeping with her again
was absolutely out of the question.

A TAP AT his door brought him back to the present. Trey quickly
stuffed the sexy thong back in his drawer.

"Come in. It's open!" he yelled out.

"What's up, boss?"

"Hey, Mason, what's up with you?"

"Got a minute?" asked the handsome young stud.

"Always." Trey extended his hand. "Have a sit down. What
brings you by?" Trey hadn't seen Mason in weeks, and was curious
as to why he was standing in his office.

"I wanted to talk to you about returning to the club," Mason
said, after settling into one of the chairs across from Trey's desk.

Trey raised his left brow. "Are you saying what I think you're
saying?"

Mason nodded his head and said, "Yep."

Trey couldn't believe his ears. Mason was one of his best
servers. He looked like a bronzed Adonis; his skin was flawless, like
a milky smooth Hershey bar. His body was muscular and toned

with hardly any body fat, and his face was handsomely chiseled like that of a Greek god with a well-groomed goatee framing his mouth. He was once the most requested server at The Black Door and made many a woman happy, but he had retired from that end of the business to focus on school. "I thought you didn't have time to serve now that you're in med school."

Mason dropped his head momentarily, as if he were embarrassed. "I didn't, but I'm not in school anymore," he said, with a tinge of sadness in his voice.

"Why?" Trey leaned his elbows on the desk. "What happened?"

"Money happened, or should I say the lack of money." He hadn't seen his sugar mama in months, and his coffers were dry. "I've used up my savings and had to take a year off. Med school is expensive as hell, and I need to restack my paper before I can go back. Being an escort is cool, but the real money, as you know, is working inside the club."

Trey paid the escorts barely minimum wage, because he knew that their "dates" doled out hefty tips at the end of an enjoyable evening. But he paid the servers who worked inside of the club full-time a handsome salary plus benefits. They were the soul of the club, and he wanted to make sure that they were compensated accordingly. Money equaled loyalty, and the turnover rate at The Black Door was extremely low.

"I'm sorry to hear that you had to drop out of school." He flashed a broad smile. "But I'm glad you're back, my man."

"I just bet you are," Mason said sarcastically.

"Hold on," he said, picking up on Mason's tone. "It's not what you think."

"Oh, yeah?" Mason said, looking doubtful.

"Yeah." Trey leaned in closer. "Actually, I've been thinking about opening a Black Door downtown, but I haven't found the right property yet."

Mason wasn't following what Trey was saying. "So, what does that have to do with me?"

"Well, I would need someone to run the club once it's open, and I couldn't think of a better manager than you." He smiled.

"Thanks, man, but I don't know a thing about managing a club."

"I know you don't; that's why I'd like you to be the assistant manger here at the club, instead of a server. That way I can personally teach you the ropes. You'll be my right hand, and by the time the new club is ready to open, you'll be an old pro."

Mason quickly warmed up to the idea. He really didn't want to service the members anymore. Some of the women were relentless, and as much as he loved sex, performing on command could be grueling. The only reason he was returning to The Black Door was the money, and nothing else. "You got a deal! When do I start?" he asked gleefully.

"I'll have my attorney draw up a contract as soon as possible, but until then, why don't we go out to dinner and celebrate. Are you free tonight?"

"Free as a bird." Mason beamed.

Trey picked up the phone. "Let me call 66 and see if we can get a reservation."

"Sounds like a plan." Mason hadn't expected to be offered a position in management, and was pleased as holiday punch.

Trey had connections with most of the trendy restaurants in the city, and could usually get a reservation at a moment's notice. He spoke to the manger at 66, a friend of a friend, and locked down a reservation for that night.

"How does eight thirty sound?" he asked Mason once he hung up the phone.

"Sounds good; let me go home and change into something more respectable," he said, looking down at his ripped jeans and

Timberlands. "I'll meet you there at eight thirty." Mason stood up and shook Trey's hand. "Thanks, Boss."

"You are more than welcome, Mason. As you know, this business is dicey, and it's good to have someone in my corner that I can trust."

"Man, I got your back. And you can take that to the bank."

When Mason left his office, Trey leaned back in his chair, folded his arms across his chest, and kicked his feet up on the desk. He had visions of expanding, but knew that he couldn't personally manage both clubs successfully. With The Black Door being a private club, he had reservations about bringing a stranger into the fold. Now he wouldn't have to worry about proprietary information being divulged to the competition.

Trey had resolved one issue, but still had Ariel on the brain. Though he knew that she was off-limits, it didn't stop him from desiring her. He opened his desk drawer and reached for the thong. He took it out and held the sexy silk underwear up to his face; even though he knew her essence had long dissipated, he took one last sniff, and then tossed the scandalous undies in the trash. "Goodbye, Ms. Vaughn," he said ever so sadly, as the thong hit the bottom of the can.

CHEF JEAN-GEORGES'S Asian-inspired restaurant, 66, in TriBeCa was a well-known destination for corporate tycoons, music industry moguls, supermodels, models in training, and just plain folk in search of a gastronomical treat. The modern interior with its monochromatic color scheme, steel mesh curtains, and oblong Lucite communal dining table near the front of the restaurant was welcoming. The rear of the space offered a more private dinning experience and a breathtaking view of its colossal aqua-blue salt-water aquarium stocked with baby sharks, moray eels, vibrant blue yellow-tailed hippo tangs, prickly porcupine puffers, and striped lionfish.

Trey arrived before Mason and took a seat in the lounge area. The section was filled with a smattering of Euro-trash, Wall-streeters, and downtown artists. Trey glanced around and perched across from him on a set of white leather cubes was a group of leggy models. They were busy poring over a portfolio and didn't see him when he sat down.

"I think my boobs look too fake in this shot," said a tall redhead.

"Well aren't they?" responded a beautiful brunette with short cropped hair.

"Yeah, but the surgeon said that after the swelling went down, they would hang just like regular boobs."

"Beth, you know good and well, that they are too damn big to look *regular*. What cup size are you now, 40-triple-E?" she mused.

"No." The redhead smiled. "I'm a 38-double-D," she said proudly, not getting the joke.

The brunette shook her head. "And you wonder why they look fake?"

Trey couldn't help but look over at the women. The first one he noticed was the redhead. She had on a white wife-beater and her breasts nearly spilled out of the deep-cut sides. She might as well have been topless, because the thin cotton tanktop barely contained her enormous jugs. He was a breast man, but hers were too damn unnatural. Instead of soft and feminine, they looked hard and synthetic. He liked the thrill of seeing a woman's nipples harden as he played with them, but this chick's nipples were already as firm as two thimbles. Trey had seen enough saline enhancements at the club that he'd become immune to the manufactured boobs.

"Sorry I'm late," Mason said, walking into the bar area.

"No problem, man. I just got here myself a few minutes ago."

Before Mason could sit down, the redhead called out, "Excuse me."

Mason looked in the direction of the trio, thinking that maybe someone in the group knew him, but he didn't recognize any faces. He pointed to himself. "You talking to me?" he asked.

She stood up and walked over to him. "Didn't I meet you at The CroBar the other night?"

Mason was always getting mistaken for someone; he had that type of face. "No, it wasn't me." He smiled.

She walked closer so that her boobs nearly touched his chest. "Are you sure? I was dancing with this guy who looked exactly like you." She reached out and touched his well-defined bicep through his form-fitting knit sweater.

Mason blushed slightly at the flattery. He got hit on on a daily basis, but he never tired of the attention. With the demands of med school and working, he hadn't had time for much of anything else. His sugar mama had disappeared, and he hadn't been laid in months, but now that he was taking a hiatus from school, he'd have time to get his freak on. Mason gave her the once-over, and his eyes zeroed in on her big-ass titties. She didn't have on a bra, so he could see her nipples as clear as day. He felt his dick responding, but didn't want to act like a hound dog in front of his boss. He extended his hand. "My name is Mason, and yours?" he asked, flashing her a sly, sexy smile.

"I'm Elizabeth, but my friends call me Beth," she flirted, relishing his firm grip. After a few seconds, she released his hand, reached inside her jeans pocket, pulled out a business card with her picture on the front, and handed it to him.

He looked at her mini head shot on the front and assumed that she was a model. Mason loved models. They were usually freaky as hell. Most of them were bisexual and loved to have sex with their girls and a random guy. He was more than willing to be that random stud. Mason turned the card over.

"That's my cell number. Give me a call. I'd love to go out sometime." She winked.

"Okay, Beth. Have a good evening." He tucked the card in his back pocket and turned back to Trey.

"Gentlemen, your table is ready," the hostess said, approaching them.

Once they were seated at their table, Trey didn't waste any time commenting on Beth. "Man, she was really vibing on you."

"What can I say? The ladies love them some Mason." He laughed.

"Spoken like a true player."

"I'm not a player." He grinned. "I just enjoy the company of a fine young lady every once in a while."

Trey smirked doubtfully. "Yeah, right."

"Good evening, gentlemen," the waiter said, approaching their table. "Can I get you sparkling or flat water?" He handed them two menus.

"Flat is fine for me," Trey said, and then turned to Mason. "Is that okay with you?"

"Evian, if you have it. I don't care much for carbonated water."

"And a bottle of Veuve Grand Dame," Trey added.

"Sure, sir. I'll be right back with your drinks."

They perused the mouthwatering menu, with its selections of nouveau Asian dishes; every item on the extensive menu was tempting, from the honey-glazed spare rib appetizer, to the succulent Peking duck and ginger-infused squab with an orange glaze. Even the coconut tapioca, winter-fruit parfait for dessert sounded totally sinful.

The waiter returned with their water and champagne. "Can I start you off with an appetizer?"

"You can bring the spare ribs, and two orders of the rock shrimp," Trey said, ordering for the table.

"And as an entrée, I'll have the roasted garlic lamb chops," Mason said.

Trey added, "I'll have the sesame-crusted salmon, medium rare."

Once their orders were placed and the champagne poured, Trey raised his glass. "Welcome to the executive suite."

Mason, clinked his glass. "Thanks, Trey. It feels good to not have to worry about finances anymore."

"Hey, wait a minute . . . Who said I was paying you a salary? This is an internship position," he said, without cracking a smile.

Mason stopped drinking and looked Trey dead in the eyes. "What? I thought—"

Before he could finish, Trey burst out laughing. "Just kidding, my man. Of course I'm going to pay you a salary. After all, 'the ladies love them some Mason,'" he said, mocking Mason's earlier words. "And I'm counting on you to increase our membership numbers by referring quality ladies who need some excitement in their lives."

Mason breathed a sigh of relief. "Done!"

The champagne was flowing and the food was beyond delectable, so Trey and Mason sat back and ate and drank like kings. After dinner, they each ordered Lagavulin, an aged, single-malt Scotch, and shared stories of the women they had loved *and* lost. Trey was tempted to tell Mason about his tryst with Ariel, but stopped himself. He realized that saying he knocked boots with his future stepmother would sound bizarre—at best—so he kept his mouth shut. When the check arrived, Trey reached in his wallet, took out his American Express Black Card, and put it on the table.

Trey's cell phone rang, and he looked at the caller ID. It was Michele. He didn't feel like being bothered, so he pressed DECLINE and sent her call into voice mail. He hadn't seen her since the cocktail party a week ago, and was trying to avoid her so that he could slowly break off their relationship. After experiencing such a cosmic connection with Ariel, Trey knew that if Michele was indeed his soul mate, he would never have been attracted to another woman. He didn't want to waste Michele's time, and realized that he needed to step up and tell her that it wasn't working out for him. But his true confession could wait until tomorrow. "I gotta take a whiz," Trey said, and excused himself to the restroom.

The bathrooms at 66 were as unique as the restaurant itself. Hidden behind silver mesh curtains was a darkened hallway lined with several individual bathrooms. Each unisex stall was private, complete with its own sink and vanity mirror. Trey tried the first door, but it was locked, so he went to the next one and knocked, but it was occupied as well. He wasn't in the mood to try each door, so he decided to wait until the person came out of stall number one. With champagne and Scotch flowing through his veins, Trey was feeling no pain. He was in a good mood and whistled lightly as he waited. He heard the lock click and stepped aside. When the door opened, he couldn't believe his eyes. Standing in front of him was none other than . . . Ariel Vaughn.

Her eyes widened when she saw him standing there. Ariel stood in the doorway motionless, practically paralyzed from shock. Trey was the last person she expected to see. She didn't know what to do, so she did nothing.

Trey's animalistic instincts took over and he knew exactly what to do. He didn't say one word, just took hold of her shoulders, walked her backward into the bathroom, and kicked the door shut with his foot.

Trey released her shoulders, locked the door, took her face in his hands, and kissed her passionately. He almost groaned. He had wanted to do this in the kitchen of his father's town house. Her lips were as soft as butter and melted into his. He then slipped his tongue inside of her expectant mouth. Their tongues met and danced together to a seductive rhythm all their own.

Ariel gently pushed Trey against the door, pressing her body closer to his. She knew it was wrong, but couldn't stop herself. Her skin craved his touch and she wouldn't be satisfied until he kissed every pore on her body.

Trey seemed to read her mind. His kisses went from her mouth down to her neck. He unbuttoned her blouse with one hand as he held her tight with the other; once her blouse was opened, he trailed his tongue down to her bra. He nuzzled his head between her breasts and traced his tongue around the edges of her tattoo. Trey loved that rose, because if it were not for that discerning mark, he would have never known that she was the woman behind the red mask. He kissed the rose, and began nibbling on the edges of her lacy bra. He bit open the front snap with his teeth, causing her bra to pop open and her breasts to spill out. Unlike the model with the saline boobs, Ariel's were the real thing. He caressed them and loved the way they felt— soft and voluptuous. He leaned down and licked each nipple with the tip of his tongue, then proceeded to suck them ever so tenderly.

Ariel's eyelids fluttered and her eyes rolled to the back of her head at his masculine, yet gentle touch. He pressed her tits together and went from one to the other with a combination of kissing, licking, and sucking. The sensation made her gasp with pleasure. She reached down to unzip his pants, but he caught her wrist and stopped her hand from going any further.

In an uncharacteristic move, Trey hooked Ariel's bra closed and carefully buttoned each pearl button on her blouse. Ariel looked disappointed, but understood why he stopped himself. This was so wrong. They had committed the ultimate betrayal and now that they knew each other's identity, the *only* choice was to stop before Preston found out.

Trey grabbed her by the hand and unlocked the door. He headed straight for the exit with Ariel in tow. They walked right past the hostess and out the door. He didn't say a word and neither did she; outside, he hailed a taxi with one hand, while still holding her hand with the other.

"Take us to 128 East Thirty-eighth, right off Park," he told the driver.

Neither spoke as the taxi weaved through traffic on the way to midtown. Remembering that he'd left Mason and his AmEx card, Trey took out his cell phone.

"Hey, man, something came up and I had to leave. Can you sign the check and hold onto my card for me? I'll get it from you tomorrow . . . Okay, thanks." Trey put his phone on vibrate, and stuck it back in the breast pocket of his blazer.

Realizing that she had abandoned Meri, Ariel took out her phone and dialed her friend. "Uh, hi. Something came up and I had to leave," she said, using the same words as Trey.

"Not to worry, daarliing. I see a handsome young thing with yummy biceps sitting all alone, and he looks familiar. I think I just might have to have him for dessert tonight," Meri said, with a devilish grin.

Ariel was glad that Meri wasn't the needy type and could fend for herself. But she knew that in true Meri style, she was going to call back at some point and drill her for the real reason as to why she left so abruptly. Ariel wasn't going to take any calls tonight, so she turned off her phone and put it back in her purse. She knew that they were breaking all the rules, but this chance encounter was fate giving them one final good-bye. She should've asked where they were going, but she didn't want to ruin the magic of the moment, so she remained silent.

Trey felt his phone buzzing against his chest, but he ignored it. Five minutes later, the phone buzzed again. He knew it could only be one person annoying the hell out of him—Michele—and he wanted to toss the phone out of the window so that he would never have to talk to her again. But that was useless, because she'd only call his house phone. He was definitely going to tell her that it was over, but not tonight.

It had begun to rain slightly, and Ariel watched the tiny droplets fall softly against the window. She loved rainy nights; they could be so sexy, especially when you were cozied up with a warm body. For the first time in a long time, Ariel felt completely relaxed. She leaned her head on Trey's shoulder, closed her eyes, and enjoyed the rest of the ride.

Within a few minutes, they were pulling up in front of his building. After paying the fare, Trey took off his sports coat, held it over his head, and got out; he then reached inside for Ariel's hand. He stood over her with his blazer held high, shielding them both from the rain, which had increased from a few drops into a torrential downpour.

Trey was so busy being the attentive gentleman that he didn't notice Michele's black BMW parked across the street. She had been calling him all evening, but kept getting his voice mail. Usually he accepted her calls, but tonight he was purposely ignoring her. She became suspicious and decided to drive over to his apartment. Michele hadn't been sitting there five minutes when a taxi eased in front of Trey's building. A couple got out, but she couldn't see their faces, because the man was holding a jacket over their heads as they rushed quickly toward the door.

"Gene, no visitors tonight," Trey instructed the doorman, before they stepped onto the elevator.

Gene nodded. He knew that meant if Trey had any unexpected guests, he was to say that Mr. Curtis was out for the evening.

Neither one spoke on the ride up to his apartment, as if words would ruin the magic between them. Even though their only communication since seeing each other at the restaurant had been nonverbal, they both spoke the same language—the language of lust. They stood hand in hand until the elevator stopped.

Trey led Ariel down the hallway to his apartment, and she willingly followed like a helpless puppy. He released her hand long enough to unlock the door. Once the door was open, he swept her into his arms and gallantly carried her inside. Not missing a step, he kicked the door shut with one foot and kept walking. He carried her into his bedroom and gently laid her across the bed.

The room was dark, with only the faint light from the street streaming through the slits of the blinds. Ariel couldn't see his face, but she saw the shadows of his movements as he pulled the mock turtleneck over his head. She heard him unzip his trousers, and heard the buckle of his belt hit the floor. Her eyes were glued to him as he stood there in his snug boxer-briefs. In anticipation of what was to come, her heart was beating as loudly as the rain that was pounding the window sills.

Trey wanted to take his time. He knew that this would be their final rendezvous, and he wanted to relish every second. He eased onto the bed, lay on his side, and pulled Ariel close to him. She curled up into a semi-fetal position, and her body molded into his. For the first time since meeting her, Trey stroked her dark raven tresses, and they felt silky smooth. He moved her hair to one side and softly kissed the nape of her neck.

Chills tickled Ariel's spine the instant he kissed her erogenous zone, and she shivered. That was the sweet spot that very few knew about—not even Preston—and his soft lips on the back of her neck made the crotch of her pantyhose moist with desire.

Trey ran his hands underneath her skirt, slowly rolled her nylons down to her ankles, and removed them along with her pumps. He leaned up on one elbow and helped her wiggle out of her skirt. Once she was naked from the bottom down, he pulled on the waistband of his underwear and slid them off in one smooth motion. Trey cradled her back into his arms, and began to rock back and forth; with each move, his penis grew an inch, until he was fully erect. Trey spread her legs and eased his hard dick into her wet vagina.

Ariel arched her back and her butt jutted out a little farther so that there were no empty spaces between them. She closed her eyes and swayed to his rhythm. They seemed to move in sync with the sound of the rain, and the sensation was extremely erotic.

AS TREY AND Ariel were upstairs making tender love, Michele was downstairs making a scene. She had finally gotten out of her car and decided to go inside.

"Hi, Gene," she said to the doorman with a forced smile. "Is Trey in?"

"I'm sorry, Ms. Richards. He's out for the evening." Gene was familiar with Michele from seeing her with Trey on numerous occasions, but his loyalty lay with the tenant.

"That's okay. I'll just wait for him," she said, taking off her rain-drenched trench and walking over to one of the leather sofas in the waiting area.

"I'm sorry, Ms. Richards, but I think it best that you come back tomorrow," he suggested strongly.

Michele spun around on her heels. "Excuse me?" She shot him a menacing look that read, *Don't fuck with me.*

"I'm sorry—"

She cut him off. "Yeah, I know you're sorry. But you're going to really be sorry if you don't leave me the hell alone and let me wait!" she shouted.

An elderly couple walking through the lobby stopped and stared at Michele as she waved her hands in the air and stomped her foot in protest.

Gene had purposely pushed Michele's buttons so that she would cause a commotion, giving him justification for putting her out. Over the years, he had seen his share of irate wannabe girlfriends and knew how to handle them. "Ms. Richards, I'm going to have to ask you to leave," he said in no uncertain terms.

"You'd better be glad I have an early meeting tomorrow. Otherwise, I'd sit right in this lobby until morning, and there wouldn't be a damn thing you could do about it!" she huffed, trying to save face.

Michele threw on her coat and dashed through the rain back to her car. Once inside, she snatched her cell phone from her purse and called Trey again, but after five rings, she was greeted by his voice mail. She was fuming. The way Gene was acting all territorial and protective, she had a sneaking suspicion that he was lying. *Trey's probably in his apartment at this very moment fucking someone else, and told Gene to keep me out,* she thought.

Well, whomever he was with had won this round, but the fight had just begun. Michele was a woman with stamina, and was prepared to go the distance to keep Trey, no matter who got hurt in the process.

25

IT HAD been a week since the cocktail party in honor of the senator, and the wheels of progress were rapidly rolling along. It was just a matter of time before the nomination was official and Preston could already taste the spoils of victory. He knew that he would have to resign his current position on the bench, which he'd gladly do, but would wait until the official nod before stepping down.

Preston and Michele were at the town house working on his relocation agenda. If he won the nomination he would have to move to Washington in the ensuing months for an easier commute, but would keep his New York residence for return trips to the city.

"Bethany, the Realtor in D.C. faxed me these listings," Michele said, handing Preston a stack of papers.

He carefully scanned through them, separating the possibilities from the impossibilities. Preston was looking for another town house; he loved the layout of the space—roomy yet cozy—it was perfect for entertaining. Once he was ensconced on the Hill, he would host a series of cocktail and dinner parties to establish his position among the in-crowd. "I'm definitely interested in these two." He held up the listings featuring two redbrick colonial town houses, gave her his choices, and tossed the other listings in the trash. "Call Bethany and schedule a showing."

"When do you want to see the listings?" Michele asked, but without her usual gusto.

Preston was accustomed to Michele's spunky personality and had never seen this side of her before. He looked at her face closely and could see tearstains on her cheeks. It was apparent that she had been crying and he wanted to know why. "Michele," he called her name softly. "What's the matter?"

She held her head down, trying to hide the pain in her eyes. "Nothing," she whispered.

Preston got up and walked around the desk. "Michele, I can see that you're upset." He put his hand on her should in a fatherly gesture. "Please tell me what the problem is; maybe I can help," he offered.

She threw her hands up to her face and began to cry softly. She attempted to speak but was choked up, rendering the words inaudible.

Preston reached over, pulled a few tissues out of the silver holder that was sitting on the corner of his desk, and handed them to her. "Now, now." He patted her back until her tears stopped and her sniffles subsided. "Well?" he asked, once she had calmed down some.

Michele wiped her eyes and blew her nose with the damp tissue. She cleared her throat and said, "It's Trey."

"Trey?" Preston asked, surprised to hear his son's name come out of her mouth. The last time he had seen them together at the cocktail party, they appeared to be very much a couple. But now thinking back on that night, he remembered that Trey seemed preoccupied, as if something heavy was weighing on his mind.

"I think he's having an affair," she blurted out.

Oh, is that all? Preston wanted to say. Trey was young, handsome, and *single*. And if he was anything like his old man—who in his youth before he married had a string of woman a mile long—had more than one pillow to lay his head on. Michele may be his main girl, but they were not married, and Trey had no legal obligations of fidelity to honor as far as she was concerned. "What makes you think he's having an affair?" Preston asked instead, playing the concerned boss and father figure.

"Because I've been calling since yesterday evening *and* all morning, and I keep getting his voice mail, and . . . !" She hesitated a second before confessing. "Last night I went over to his apartment but he wasn't there. I wanted to wait in the lobby until Trey came home, but the doorman wouldn't let me. He was quite nasty about making me leave."

"I'm sure he's just busy with work. Besides, do you think it was a good idea to show up unannounced?" he asked, giving her a "you know better" look.

Michele bristled. "I'm his girlfriend and should be welcomed *anytime* I show up, announced or *unannounced*!"

"Don't get all riled up. All I'm saying is that there's probably a legitimate reason why he's not picking up his phone. I'm sure you're making something out of nothing," he said, trying to be the voice of reason.

"Yeah, I guess you're right," she said hesitantly, willing to give Trey the benefit of the doubt.

Preston could sense that she was still uneasy with Trey's behavior, so he said, "If you want me to, I'll have a talk with him."

Michele instantly perked up. "Would you?" she asked, hoping

that Preston would chastise Trey like a naughty child and make him act right.

"Sure no problem," Preston lied in an effort to squash the conversation so they could get back to the business at hand. He had no intention of browbeating his son about his relationship with Michele. Trey was a grown man and what he did in his personal life was his business.

The phone rang just in the nick of time. Preston was eager to get back to work; he had wasted too much time already on Michele's nonissue.

Michele cleared her throat and answered his desk phone. "Good afternoon, Judge Hendricks's office, Michele speaking. How may I assist you?" she asked in her most professional voice.

"Hello, Michele, how are you?"

She recognized the voice immediately. "Oh, hello, Senator Oglesby, I'm fine, and yourself?"

"Fine, thank you. Is Preston available?"

"Of course, hold on please." She handed Preston the phone and walked out of his office to give him some privacy.

"Robert," Preston greeted him cheerfully, "how are things going?"

"Well, that's why I am calling. The investigation is under way and some questions have been raised about your son," he said point-blank, wasting no time getting right to the point.

"Trey?" Preston found himself asking twice in one afternoon.

"The investigators are having a hard time finding out the exact nature of his business. He told me at dinner that he was into equity and real estate investments, but we can't seem to locate the brokerage firm or realty office that he's associated with. Do you know the name of company that he works for?"

Preston had been so self-absorbed lately that he hadn't followed up with Trey regarding which brokerage firm he had signed on with, or if he was making real estate deals on his own or with a realty company. For all he knew, Trey was working independently.

"Senator," he said, in business mode, reverting back to Robert's professional title, "I'm sure there's nothing to worry about." He chuckled nervously.

The senator detected Preston's uncertainty. "How sure are you? Listen." He lowered his voice slightly. "Preston, this isn't the time for doubts. I suggest that you find out exactly what your son is doing professionally."

"I'll have a talk with him today, Senator," Preston said, trying to appease the senator.

"Good. Have him give you all the necessary details of his employment; how long he's been with the company, address and phone number, his exact title, his direct report's name, etcetera. The sooner we can address the questions regarding Trey's professional background, the better. Rest assured the investigators won't stop digging until they uncover everything about everyone within your inner circle. The whole point of this preliminary investigation is to try and do damage control if necessary."

When Preston heard the words *damage control,* his heart skipped a beat. It never occurred to him that Trey could be involved in anything unsavory that might jeopardize his chances of sitting on the Supreme Court. He quickly ended his conversation with the senator, put on his suit jacket, and headed over to Trey's apartment for some much-needed answers.

"THE MORNING after" had taken on a whole new meaning for Trey and Ariel. With the glare of the sun cutting through the blinds, they woke up to the harsh reality of what they had done. It was one thing to fuck anonymously at the club, when neither knew the identity of the other. But now that the masks were off, there was no way to hide from the truth, and the truth was that they had committed the ultimate betrayal!

Trey was resting on his elbow, looking down at Ariel. He had been watching her sleep for the past twenty minutes, and even in her slumber, she was beautiful. Her skin was flawless, and her lips were perfect, not too small and not too big; just right for kissing. He couldn't keep his eyes off of her, and he now understood why Michele was obsessed with staring at him on and off during the night. There was something angelic about looking at someone you desired in a peaceful state. It was as if they belonged solely to you and no one else. And Trey wished that were true now more than ever. He wished they were alone on a deserted island, with no one to answer to but themselves—nothing to do all day but eat, swim in a tranquil blue lagoon, and make love all night into the early morning. They would wake up the next day and do it all over again. Then he wouldn't have to face his father and tell him that he'd made love with his fiancée, not once, not twice, but three times. However, that was one wish that would never be granted, because there was no way on earth that he could form his lips to tell his father the truth. Besides, what was the point? This was their last hurrah, their last visit to the land of deceit.

With the sun's rays beaming down on Ariel's face, she began to stir. She blinked open her eyes and looked up directly into Trey's handsome face. They hadn't spoken the entire night, and now Ariel didn't quite know how to begin. Guilt covered her like a wet wool blanket, and she felt uncomfortable all over. "Good morning," she said in a soft whisper, finally finding her voice.

Trey leaned down and kissed her on the forehead. "Morning, sleepy head."

Ariel had slept like a baby, and had no clue what time it was. She popped straight up, looking for a clock, but didn't see one. "What time is it?" She panicked, thinking that she had overslept.

He glanced down at his Rolex, which was the only thing he was wearing. "Relax, it's only seven-thirty."

"I've got to go, I have an eleven o'clock meeting," she said, throwing her leg over the side of the bed.

Trey didn't want her to leave so soon. He knew that once she walked out his door, she would never walk back in, and so he gently touched her arm. "Don't rush off. You have plenty of time to make your meeting."

His touch stopped her cold. Ariel's mind told her to leave before she got in any deeper (if that was possible), but her body had a mind of its own and was telling a different story. She slumped back on the pillows and sighed hard. As much as she tried, she couldn't exert any willpower when it came to Trey. Just one touch from him and she melted like whipped butter on a toasted bagel.

Trey eased over and partially covered her body with his. His appetite for her was insatiable and he needed more of her loving before she walked out of his world, back into his father's. He wedged open her legs with his, and began fingering her vagina with one hand, while fondling her breasts with the other. Her areolas turned a shade darker and her nipples became as hard as two small pieces of lead. Just watching them firm to his touch had awakened his limp dick. He stroked her clit with his thumb, while engaging her pussy with his index and middle fingers.

Ariel moaned with each rub of her G-spot, wanting more. His fingers were stimulating, but they didn't compare to his long, thick penis. She opened her legs wider inviting him inside. When he didn't take the hint, she reached down and found the object of her desire, which was only semihard. In an effort to help him reach his full potential, Ariel gripped his dick and firmly ran her hand up and down the shaft until she felt his penis expand. She looked down and saw clear juices ooze out of the tip. She rubbed the pre-cum around the head of his cock and it glistened like a thin coat of shellac across the pulsating surface.

"That's it, baby," Trey whispered in her ear. She had the Midas touch, and he responded immediately. Now fully erect, he was ready for penetration. He got on his knees and then pulled her down to him. "Bend your knees, baby," he directed her.

Ariel followed his instructions and when she did, her pussy opened just a little wider for him.

Trey's dick was now as hard as a jackhammer and ready to go to work. He pressed her inner thighs down ever so slightly, and then fed her hungry pussy. The lips of her vagina nibbled on the head of his penis as he inched inside.

"Give it to me!" she pleaded.

He held back. "Tell me how bad you want this big dick."

"Trey." She sang his name for the first time. "I want it so bad that if you don't fuck me right now, I'm going to go crazy," she said in between clenched teeth.

He stuck his dick in another inch. "We can't have that, now can we?" he said, looking down at her.

The expression on Ariel's face was that of lust mixed with frustration. She couldn't believe that he was teasing her. She was dripping wet and wanted him to finish what he had started. When he was inside of her, she felt whole for the first time in her life, and the feeling was beyond addictive.

Trey read her face, and it said that she was ready, so he gave up the goods.

"Yeah, that's it," she moaned, as he fed her the full length of his shaft.

Trey raised her ass up with both of his hands and held her cheeks tight as he increased his pace.

Ariel met his thrusts with hers, and they bucked back and forth like untamed thoroughbreds. "I'm—I'm—I'm cumming!" Ariel panted.

Trey gave her another deep thrust. "I want you to cum all over this big dick," he said, dropping his voice into a lower Billy Dee–type register.

His deep sexy voice was the cherry on top of her icing, and she screamed, *"I'm cumming!"*

Her screams were music to his ears, and he couldn't hold back any longer. Trey didn't care about his neighbors. All he cared about at the moment was climaxing. He quickly pulled out, came all over her stomach, and slumped down beside her in sheer exhaustion. He lay there for a few seconds to catch his breath. Once his breathing was under control, he got out of the bed and walked into the bathroom. Trey returned with a fluffy terry-cloth bath towel and carefully wiped his secretions off of her stomach.

Ariel smiled as he cleaned her up. The gesture was so sweet that she couldn't help but rub his head as he dabbed away the milky substance. "That's okay, I need to take a shower anyway."

"Mind if I join you?" He winked suggestively.

"Only if you promise to be good." She winked back.

"I'm always good." Trey held out his hand and helped her out of the bed.

Ariel trailed him into the bathroom and stood back as he adjusted the water to the perfect temperature. Seeing his dick hang between his legs as he bent over the tub made her want to fuck him all over again.

He held his hand underneath the water. "That's perfect." He climbed in first, and she followed.

Ariel stood in front of him and allowed the warm water to run down her face, traveling south to her breasts and down to her Bermuda triangle. Her eyes were closed so she didn't see him reach around for the shower gel.

Trey squirted the cool gel on her back, and she jumped. "Sorry, I didn't mean to startle you." He rubbed the gel into her back until it lathered. He massaged her back and shoulders, relaxing her.

Ariel eased back into his touch. "Hmm, that feels so good."

Trey squirted more gel into his hands and reached underneath her arms. He began massaging her breasts, and his hands slid up and down her luscious titties. The slick feel of the gel against her skin felt so sensuous that his dick sprung to attention. He held her breasts from underneath, and pulled her nipples downward, causing her to bend over. He then put one foot on the side of the tub, removed his hands from her breasts, held onto her waist, and rammed his dick deep within her.

Ariel held onto the side of the shower as he made love to her underneath the pulsating spray of the water, and her body twitched from the electrifying experience.

After cleansing their bodies, Trey stepped out of the shower first, and left Ariel in the bathroom to wash her hair. He wrapped a towel around himself and closed the door.

The moment he toweled off and put on his boxers, someone knocked at the front door. *That's odd*, he thought. The doorman always announced his visitors before they came up. There was only one person who knocked on his door unannounced at this time of the morning, and that was his housekeeper. Trey had forgotten that this was her day to clean. He was usually dressed and ready to head out once he let her in, but today he had been pleasantly distracted. He reached for the pants from last night that were balled up in a heap on the floor, quickly pulled them on, and walked to the door. He planned to tell her to go across the street to Starbucks, have a latté or two, and come back in an hour. That way it would give him and Ariel time to say their final good-byes.

"Rosa, can you—" he started to say as he opened the door, but it wasn't Rosa.

"Son, we need to talk," Preston said, bursting into his apartment.

Oh shit! was Trey's first thought. *He knows about me and Ariel*, was his second thought.

Preston marched into the living room and began pacing back and forth. "Tell me the truth, son."

Trey looked toward his bedroom. He had left the door slightly ajar, but thankfully had shut the bathroom door. He hoped Ariel wouldn't come out of the shower anytime soon. "The truth about what?" he asked. He decided to play dumb, until his dad flat-out accused him of sleeping with his fiancée.

Preston stopped pacing and stared Trey directly in the eye. "The truth about the equity and real estate ventures you're involved in."

"What?" Trey didn't have a clue what his dad was talking about.

"You told the senator that you've been investing in stocks and real estate, but the investigators can't find any proof of that. What's the name of the company you're with, the name of your supervisor, and where are their offices located? And I'll also need their phone and fax numbers," Preston blurted out, making sure that he didn't miss any of the details that the senator had requested.

Trey exhaled deeply. Questions about his livelihood he could deal with, but he wasn't ready for a confrontation about Ariel, especially since their affair was over. "I'm not with a realty company or brokerage firm. I'm investing on my own," he said calmly.

"Do you have an office, and a list of properties and stocks that you've bought recently?"

Seeing the panic in his dad's eyes made Trey nervous. Obviously the inquiry was coming directly from the senator, who was probably conducting a preliminary investigation. Trey was so preoccupied with running The Black Door that he didn't realize the investigation process had started. If he had known, he would have called in a few favors to carefully cover his lies. Luckily, he had used "Curtis," his mother's maiden name, when he bought the building that The Black Door occupied. Realizing that this was serious, Trey broke out in a light sweat. Though the club was legit, there was no way on this green earth that he could tell his father that he owned The Black Door. Being an officer of the court, his dad would think that being affiliated with a sex club was an unacceptable business for his only son. Trey never suspected that his occupation would interfere with his father's career. "Uh, no, I don't have an outside office. I work right here in my apartment."

"What about a list of stocks and properties? I know the senator is going to want details."

Ariel heard Preston's voice the second she opened the bathroom door and panic instantly set in. *We've been caught.* She stood naked in the doorway, as quiet as a church mouse, and listened closely.

"Uh, I haven't bought any stocks yet, and I'm looking at a couple of properties in the Meatpacking District. Why does the senator need to know about me anyway? I'm not the one seeking the nomination."

"I know. I thought it was strange too. My guess is that he wants to be certain that there will be no surprises cropping up once the official investigation gets under way," Preston said.

Ariel, holding her breath, let it out slowly, but her heart was still pounding wildly against her chest like a tom-tom. At first she thought that Preston had found them out, but she should have known that he was there about his *damn* nomination. She had half a mind to strut into the living room, buck naked with her titties swinging from side to side, and tell him that it was over. He would probably care less. The only thing he cared about was his *fucking* career. Realizing that she was being paranoid, she calmed down and continued to listen to their conversation.

"Tell the senator not to waste his money. There's no dirt to be found here. I'm clean as the driven snow." Trey smiled, trying to hide the panic he felt inside.

Preston sighed. He had come there for answers, but still didn't have anything concrete to tell the senator. "Well, son, I hope you're right. I have a lot riding on this nomination. I've never wanted anything so badly. I've wanted to be a justice ever since I saw pictures of lynched men hanging from trees like forbidden fruit, with no one to right the injustices that they suffered. Sitting on the Supreme Court is *the* single most important thing in my life, more important than anything or *anybody*. I can finally be that voice for the voiceless victims of this world," he said adamantly.

All Ariel could hear was that sitting on the Supreme Court was more important than anything and anyone to Preston, and she almost hit the ceiling. The vein in her forehead was pulsing so hard that it felt like it was going to pop. She knew where Preston's priorities lay, but hearing him actually say the words hurt her to the core. Suddenly she felt like the little orphan girl that nobody wanted. She had felt horrible about fucking Trey, but now she didn't regret one single second she had spent with him.

Trey walked toward the door. "Don't worry, Dad. I'm sure everything will be okay. I hate to end this conversation, but I have an important meeting and have to finish getting dressed," he said, rushing his father out of his apartment. He was certain that Ariel was out of the shower by now and didn't want her to overhear any more of their conversation than necessary.

"Oh, okay," Preston said, slightly defeated. "See you later."

Trey slumped down on the sofa once his father was gone. He couldn't believe the sudden turn of events.

"That was close," Ariel said, coming out of the bedroom wearing only a towel. She walked over to Trey and stood in between his legs. "Look . . . maybe we should tell him about us," she said. Ariel was stunned by her own words once she heard them float through the air. Telling Preston was the worst thing they could do, and she knew it was just that hurt, orphaned little girl, afraid of being abandoned once again who was lashing out.

"What?" He looked up shocked. As far as he was concerned, there was no "us." "I don't think that's a good idea. He has too much on his plate." Trey couldn't think straight. Not only was he fucking his dad's woman, he was fucking with his chances of sitting on the Supreme Court. Suppose the investigators found out about The Black Door? What then?

THE LAST time Mason roamed the salacious corridors of The Black Door, he had been a server, whose only purpose was to keep the client smiling, which could mean anything from an intelligent conversation over a glass of champagne, to licking clits or pleasing multiple women at once. Thankfully, the only person Mason had to please this time around was his boss. As the assistant manager, he didn't have to perform on demand, which made returning to the club a dream job instead of a chore. One of the fringe benefits of working at The Black Door was easy access to the punanny. Now if he wanted to indulge in a little extracurricular activity, it was his choice—not theirs—and that made the prospect of fucking a member or two even more appealing.

With the bronze-toned mask tied securely around the upper portion of his face, concealing his eyes and nose, Mason strolled casually through the club. He hadn't been in the inner sanctum of The Black Door in a while, and he wanted to peruse each chamber to see where they could make improvements. He not only wanted to help increase membership, but planned to add value to the club by expanding on its theme of erotic suites. He thought about adding a Brazilian wax room, where members could get their pubic hairs removed and at the same time get their clitoris stimulated; or a Mani/Pedi Suite where members could indulge in toe-sucking pedicures. However, there was one thing he definitely wouldn't change and that was the main floor. Elegant and inviting, the parlors with their posh, ultramodern Louis XVI furnishings were the perfect introduction to the club. The parlors were nonthreatening, which was important, especially for new members who could be intimidated if confronted with too much stimulation too soon. The rooms on the ground level lured members in with soft music and soothing drinks in a relaxed environment. With half-clad, buffed male servers and horny, scantily dressed women, the air was heavy with sexual tension, but it wasn't overwhelming like some of the rooms on the upper floors.

Mason nodded at a server wearing a hunter-green mask who was standing beside the vodka fountain engaging two members with a witty tale. He didn't hear the entire joke, but it must have been funny, because the women were howling with laugher. Mason knew exactly who was behind the green mask. Rodney was a budding comic and used every opportunity to practice his craft. He loosened members up with his wry sense of humor before taking them upstairs to tickle their vulvas.

Mason crossed the parlor floor and made his way through the crimson velvet drapes and up the narrow staircase that led to the second floor. Tonight the sounds of sex overshadowed the smooth jazz playing in the background, and hearing the moans of pleasure floating through the atmosphere was extremely arousing. Mason's cock immediately reacted to the hedonistic groans as he strolled down the darkened corridor. He was way past horny—it had been

months since he had seen a pussy up close and personal—and ready
to fuck anything moving. Tonight his mission was twofold: one, to
look for ways to improve the club, and two, to get his freak on. He
figured it was far safer to get laid at the club. The members were
all screened for sexual diseases, so he didn't have to worry about
catching an STD from a random stranger. He could have made a
booty call, but didn't want the complications of screwing someone
he knew. He wanted to fuck without feelings, and all the women
he knew were ready for monogamous relationships. He didn't want
to chance someone misconstruing his middle-of-the-night call,
thinking that he too wanted a relationship. Settling down was the
last thing on his mind. Mason liked variety—young, old, skinny,
plump, short, tall, black, or white—and planned to experiment
with as many pussies as he could get his cock into before reciting
vows at the altar.

Mason stopped at the Voyeurism Room and peered through the
window. He enjoyed watching people having sex, almost as much
as he enjoyed the act itself. On the other side of the glass were two
women and a server. One woman was on all fours in the middle of
the king-size bed, while the server stood on his knees behind her,
rubbing his pole-sized dick against the inside of her thighs. The
second woman lay still on her back, spread eagle, directly underneath the first woman. At first glance, the scene didn't look excit-
ing at all. It just appeared as if the guy was masturbating, but
Mason knew better and stood there until the real action kicked off.
And sure enough, seconds later, the server pushed the woman
down onto her elbows, so that her mouth landed on the other
woman's bushy triangle. Now with the woman's ass high in the air,
he spread her cheeks apart and slowly inched his rod into her anus.
The woman backed up and wiggled her ass toward him for easier
access. Once he was all the way inside, he arched his back and began ramming in and out of her tight ass. She bent down even far-

ther, stuck out her tongue, and started licking the perimeter of the other woman's vagina. She trailed her tongue down to the hood of the woman's clit, lifted it back, and began hungrily munching the woman's hidden treasure. Mason salivated as he watched the woman getting butt-fucked, while at the same time eating out another woman's pussy. He rubbed his own throbbing cock as the three came simultaneously. He was so horny that he nearly came in his pants right along with them. He wiped the drool from the corner of his mouth and swallowed hard. His throat was parched from quietly panting as he watched the heated action.

I need a drink, he thought, and walked toward the Leopard Lounge. Mason nodded to the bartender as he made his way to one of the leopard-print booths. He had a massive hard-on and wanted to sit in the back in one of the private booths so that he could soothe his aching cock.

A waiter came over and he ordered a single-malt Scotch. The bar was dimly lit, and was even darker in the back where the booths were, allowing discretion for those indiscreet moments. Once the waiter returned with his drink, Mason told him that would be all for now. He wanted to stroke his throbbing cock and didn't want to be disturbed. Mason unzipped his leather pants and let the head of his dick peek through the opening of the zipper. He closed his eyes and rubbed the tip with his thumb. Mason needed a good fuck and opened his eyes to see if there were any prospects in the room. When he had walked in, no one was sitting at the bar, but now there was a woman with her back to him. He squinted so that he could see better, and from where he sat, he could tell that she had short blond hair and was wearing a back-baring halter dress. One look at her precision haircut and he knew exactly who it was.

She swiveled around on the stool with an ornate flute in her hand. Only one cocktail was served in a handblown crystal glass and it was The Black Door, named appropriately after the club.

The drink consisted of champagne with a splash of vodka, iced-cold, and garnished with a black seedless Chilean grape.

Mason watched as she sipped the effervescent cocktail, and when she neared the end of the drink, she tilted the flute upward, causing the grape to tumble gently to her lips. She caught the plump piece of fruit between her front teeth and took it out of her mouth. She began expertly peeling the delicate skin from the grape. Her long manicured nails sliced into the dark outer layer, pulling back piece after piece until the fruit's firm pale flesh was revealed. She seemed to sense that he was watching and really began to put on a show.

Mason unbuttoned his pants, took his cock all the way out, and stroked himself as she slowly and seductively sucked the naked fruit. The way she wrapped her lips around the grape, as if it were her most precious possession, was enticing and made him wish that he could replace that grape with his cock.

After she had finished with the decadent fruit display, she popped the grape into her mouth and savored its sweet juices. She then put the empty flute on the bar and got up from the stool.

Mason thought that she was leaving, but to his delight, she sauntered knowingly toward him. She was a classy woman who knew exactly what she wanted, and at the moment she wanted him. With each one of her steps, his cock pulsated, aching to be inside of her.

"Long time no see," she said, eying him up and down. "Want some company?" She licked her lips seductively, standing before him.

Mason looked up and his eyes were instantly drawn to her neck. She was wearing her signature diamond necklace, whose graduated, faceted stones sparkled underneath the overhead penlights. The diamonds were blinding and he blinked from the glare. "Too long. Where have you been hiding?" He hadn't seen her since their heated night of fucking at The W Hotel.

"In D.C.," she simply said.

"Welcome back to the city. We've missed you," he said, stroking Mr. Big.

She licked her lips again at the site of his mammoth member. She hadn't had mind-blowing sex in months; though she loved her husband dearly, his equipment wasn't big enough to satisfy her needs. "And I've missed the both of you," she said, sliding into the booth beside him.

Mason rubbed her bare back before slipping his hand though the left side of her halter dress and caressing her breast. She scooted closer and put her hand on top of his pulsating cock.

"Hmm . . ." She moaned as she began kneading the head of his penis. "Oh, how I've missed Mr. Big."

"And he's missed you too," he said, slowly raising up her dress until the hem was past her waist, exposing her naked bottom. He fingered her labia and felt the soft lips swell with his touch. After a few minutes of teasing her outer vaginal area, he stuck two fingers inside of her moist, juicy canal. Now that they were both primed and ready, he whispered in her ear, "Sit on my cock."

She didn't say another word, just lifted herself off of the seat and straddled him. He firmly gripped her waist and pushed her farther down on Mr. Big. The moment he penetrated her, she threw her head back, and grabbed hold of his shoulders for support, then slowly rode him up and down. His cock was so big and thick, unlike her husband's puny penis, and she loved how it filled up her pussy, something her husband could never accomplish.

She threw her head back and whispered, "Fuck me harder, Mr. Big."

Mason raised his hips and thrust his dick in deeper and harder until she was on the brink of orgasm.

She held on to him and rode them both into ecstasy. Once they both came, she climbed off as easily as she had mounted him. "I see you still have the magic touch." She smiled, pulling her dress down. "Now I can go home a happy woman."

"When are you leaving?"

"I'm taking the Acela back to D.C. tomorrow," she said, getting up to leave.

"How about we meet for some love in the afternoon?" he smiled suggestively.

"Oh, I wish I could, but I'm leaving on the 8 A.M. train." She leaned over and kissed him full on the lips. "But trust me, I'll see both of you," she nodded to his crotch, "real soon." And with that she was gone.

Totally satisfied, Mason leaned back in the booth and watched her disappear into the darkness.

28

IT HAD been a few days since Ariel had seen or talked to Trey. She didn't like the way they had left things the other morning. The more she thought about it, the more she thought it was time to come clean with Preston before the truth came out in some uglier way, especially since Preston had so much more to lose. But Trey strongly opposed the idea, saying that his father had too much on his plate, and that now was not the right time to expose their affair. His excitement over their relationship also seemed to have cooled overnight and Ariel didn't know where she stood with him. The initial shock of sleeping with Preston's son had long worn off, and regardless of what happened she planned to call off the engagement. Ariel glanced at the diamond sparkling on her left hand, slowly twisted the ring off, and put it in her desk drawer. Their relationship was a farce, and she didn't feel the need to put on a front any longer, especially after Preston had told Trey that securing the nomination was "*the* single most important thing in my life." His words cut her to the quick, and just thinking about that morning made her stomach churn. And while she didn't know what would happen with Trey, Ariel knew she needed a man who appreciated all of her and everything she had to offer.

Ariel picked up the phone to call Preston's office, but JoAnne's voice interrupted her through the intercom.

"Ms. Vaughn, a Mr. Trey Curtis is on line two."

"Trey Curtis?" she asked herself. She had assumed that Trey's last name was Hendricks like his father's, but obviously it wasn't. "Put him through, JoAnne." Ariel exhaled to calm herself before depressing her second phone line. "Well, hello Mr. *Curtis,*" she said, emphasizing his surname.

He picked up on her tone and said, "I use my mother's maiden name for business purposes." He paused for a second. "I'm sure you can understand why."

Ariel knew exactly what he was talking about and didn't push the subject. "I was just thinking about you." She smiled into the receiver.

"Is that right?" he asked, unenthusiastically.

"Yes. I need to see you." As soon as those words left her lips, Ariel regretted saying them. She sounded like some needy school-girl begging for attention. "Well, what I mean is—"

"I know what you mean. I need to see you too. How about to-night?"

She had planned to call Meri for a girls' night out, but would rather have a girls' night in with Trey. "Tonight's good." This time around, Ariel wanted him in her bed. They had made love at the club, and at his apartment, now it was her turn to play hostess. "Why don't you come over to my place, say around seven thirty?"

"Okay," he agreed. "What's your address?"

Ariel rattled off her address, and then said, "I can't wait to see you."

It took a few seconds for Trey to respond. "Okay, see you to-night."

The rest of Ariel's afternoon went by at a snail's pace. Every five minutes, she found herself looking at the clock, which only made the minutes tick by even slower. She thought about leaving early, but she'd been slacking off at work lately and didn't want to arouse any suspicions. Most of the partners were workaholics who came in early and stayed late, and expected their colleagues to do the same. She didn't need Bob breathing down her neck about billable hours. Anyway, she had a three thirty deposition scheduled and couldn't leave early even if she wanted to.

Ariel rushed out of the office at six forty-five and hailed a taxi. The deposition had taken longer than she had anticipated, and had put her behind schedule. She'd planned on whipping up a light meal of grilled pork chops, sautéed spinach, and mashed potatoes. She wanted to show off her culinary skills. Ariel was going to prove to Trey that she could cook in the kitchen as well as in the bedroom. He was a man after all, and men loved a woman who could satisfy their taste buds *and* their sexual desires. But at this point, she'd only have time to order carry-out from Table for Two, so she took out her cell phone and ordered an assortment of aphrodisiacs—oysters, caviar, mussels, and chocolate-dipped strawberries—to enhance their lovemaking.

With the evening midtown traffic clogging up the avenues and streets, Ariel didn't get home until almost seven thirty. She peeled off her suit jacket and blouse on the way to the bedroom. She wanted to shower and change before Trey arrived, but now she would have to settle for a quick wash-up instead.

The second she turned on the water, the phone rang. "Damn," she hissed, running from the bathroom back into the bedroom to answer the call. "Hello?"

"Hi, Ms. Vaughn. A Mr. Curtis is downstairs," said the doorman.

"Thanks, Pete. You can send him up."

Ariel hung up and ran back into the bathroom. She dampened a hand towel and quickly dabbed her armpits. After her brief bird-bath, she jetted into her closet, kicked off her pumps, and took her nylons and skirt off. Ariel stood there naked for a second trying to decide what to wear. She snatched a black negligee off of its hanger and slipped it on. She then dashed over to the vanity table, took the bobby pins out of her bun, and shook her hair loose. As she spritzed her neck with ENJOY, the buzzer rang.

"Perfect timing," she said, looking in the mirror. The see-through negligee left nothing to the imagination. Her 38-Cs, taut waist, and shapely hips looked delectable in the sheer silk fabric. Ariel got horny just looking at herself. She rubbed her hands over her boobs and felt her nipples harden. She couldn't wait for Trey to suck her tits. The doorbell buzzed again, and she raced to answer it.

Ariel swung the door open and stood in the doorway with her legs slightly spread apart so that he could get an eyeful.

Trey had come over to talk, but looking at Ariel standing before him in a sexy, "come fuck me" outfit, he lost his train of thought, as the head on his shoulders shut down, and the head in between his legs took over. "You look good enough to eat." He licked his lips, walked into the apartment, and shut the door behind him.

Ariel jiggled her boobs, causing them to do a little dance, and she then turned around and wiggled her behind. "Where do you want to start your feast?" She stepped closer, wrapped her arms around his neck, and gave him a deep French kiss.

Trey was hypnotized by the movement of her tongue as it danced around the inside of his mouth, tickling his tongue, teeth, and the roof of his mouth. After a few minutes of giving into the moment, he pulled back.

"Why'd you stop?" She looked perplexed.

He reached up, took her arms from around his neck, and

coughed nervously. "Well, I really didn't come over here for sex, but when you opened the door in that sexy getup, I lost my train of thought," he said, turning his back to her and walking into the living room.

Ariel stood in the foyer, shocked; she couldn't believe that he wasn't eagerly jumping her bones like the other night. Paranoia began to creep up from the soles of her feet, up through her legs, traveling to her consciousness, bringing her out of her lust-induced state of mind back to reality. Suddenly she felt self-conscious and crossed her arms in front of her breasts, before joining him in the living room. "So what did you come over here for?"

"Have you spoken to my father yet?" he asked out of the clear blue sky.

She looked surprised. "No I haven't, but I plan to."

"Well, that's what I wanted to talk to you about." He looked down, and then back up at her. "I don't think you should mention anything about us." He looked away again. "Because there's really no 'us,' Ariel." He looked her in the eyes. "We got caught up in the excitement of The Black Door, but now that the masks are off, there's no way we can continue seeing each other."

"Funny, you didn't say that the other night when you fucked my brains out," she said, anger beginning to heat up her tone.

"Whoa, don't you think you're being a bit melodramatic? You know as well as I do, that this is an impossible situation. After all, you're—"

She cut him off. "Why is it *impossible*?"

"Because you're engaged to my father, and he's embarking on a new career, a career with an extensive investigation in progress. And if anyone finds out about me, you, and The Black Door, the nomination will be over before it gets started."

Ariel threw her hands in the air out of frustration. She was at a loss for words. She didn't want to ruin Preston's career, but she wasn't ready to cut Trey out of her life yet. "Well, maybe we can just meet at The Black Door. Since everyone's in a mask, nobody will have to ever find out," she pleaded, trying to salvage the no-win situation.

Trey had to admit that their initial encounter was thrilling and mysterious, but now that reality had settled in, the thrill was gone. Seeing how selfish Ariel was acting, Trey knew that he had made a huge mistake by taking her back to his apartment and making love to her. Obviously she wanted more than he was willing to offer. Now he'd have to put on kid gloves and handle her with extreme care, so that she wouldn't go rushing to his father with half-truths. "I hear what you're saying." He stood up, grabbed her waist, and pulled her close to him. "But please do me this one favor and wait until the investigations are over before you come back to The Black Door."

Ariel's knees buckled and she felt weak in his arms. It was like he had cast a spell over her and she was defenseless against his charms. She wrapped her arms around his neck and pressed her groin into his, trying to get him aroused. "Anything for you, Trey." She began to grind her hips into him, but he pulled away.

"I gotta get back to the club," he said, heading for the door.

Ariel started to follow him, to convince him to stay, but was stopped by the ringing phone.

LITTLE DID TREY know, but Michele had been following him the entire day, and was shocked when he walked into the lobby of Ariel's building. She recognized the exterior from when she and Preston had picked her up for their drive to Washington.

She stood across the street, behind a light post, and asked herself, *What the hell is going on?* Through the glass door, Michele watched Trey stop at the doorman's podium and then walk to the elevators.

"I've got to get upstairs." She knew firsthand how protective doormen could be, and didn't want to chance being turned away like the other night.

Michele paced back and forth, trying to hatch a scheme to get past the doorman. And as she watched a parade of delivery people coming in and out of the revolving doors, the idea hit her. "That's it!"

"Hey!" she yelled across the street to a young man wearing a Table for Two uniform. "Can you come here for a second?"

"Yeah?" asked the delivery guy once he had crossed the street.

Michele took her wallet out of her purse, took out two crisp, one-hundred-dollar bills, and waved them in the kid's face. "These are yours if you let me borrow your jacket and cap and let me take that delivery upstairs."

His eyes popped wide open. "Yeah, okay, but I'll need my jacket and cap back," he said, reaching for the money and stuffing the bills into the back pocket of his tattered jeans.

"No problem; I won't be long." Michele traded her tailored blazer for the loose-fitting jacket, stuffed her hair underneath the cap, and took the thermo-sealed box from his hands. She looked down at the name on the delivery slip. "Eureka! It must be my lucky day!" she wanted to shout. Printed in clear view was Ariel's full name and apartment number.

"Food delivery for apartment 1623," she told the doorman once she entered the lobby.

He had never seen her before and looked at her strangely. Pete knew most of the guys who delivered to the building. "I've never seen you around here before."

Michele began to mildly perspire. "That's because it's my first day on the job," she explained.

"Oh," was his response. He picked up the house phone and called up. "Ms. Vaughn, you have a food delivery coming up."

"Okay, Pete."

By the time Ariel had hung up the phone, Trey was at the door and had it partially open. "I hate to run, but I need to check on my new assistant manager."

Ariel ignored what he was saying, walked directly up to him, and planted a big juicy kiss on his full lips. She wasn't about to let him go without a proper send-off, and wrapped her arms around his neck, pulling him in closer. She could feel his cock getting hard, and reached down and began massaging his manhood. "Are you sure you have to go?" she asked, in between kisses.

Trey was getting horny and thought that maybe one last fuck wouldn't hurt. He reached up, put his hand underneath her negligee, and began playing with her nipples. She had an awesome rack and he couldn't resist feeling her big jugs. He lifted her right breast, leaned down, and began sucking her nipples like they were his life source.

Ariel closed her eyes and moaned. "Ooh, *Trey*, that feels sooo good," she purred.

"Yeah, *bitch*, I just bet it does!!!"

Ariel's eyes popped open and Trey stopped midsuck. Standing there watching the entire scene was Michele. At first they didn't recognize her face underneath the brim of the cap, but Trey looked closer and said, "Michele, is that you?"

"Yeah, it's me, you asshole!" she shouted. "I knew you were fucking somebody, but I didn't think it was your father's fiancée. How could you, Trey?" she asked, with tears forming in the corner of her eyes.

He took two steps away from Ariel. "Wait a minute, Michele. It's not what you think!"

Ariel didn't say a word; in a way she was glad that they had been caught. Now she wouldn't have to tell Preston, because she knew that his eager-beaver assistant would run screaming over to his town house and fill him in blow-by-blow on what she had just witnessed.

Michele turned away in disgust and took off down the hallway.

"Wait!" Trey screamed after her.

"Let her go," Ariel said, grabbing hold of his arm.

"No." He broke away. "I can't let her leave, not like this," he said, as he chased after Michele.

Ariel stood in the doorway and watched the two of them talking. Trey wrapped his arm around Michele to console her as she put her head on his chest. Ariel couldn't hear what they were saying, but she had a hunch that he was coaxing Michele to keep her mouth shut.

"Well, if she won't spill the beans, then I will," Ariel said underneath her breath and slammed the door.

She was sick and tried of playing second string. First Preston had put her off, and now Trey was doing the same thing. She couldn't believe that both father and son were putting her on the back burner. Well, she'd be damned if she let that happen to her twice. Ariel needed to get her power back, and she would start by telling Preston that it was over, and then deal with Trey.

29

TREY HADN'T been busted since college. He didn't like it then as a teen, and he sure as hell didn't like it now that he was a grown man. He should have never broken his cardinal rule by fucking a client, but that was in the past; now he'd have to deal with the present. Luckily for Trey, he was used to putting out fires on a daily basis and was able to extinguish Michele's fiery temper. He calmed her down long enough to convince her to come over to his apartment. Trey knew that he would have to do some fast talking to persuade her from going to his father with her discovery. And he was willing to do or say whatever it took to get his way. Trey had always been as smooth as Teflon, and prided himself on getting out of sticky situations. He wasn't an angel by any means, just careful; that was, until now. Now he had a major mess on his hands, but it wasn't anything that he couldn't clean up.

"Sit down, baby." He led Michele to the sofa. "Can I get you something to drink? Green tea, brandy, or maybe some port?" he offered.

She averted her eyes from him and shook her head no. In her haste to flee Ariel's building, she had forgotten to return the cap and jacket to the delivery guy, and sat wedged in the corner of Trey's couch looking disheveled in the oversized uniform.

He sat down next to her. "Come on, baby, take that off," he said, removing the cap from her head. He gently ran his hand through her hair and fluffed it out. "Now that's better."

Michele jerked her head away. "Trey, don't."

This is going to be harder than I thought. His plan was to sweet-talk Michele right into bed, fuck her brains out, and make her forget about blabbing to his father. If anyone was going to tell his business, it was going to be him. He realized that he would have to work a little harder, because he wasn't about to scrap his plan of seduction. "Michele, please let me explain," he said, almost pleading.

She didn't say a word, just looked at him out of the corner of her eyes, and defensively folded her arms in front of her chest. She had heard her fair share of sob stories over the years, and wanted to hear Trey try and talk his way out of this.

"Remember the night of the engagement party?"

Michele shook her head yes, and waited for him to continue.

"Well, that's when Ariel came on to me." He paused for a response, but she didn't say a word. "Anyway, I went over to ask her why she was crying, and she told me that things between her and Dad were not going well." Trey looked at Michele for a reaction, but her face was blank, so he continued with his lie. "I *innocently* put my arm around her shoulders to comfort her, and that's when she reached up and kissed me lightly on the lips. She said it was just a thank-you kiss and, to be honest, I really didn't think much about it."

"That's when you should have told your dad," she said, finally opening up, "because he has the right to know that he's engaged to a two-timing skank."

Trey hung his head to hide the slight smirk spreading across his face. *Good, I got her now.* "You're right. I should have told him, right then and there."

"Why the *hell* didn't you?" she shouted, and slapped him on the back, now back in full Michele mode.

Trey jerked his head up. He hadn't expected her to raise her voice, let alone hit him. "I, uh——" He stalled, trying to come up with the right answer.

She cut him off. "And furthermore, what the *hell* were you doing at *her* apartment, sucking on *her tits?*"

"She called me and said that she wanted to talk about my dad, and when I got there she was dressed to seduce me in that see-through number." Trey forced a lone tear to drip from his left eye, and dropped his head into her lap. "I . . . I . . . was just weak." He sobbed, making more noise than actual tears.

Michele had never seen a grown man cry, and his vulnerability tugged at her heartstrings. She rubbed his back, on the exact spot where she had slapped it a few minutes before. "Don't cry, baby. I'm sure *she's* been after you from the start. I mean who wouldn't? You're such a good catch."

With his head buried deep in her lap, Trey smiled a smile of victory. *Jackpot!* Now he knew that he had Michele exactly where he wanted her—back under his control. He sniffled for effect, slowly sat up, and wiped the lonely tear from his eye. "I'd been working too hard and missing you, and my hormones got in the way of my thinking and I lost control." He sniffled again. "Can you ever forgive me?"

"I'll forgive you on two conditions," she said, sounding like she was calling all the shots.

"Anything, just name it," he said, playing right along, knowing good and well that he had no intention of letting her direct his program. He still planned on ending their relationship, but now he'd have to prolong the inevitable until the timing was right, and it wouldn't be right until after the nomination was secure.

"One, you promise to never see that *bitch* again, and two, we tell your father what she did to you," she demanded.

Damn, not that again, Trey thought. He had assumed that Michele would be a pushover and that he could sway her with his fake waterworks, but he was sadly mistaken. Now he would have to pull out the *big* gun, and fire at her with both barrels. "We will, baby, but I need to take some time to wrap my mind around what happened. I think we should go away to de-stress. This ordeal has been traumatic for both of us, and I know this great little resort in the Cayman Islands where we can sort everything out in peace and quiet."

She perked up like a peacock. "Oh, Trey, I would love that!" Michele had never been whisked away before; it was always her sister who went on exotic trips. Now it was her time in the sun and she was ecstatic—even though the trip was under these circumstances.

"Okay, I'll book the reservations this evening and we can leave tomorrow for a long weekend." His plan had worked brilliantly, although he hadn't expected on spending a small fortune on last-minute reservations; but considering what was at stake, the money would be well spent.

"So soon? I've got a million and one things to do before we leave, I've got to—"

He kissed her lips to stop her chatter. "Baby, the only thing you need is your passport. Everything else we can buy once we land."

"But—"

"No buts." He kissed her again. "We'll stop by your apartment in the morning on the way to the airport and get your passport."

"Trey, I need to at least go home and change clothes," she protested.

He put his hand on her breast and began massaging it. "You can change in the morning. Please, don't leave me tonight. I need you." Trey wasn't about to let her out of his sight for fear that she would hightail it over to the town house and fill his father in on the sordid details.

Michele's mind was reeling, and she didn't know what to do. She didn't want to skip out on Preston without notice, but things were going smoothly with his nomination and he could hold down the fort until she came back. As she was weighing the pros and cons of going on a dream vacation with her dream man, Trey was nibbling on her nipples, making it easier and easier for her to say yes.

She knew that he was manipulating her, but she didn't care; she wasn't about to push him away in case he went back to that *bitch*, so she did what came naturally. Michele began unbuttoning her blouse so that he could have easier access to her nipples.

Trey unsnapped her bra and eagerly sucked away, hoping that he could make her forget about tonight and focus on going away with him tomorrow.

"I love you so much, Trey," she moaned.

"I love you too," he lied, to seal the deal.

Michele eased out of the oversized jacket and took off her blouse and bra. "Wait a minute." She stood up, unhooked her skirt, and removed her pantyhose. Now totally nude, she lay back down, and draped one leg over the back of the sofa so that she was spread eagle.

Trey knew exactly what that meant. She wanted him to feed the pussycat. He scooted down between her legs, spread her lips apart, and gingerly kissed her clit. He then stiffened his tongue and darted it in and out of her hungry pussy, while at the same time fingering her ass. He was sucking and finger fucking her at such a fast and furious pace that she screamed.

"Oh, yeah, baby, I'm cuming!"

Trey didn't stop until her body was twitching from multiple organisms. His tongue was magical and worked like a charm and now she was once again under his control. Trey would spend a few days fucking her in the sun and by the time they got back to the U.S., he would tell his dad about him and Ariel . . . his version of the events, of course.

IT WAS after eight thirty in the morning and Michele was nowhere in sight. She was usually at the town house before eight with two steaming cups of coffee from Starbucks—a low-fat latte for her and a double espresso with one sugar for Preston.

"Where is she?" His body was craving his daily dose of caffeine. Besides, he wanted to get the day started. He needed Michele to call the senator's assistant and ask her if his calendar was clear for a meeting the following week. Preston hadn't spoken to Robert in a few days, and he was on pins and needles wondering about the status of the investigation. He preferred a face-to-face with the senator and not another telephone confrontation like before.

Preston sat behind his desk and spread open the pages of *The New York Times*. His morning ritual was to read the *Times* while he drank a cup of coffee. Well this morning, he would have to deviate slightly from his habit while he waited for Michele. He had finished reading the first half of the newspaper and was on to the business section when the telephone rang. He snatched up the receiver, slightly annoyed at having to answer his own phone. "Hello?"

"Good morning, Judge," Michele said sheepishly, using his professional title instead of addressing him by his first name like she normally did.

"Where are you? I was expecting you here over an hour ago. I need you to call the senator's office, and . . ." Preston began barking out orders.

"I'm so sorry, but I won't be in today," she said hesitantly.

"Oh." He calmed down. "Are you sick?" he asked, concerned.

"No, I'm not sick. Trey and I are on our way to the Cayman Islands for a long weekend," she said, sounding totally elated.

"What? You're on your way where? Did you say the Cayman Islands?" he asked, nearly running one question into the other.

"Yes! Can you believe it?" She squealed with delight.

Preston knew that Michele and Trey were having problems, and that she suspected him of cheating. She probably caught him in the act, and as a peace offering he invited her to go away for a romantic weekend. Preston knew that sly move all too well, because he had paid dearly for a few guilt trips himself. He knew that if his son had booked a spur-of-the-moment trip, the situation must be dire. He decided not to give Michele any grief about missing work. "You sound excited."

"Yes, I am," she gushed. "I know this is totally unexpected, and I'm sorry to leave you in the lurch, but all of your affairs are in order. And I'll be back in the office bright and early Tuesday morning," she said, always the efficient assistant.

"Don't worry, Michele. It's already Friday, and since you'll be back on Tuesday, I'm sure I can manage by myself for two days. You just concentrate on having a good time. Let me talk to Trey," he said, wanting to clear a few things up with his son.

"Hold on. Here he is."

"Uh, hey . . ." Trey said nervously, wondering why his dad wanted to speak with him. Maybe Ariel had told him everything.

"I know you can't really talk, so just listen. Did Michele catch you with your hand in the cookie jar?" he asked knowingly.

"Yep," Trey said, but didn't mention that it was his dad's private stash that he had been dipping into.

"So this is literally a guilt trip?"

Trey was guilty on so many different fronts. He was guilty of seducing his father's fiancée; guilty of cheating on Michele; but most of all guilty of jeopardizing his dad's Supreme Court nomination. "You have no idea," he said sorrowfully.

Hearing the despair in Trey's voice, Preston said, "Son, I've been where you are. Don't worry, things *will* work out fine."

If you knew what I knew, you wouldn't be comforting me, you'd be trying to strangle the life out me, Trey thought. "I hope that you're right, Dad."

"I know I am. Trust me. Time and distance will make any situation better, so go ahead and have a good time. I'll see you when you guys get back."

"Okay." Trey paused a second as if contemplating his next words. "I love you, Dad."

Preston was taken aback. Trey hadn't told him that he loved him since he was a boy. "I love you too, son."

Trey hoped that the love that they shared as father and son would supersede all the turmoil that he had caused. "Okay, talk to you soon," he said, and hung up.

Preston leaned back in his chair with a broad smile decorating his face. Like most parents, he was proud of his son no matter what he did. After all, Trey was the fruit of his loins and could do no wrong in his eyes.

As Preston was basking in the glow of fatherhood, he heard the hum of the fax machine, and he looked over and saw it spew out two pieces of paper forward. He got up, walked over, and retrieved the fax. Preston read the cover page.

Thought that you should see this in black and white, Robert

Preston reached for the second page, which was also written in the same script, and carefully read the brief note.

The Black Door
an adults-only club
exclusively for women.
Owned and operated by
Preston Hendricks III
aka
Trey Curtis

"What the hell is this?" Preston shouted into the empty room. He reread the fax. "An adults-only club?" He scratched his head. "Trey's got some explaining to do." He stormed back to his desk and dialed his son's cell phone, but it went straight to voice mail. *"Damnit!"*

Trey and Michele were already in flight. He didn't know where they were staying, which meant that he wouldn't be able to talk to Trey until Tuesday, but he couldn't wait that long. He needed some answers now, so he called Robert.

"Senator's Oglesby's office, Natalie speaking. How may I help you?" asked his chipper assistant.

"Natalie, it's Judge Hendricks. I need to talk to the senator right away," he huffed.

"Actually, he's expecting your call. Hold on please," she said, and put him through.

"I see you got my fax," Robert simply said.

"What is this?" He waved the paper at the phone as if the senator could see it fanning in the air.

"My investigators found out that your son is the sole owner of an adult entertainment club called The Black Door, where mask-wearing members enjoy carnal pleasures of various kinds," he explained.

Preston's jaw dropped wide open, and he was stunned into silence. Never in his wildest dreams did he think that his son would be involved in the sleazy adult trade. Trey never even mentioned going to a strip club, let alone owning one. His resolve about his son doing no wrong quickly dissolved, along with the fatherly pride that he had felt only moments before.

"From your response, I take it that you didn't know anything about the club."

"Not a thing. I swear!" Preston said defensively. "I met with Trey the other day and he assured me that he was in the equity and real estate business."

The senator chucked. "Well, I've made some calls of my own, and it turns out that Trey is a very clever boy. He owns the building uptown out of which the club operates, so he didn't actually lie about being into real estate; he just failed to tell you the whole truth."

"I'll just have the damn club shut down!" Preston shouted adamantly, slamming his fist on the desk.

"That'll be nearly impossible. My sources tell me that his membership register is full of some of the most powerful and influential women in the country. There are even a few foreign dignitaries who are active members. Actually, the club is registered as a legal adult entertainment establishment so trying to shut it down would cause you more trouble than it's worth."

"So what are we going to do now?" Preston asked, hoping that there was a solution to this unsuspected problem.

"Well . . ." The senator exhaled into the receiver. "I hate to be the bearer of bad news, Preston, but with your son operating a risqué business, it'll be too embarrassing if—"

Preston cut him off. "That doesn't have anything to do with me," he said frantically, trying desperately to hold onto his dream before it slipped through his fingers.

"Well, actually it does. If we went ahead with the proceedings and I threw your name into the ring as a viable candidate, the official investigation would begin. They would uncover Trey's ownership of The Black Door before you could say, 'I didn't know.' The scandal would be headline news and spread across every newspaper and tabloid in the western hemisphere. You would be crucified in the press and would lose the nomination before it even began. You understand, don't you?"

There was dead air on the opposite end of the phone. Preston couldn't believe that his lifelong dream had been dashed, and through no fault of his own.

When the senator didn't get a response, he continued. "I'm so sorry, Preston, but we gave it the good ole college try. Take care and I'll talk with you soon," he said, and hung up.

Preston let the phone drop from his ear, and it hit the desk with a thud. He sat motionless, trying to digest what had just happened. A neutron bomb had just exploded in his lap, and the debris from the carnage was falling all around him. He didn't know how to put the pieces back together. After an hour of marinating in the devastation, he realized that he needed to see his woman. She could console him with a night of lovemaking, which he needed desperately to get his mind off of his troubles. Preston wearily rose from his chair and tossed the incriminating fax (which was still clenched in

his fist) into the air, and as it floated to the floor, he calmly walked
out, leaving his hopes and dreams behind.

ARIEL HAD TAKEN the day off. She wasn't in the mood for work,
or much of anything else. She was still reeling from last night
when Trey had walked out on her to console Michele. She tried
calling him, but only got his voice mail. She was also furious at
herself for practically begging him to stay. Her hormones had gotten the best of her and she realized now that she had made a complete fool of herself. To ease the pain, she had started the day with
mimosas, and by lunch had tossed the orange juice aside and was
drinking straight champagne.

She was on her second bottle of Veuve when the telephone
rang. Ariel wasn't in the mood to talk so she let the call go to voice
mail, but it rang again, and again, until she picked up. "Hello?"
she said, annoyed that someone was interrupting her pity party.

"Ms. Vaughn, Judge Hendricks is downstairs," Pete informed her.

He knows, was Ariel's first thought, and her heart began to pal-
pitate. She took a deep breath to slow her pulse.

The doorbell buzzed and she staggered to open it. The champagne was flowing freely through her bloodstream, making it hard
for her to keep her balance. She flung the door wide open.

"If . . . if . . . you're here to talk about Trey, then come right on
in," she stammered. Ariel hadn't showered and her hair was all
over her head. She looked like a madwoman as she waved him in
with her arm.

"As a matter of fact, I am," Preston said, wondering how she
knew about Trey's involvement with The Black Door. "What's
wrong with your hair?" he asked, giving her a questioning stare. In
all the years that he had known Ariel, he had never seen her look
so wild and out of sorts.

"I don't care about my hair," she spat out, and slammed the door. She spun quickly around, almost falling flat on her face. "You didn't come here to talk about my hair. You came here to talk about Trey, and all of it is true, every single detail," she slurred.

Preston looked baffled. "What do you know about The Black Door?"

"That's where I made love to your son! Didn't Michele tell you everything?" Ariel put her hand on her hip. "Well, I guess she only told you what she saw last night." She looked up at the ceiling and then began mumbling. "Michele couldn't have known about the club unless Trey told her——"

"What, what did you say?" Preston interrupted.

"I slept with your son, that's what I said!" Ariel's thinking was completely skewed. The alcohol was talking for her, mixing up her words, but at the same time saying things that she would never have the courage to confess if sober.

Preston took hold of Ariel's shoulders and looked her dead in the eyes. "*You're* a member of The Black Door?"

"No, I'm not a member. I went disguised as Meri, and at first I was just an innocent bystander, but then I met Trey and he rocked my world, something you haven't done in a long time."

First the nomination was taken away, and now his woman. Taken away by the same person—his son! The betrayal was too much to bear, and he broke out in a cold sweat. Suddenly, he felt a sharp pain shoot up the left side of his body, from his fingertips to his shoulder. The twinge quickly traveled to his frontal lobe, causing a severe headache. He tried to speak, but his tongue wouldn't cooperate, causing his words to spill out of his mouth in garbled inaudible blurbs. He staggered toward the living room, but before he could reach the sofa, he stumbled over his feet and then collapsed face first on the floor.

"*Oh my God!*" Ariel screamed. "Preston! Preston!" She kneeled down beside him. *"Preston!"* She yelled at the top of her lungs while shaking his shoulders, but he didn't respond. The alcohol surging through Ariel's bloodstream was clouding her judgment and she couldn't think straight. She stared at him intensely, willing him to move, but the only thing that budged was his head as it slumped slightly to one side. *"No, no, no!"* she wailed, and flung herself onto his lifeless body.

Epilogue

LIMOUSINES STRETCHED for miles down Fifth Avenue, inching their way toward Saint Patrick's Cathedral, the majestic Gothic-style church where services were held for New York's who's who. And it seemed that every dignitary and socialite in the city had shown up for today's service. Ariel sat nervously in the back of her limo, praying that traffic would ease so she wouldn't be late. Though she had left in plenty of time, the seconds were dragging by at a snail's pace, and the longer she sat, the more anxious she became.

"How much longer before we get to the church?" she asked the driver.

"Just two more blocks, but in this traffic that might take five to ten minutes," he said over his shoulder.

"Let's hope not," she said, and then focused her attention on the crowded sidewalk. People were busy with their daily routines, rushing to and from work, shopping in the boutiques that lined

Fifth Avenue, and lunching casually with friends. She marveled at how normal everything seemed, how the world didn't stop when life threw you a curveball or two. Ariel closed her eyes for a second to collect her thoughts, but before she could take a trip down memory lane, the driver spoke.

"We're here, miss."

Ariel opened her eyes and saw familiar faces filing into the church one by one. She wasn't in the mood to speak, so she waited for a few minutes until most of the people were inside before exiting the car. She climbed the alabaster marble steps to the grand entrance and walked through the ornate double doors into the sanctuary. A pipe organ was playing softly, the melody wafting through the flying buttresses overhead and echoing gently off of the rose stained glass. Ariel stood for a moment and took in the beauty of the century-old church. As she inhaled, she could smell the scent of orchids and calla lilies, with undertones of frankincense and myrrh. As she slowly exhaled, a sense of calm washed over her, settling the butterflies fluttering in her belly.

"Are you ready?" asked the assistant priest.

"Yes." She nodded.

He took Ariel by the elbow and escorted her to the front of the church. She was grateful for his support, because her legs were so wobbly that she thought she would stumble forward at any second. From the distance, she could see Preston, as stiff as a board, and tears began streaming down her face.

When she reached the altar, his stoic expression softened into a warm smile, and he took her hand. "You're the most beautiful bride I've ever seen." He reached into his tuxedo jacket, took out a white handkerchief, and dabbed the tears from her cheeks.

"Dearly beloved, we are gathered here today to witness the union of Ariel Renée Vaughn and Preston Hendricks II into the state of holy matrimony," the priest said, beginning the wedding of the year. After an hour of singing, receiving communion, reciting of vows, the blessing and exchanging of rings, and lighting of the unity candle, it was official.

"May I introduce to you Mr. and Mrs. Preston Hendricks II," the priest announced after the ceremonial kiss.

Ariel—in a flowing, pearl-white, strapless Elie Saab wedding gown with satin, opera-length gloves—and Preston, in a tailored Armani tuxedo, were the picture of perfection as they strolled down the center aisle of the cathedral. Their faces beamed with happiness as they waved to well-wishers on the way to the waiting limousine.

The reception was held at Cipriani in the landmark Bowery building on Forty-second Street. With its soaring sixty-five-foot ceilings, Corinthian columns, inlaid Italian marble tiling, and dazzling chandeliers, Cipriani was the perfect venue in which to celebrate such an auspicious occasion. Tuxedoed waiters were standing at attention—Buckingham Palace–style—armed with trays of beluga caviar, carpaccio, crab croquettes, asparagus wrapped in prosciutto, grilled shrimp bruschetta, and baby lamb chops. There was also an army of waiters ready to serve chilled flutes of Cristal champagne.

Ariel and Preston arrived ahead of their guests and positioned themselves near the entryway, forming an abbreviated receiving line. First to greet the happy couple was none other than Ariel's foster mother, Mrs. Grant.

"Oh, baby," she gushed, grabbing both Ariel and Preston in a tight bear hug. "I'm so happy for you two. The ceremony was beautiful. You know I've never been to a Catholic wedding, and I thought it was going to be boring, but it was much better than I expected," she said, without mincing words.

"Thanks, Mom," Ariel responded, kissing her on the cheek. "You're sitting at the bridal table." She pointed to a white, linen-draped table over to the right.

"Okay, baby." She kissed Ariel on the cheek. "I'll see you later."

Preston and Ariel shook hands, air-kissed, and greeted a parade of some of their closest friends, local politicians, and business associates. Ariel's toes were beginning to ache from standing on her feet for hours on end, and she was ready to sit down and enjoy the reception, but there were a few more people to greet.

"Congratulations, Dad," Trey said, shaking his father's hand.

He clenched Trey's hand with both of his. "Thanks, son."

"Judge Hendricks, I hope you'll be as happy the rest of your life as you are today," Michele said, looking cuttingly at Ariel.

"Thank you so much." He hugged Michele. "Hey, who knows? Maybe you guys will be next to walk down that aisle." He winked.

Ariel wanted to gag, but she just smiled politely, hoping that they wouldn't linger longer than necessary.

"Excuse me, darlings," Meri said, interrupting the pseudo-love fest, "but I must kiss the bride *and* groom."

Ariel couldn't have been happier to see her old friend, and she reached out and pulled Meri in closer. "Thanks for saving me. I didn't know how much longer I could stand listening to Michele's phony well wishes," she whispered.

"Anytime, darling, but I need to talk to you privately. You've been so busy planning your wedding that we've missed our weekly chat sessions. And though I just witnessed you getting hitched, I'm still having a hard time wrapping my mind around everything that's happened in the past few months," she said softly, to keep Preston from hearing.

"Okay, just give me a minute and I'll meet you in the back."

WHEN ALL THE guests were seated, drinking and chatting among one another, Ariel took the opportunity to steal away.

Meri was seated alone near the rear of the room, far away from the rest of the guests. At her side was a champagne stand with a chilled bottle of Cristal; she handed Ariel a flute of bubbly when she sat down. "Lucy . . . you got some 'splaining to do!" she sang in a Spanish accent, perfectly mimicking Ricky Ricardo.

"I know. This has been one hell of a crazy whirlwind." She exhaled, taking a sip of champagne. "I don't even know where to begin."

"You can skip all the boring stuff and get right down to the nitty-gritty." Meri scooted her chair closer and perched both elbows on the table, eagerly awaiting the juicy details.

Ariel chuckled slightly. "But of course. Well . . ." She paused and looked toward the ceiling as if recalling the events that led to this day. "You already know that Preston had a mild stroke, but what you don't know is that the stroke short-circuited his short-term memory."

"Are you telling me that he doesn't remember your blatant confession of fucking his son?"

Ariel had called Meri right after she called the paramedics the night Preston collapsed. While in the waiting room, Ariel told Meri verbatim what happened minutes before Preston's stroke. After a few hours of waiting, the doctors told them that Preston was stable and sleeping comfortably. Meri insisted that they both go home and get some rest, but when Ariel returned later that day, the doctor told her that Preston had lost his short-term memory. He said it wasn't uncommon with the type of stroke that he had had, and that his memory would probably return in a few months, if not sooner. Ariel realized right then and there that she had a second chance with the one man in the world who truly loved her unconditionally. She couldn't believe how stupid she had been to believe that Trey loved her. He may have loved sleeping with her, but he surely didn't love her in the true sense of the word. Their connection was purely physical and nothing more. Ariel had let her feelings of abandonment cloud her judgment. Her mother had left her as a child, and Preston's preoccupation with his career had brought back those same unworthy feelings. She got involved with the first person who showed her any attention, and unfortunately, that person was Trey. But now the past had momentarily been erased, and she didn't waste any time getting Preston to the altar before he regained his memory.

"Fortunately for me, he doesn't remember the last forty-eight hours prior to the stroke, but the doctor said that his memory could return at any given moment," she said, with a sense of panic.

"What are you going to do when he remembers the events that led to his stroke?"

"Deny, deny, deny." She laughed nervously.

Meri looked at her like she had lost her mind. "You don't honestly think that Preston will simply take your word that none of this happened, do you?"

"It won't only be my word." She raised her brow.

"What do you mean?"

"Trey and Michele have both agreed to back up my story," she said, matter-of-factly as if they were best friends sworn to a secret pact.

"What?" Meri cocked her head to one side, trying to make sense of what she had just heard.

"I know it sounds bizarre, but once Trey found out about his dad's stroke, he came directly to the hospital from the airport. Apparently, he and Michele had gone away for a long weekend. Anyway, Preston was asleep when he arrived, so I took the opportunity to tell Trey everything that had happened—"

"What did he say?"

"At first, he was mortified that I had confessed our affair, and saddened when I told him that his dad had lost any chance of sitting on the Supreme Court because of his ownership of The Black Door. Once that information sank in, he became furious and—"

"At you?" Meri asked, interrupting.

"Thankfully no. He was furious at the senator for not recommending his dad for the nomination."

"Why? It's not like the senator was the man behind The Black Door. Trey was the one who ruined his dad's chances, not the senator," Meri said, without of any remorse for Trey.

"I know." Ariel nodded in agreement. "That's why Trey called in a huge favor."

"A favor from whom?"

"Remember that guy who escorted me to the Lancaster benefit a few months ago?"

"How could I forget the good 'doctor'?" Meri said, referring to Mason's cover for the evening.

"Apparently, one of Mason's clients is none other than . . ." She paused for effect. "Are you ready for this?" she asked, lowering her voice so that she wouldn't be overheard.

Meri scooted her body closer to Ariel, "Who? Who is it? Wait, don't tell me. Let me guess," she said eagerly, as if she were on a game show. She thought hard for a moment, and then said, "Libby Lancaster," referring to the millionaire matriarch.

Ariel shook her head, but before she could continue, Meri spouted out another name. "Bitsy Reynolds?"

"No, it's not Bitsy; she's too busy spending her husband's money on lavish social events to be involved with The Black Door. Mason's undercover client is none other than Angelica Oglesby," she whispered.

"Who?" Meri knew all the New York socialites, but this name didn't ring a bell.

"Angelica Oglesby," she repeated. "You know, Senator Oglesby's wife!"

Meri threw her hand to her mouth, her eyes widened with shock. "You've got to be kidding me!" she shrieked softly.

"No, I'm not kidding. It seems the senator's loving wife has been busy loving Mason. Anyway, Trey used Angelica's membership to convince the senator that it would be in his best interest to keep The Black Door under wraps and reconsider his dad for the nomination. Can you believe it?" she asked, still finding it hard to believe the story herself.

Meri exhaled. "Wow, what a story! But what happens once Preston regains his memory?"

"Well, that's the million-dollar question," Ariel said, with a tinge of sadness in her voice. "Hopefully, when that day comes, Preston will be a justice and he'll be so ecstatic about finally achieving his lifelong dream that he'll forgive me and Trey for deceiving him."

"What about Michele? Aren't you afraid that she'll help Preston refresh his memory sooner rather than later?"

"She's so happy about being with Trey that she'll keep her mouth shut in order to keep him. Besides, working for a Supreme Court justice is much more impressive than working for a county judge, and we both know that Michele is quite the little social climber. So you see, with Trey, Michele, and me working together on the same agenda, everything should be fine . . . at least for now." And with that said, Meri and Ariel rejoined the festivities and partied like everything was right with the world.